"Mind if I jo[...] a deep voice as[...]*

Maureen's gaze traveled up the arm beside her, to wide shoulders, then to gold-brown eyes and hair silvered at the temples. "Of course not." Her response was automatic; her indrawn breath was not.

"I'm Bailey McGuire," he said, sitting down. "I'm a student here."

Maureen made it a practice *not* to respond to masculine charm, but her usual control seemed to be on the blink, if her present pulse rate was any indication.

"No reason we can't all go on learning," she replied politely.

"That's right," Bailey agreed with a grin.

Maureen was sure he knew exactly how that dashing grin affected women, was even now affecting her.

"I learn something new every day," he added. "How about you?"

"One has to have an open mind," she murmured.

"Open to new experiences, right?"

She mentally shook off the spell his voice was spinning. "Like what?"

"Like meeting me back here later tonight."

Dear Reader,

Welcome to the Silhouette **Special Edition** experience! With your search for consistently satisfying reading in mind, every month the authors and editors of Silhouette **Special Edition** aim to offer you a stimulating blend of deep emotions and high romance.

The name Silhouette **Special Edition** and the distinctive arch on the cover represent a commitment—a commitment to bring you six sensitive, substantial novels each month. In the pages of a Silhouette **Special Edition**, compelling true-to-life characters face riveting emotional issues—and come out winners. All the authors in the series strive for depth, vividness and warmth in writing these stories of living and loving in today's world.

The result, we hope, is romance you can believe in. Deeply emotional, richly romantic, infinitely rewarding—that's the Silhouette **Special Edition** experience. Come share it with us—six times a month!

From all the authors and editors of Silhouette **Special Edition**,

Best wishes,

Leslie Kazanjian,
Senior Editor

PAMELA TOTH
Old Enough To Know Better

Silhouette Special Edition

Published by Silhouette Books New York
America's Publisher of Contemporary Romance

This book is dedicated to Janice Kay Johnson,
a true friend who keeps me headed
in the right direction

SILHOUETTE BOOKS
300 East 42nd St., New York, N.Y. 10017

ISBN: 0-373-09624-0

First Silhouette Books printing September 1990

Books by Pamela Toth

Silhouette Romance

Kissing Games #500
The Ladybug Lady #595

Silhouette Special Edition

Thunderstruck #411
Dark Angel #515
Old Enough To Know Better #624

PAMELA TOTH

was born in Wisconsin but now makes her home near Seattle, Washington, with her husband and two daughters. When not busy writing, she enjoys bowling, roller skating and camping with her family.

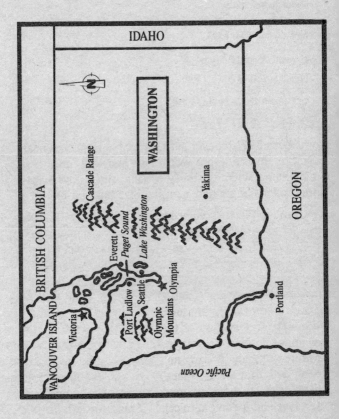

Chapter One

Maureen Fletcher glanced around the crowded cafeteria, looking for an empty table. When she finally spotted one, she shifted her purse and briefcase, picked up her coffee, and threaded her way through the crowd of returning night students.

She set down her cup and sank gratefully into the empty chair, glad of a few moments' respite before she had to begin the first session of the class she was teaching that evening, Foreign Language Review. During the daytime Maureen taught French and Spanish. She had already dealt with four classes that day, as well as joining several other teachers during a break in their afternoon schedule for cake and ice cream to celebrate her fortieth birthday.

She wasn't dealing with that quite as well. The milestone evoked feelings she hadn't been able to sort through yet, feelings that perhaps her orderly, rewarding life wasn't quite as satisfying as she had always told herself it was. Feelings of restlessness she usually had no trouble ignoring. Perhaps later at home she would find the time and the quiet to examine the nameless longing this particular date had stirred up.

Night school was something Maureen especially enjoyed. The students were often older, sometimes more serious, and usually interesting. Their reasons for taking classes were varied, but they were almost always eager to learn. That was the main reason Maureen had happily spent the past six years teaching at Port Gardner Community College in northwestern Washington State. As tired as she was this first evening, she was still glad to be back.

Maureen took a sip of the weak coffee that seemed to be a college specialty and opened her briefcase, remembering with a smile the male stripper who someone had hired to serenade another teacher right there in the cafeteria on *her* birthday. When one of the empty chairs was dragged away from the table, she glanced up.

"Mind if I join you?" The man's hand was still on the chair. Her gaze traveled up his arm to wide shoulders and then to his face. He was smiling, his gold-brown eyes narrowed between dark, thick lashes.

"Of course not." Maureen's response was automatic. Her indrawn breath was not.

He dropped a pile of books and binders onto the table. On top was a small cassette recorder. Maureen stared, remembering again what had happened to Cathy Anderson.

Her friends wouldn't have done anything as embarrassing as hiring a stripper for *her* birthday, would they?

Heat spreading through her cheeks, Maureen studied the man suspiciously. He looked too mature for that kind of job, but his rugged build would qualify him in a minute despite the threads of gray in his dark hair.

Please not in the crowded cafeteria, she prayed, glancing around wildly. He picked up the cassette recorder and her mouth flew open, but before she could protest, he merely set it back down next to his books before folding his tall frame into the chair across from her.

"I'm Bailey McGuire," he said quickly, as relief poured through her. "Are you a student here?"

"Are you?" she countered, short of breath. Her heart was still tripping in double time and she was glad she hadn't said something utterly stupid.

His narrowed eyes glinted. "Yes, I'm a student. Why, do I look too mature? More like a teacher, perhaps?"

Maureen braced her chin on one finger and studiously considered the man's appearance for a moment. His dark hair was combed back from a broad forehead and silvered at the temples. His nose was straight and his mouth intriguing below a thick mustache that any pirate would have been proud to wear.

Actually, he probably *could* pass as a teacher, even in the casual plaid shirt, except that she already knew he wasn't on the staff. She would have remembered a man who looked like Bailey, and she was positive she had never seen him before. He reminded her of someone, but she couldn't think who. To Maureen's surprise, she felt a tingling response to his presence across the table.

Student or not, he would certainly make one devastating birthday present, if her reaction to him was any indication. Maureen made it a practice *not* to respond to masculine charm, but her usual calm control seemed to be on the blink, if her present pulse rate was any indication.

"There are a lot of more mature students here," she finally managed to reply, "especially in the evenings. No reason we can't all go on learning." Her mouth formed a stiff little smile.

"That's right," Bailey agreed with a beguiling grin of his own. A dimple dented his lean cheek, then disappeared as Maureen stared, fascinated. "I learn something new every day," he added in a teasing voice. She tore her attention away from Bailey's mouth, as his thick brows rose in question. "How about you?"

For a moment Maureen was lost, and then she vaguely remembered what they'd been discussing. "One has to have an open mind," she murmured, noticing that the lone dimple in his cheek reappeared each time he smiled. She was sure he knew exactly how that dashing grin affected women, was even now affecting her.

"I agree. Open to new experiences, right?" Now his eyes were clearly laughing.

Maureen saw the trap but was powerless to avoid it. "Like what?" She straightened her shoulders and raised her chin, mentally shaking off the spell his deep voice was spinning.

Bailey tipped his head to the side, studying her, and she realized with a shiver who he reminded her of. His dark coloring and undeniably good looks were not unlike those of her ex-husband, a man she had been unable to resist from the beginning. A man whose ultimate betrayal had almost destroyed her.

"Like what?" Bailey echoed. "Like meeting me back here at the break." His voice curled around her like tendrils of smoke. Hypnotic, elusive. She found herself hoping he wasn't in her class. All she needed were those eyes of his watching intently as she demonstrated conjugating an irregular verb in French. She'd end up counting in German instead and never notice.

Maureen swallowed painfully, ignoring his question. "What subject are you taking tonight?"

"Basket-weaving," Bailey drawled.

She blinked. "I didn't think that was offered this quarter." Beneath the table, her hands gripped each other tightly.

Bailey laughed, a husky, intimate sound that invited her to join in. Maureen resisted. "Do you always take everything so literally?"

His question confused her. "I beg your pardon?"

"I didn't mean basket-weaving, actually," Bailey explained in a patient voice. "I meant it in a general way, a class that's supposed to be a snap. I'm taking Spanish for my foreign-language requirement. I heard it was an easy A."

Maureen's eyes widened at his comment. "That's good to know," she murmured, glancing at her watch. "Do you need an easy A to pass?"

"Probably not, but foreign languages aren't my main field of interest."

"What's your major?" Maureen asked, knowing she should leave, but not quite being able to make herself do so.

"I'm not sure yet. So far I've been taking general subjects, but I may eventually switch to engineering."

"You're ambitious," she said, her gaze wandering over his wide shoulders before she forced her attention back to his face.

Bailey was returning her scrutiny with interest. Maureen determinedly pushed back her chair. Classes didn't start for another quarter of an hour, but she liked to be early. Besides, a man such as Bailey was too dangerous a distraction when her thoughts were supposed to be on the class at hand. She wasn't used to being rattled like this. Scooping up her belongings, she stood abruptly.

"Good luck with your basket-weaving. I have to go."

"Wait. What about later?" Bailey rose, too, towering over her.

When Maureen dropped her gaze, it landed unerringly on the well-fitting crotch of his worn jeans. Thoroughly disconcerted she tore her attention away, finally settling it on his face. What on earth was wrong with her?

"I'd better not commit myself," she gasped, seeing the flare of disappointment in his eyes before he masked his expression. "We'll probably run into each other again." Not if she could help it!

"I guess I'll have to be content with that for now," he said graciously. "But at least tell me your name."

It would be insufferably rude to refuse. "My name's Maureen," she replied. "Nice talking to you, Bailey." She slung the strap of her purse over her shoulder, freeing the strands of straight blond hair that were caught beneath it, before she grabbed her briefcase. Several women at neighboring tables had been watching them openly. No doubt if Bailey wished it, he could have another companion before she was out of the room.

He glanced down at her bare hand. "Not married?" he asked.

For a moment, some deep-rooted survival instinct tempted Maureen to lie, then she shook her head.

"Significant other?"

"No."

"That's good," he murmured.

There was nothing left to say, so Maureen darted around him and fled, taking deep breaths to slow the rapid patter of her pulse as she hurried across the room. Where were the barriers she'd spent years perfecting, when she needed them? Bailey had stormed her defenses and shattered them as easily as if they had never existed.

Behind her, Bailey remained standing, watching her make her way between tables. The pale hair that curved smoothly under, just barely brushing the collar of her light blue sweater gleamed in the overhead light as her narrow hips swayed enticingly in the slim navy skirt. The outfit was dressier than what most of the female students wore, but he liked it. The length of her elegant legs drew his gaze downward, past delicate ankles to her mid-heeled shoes, and then his view was cut off as she passed a crowded table.

Bailey remembered her mysterious smile and the challenge in her uplifted chin. There was something about her—she intrigued him as no one had in quite a while, but his timing certainly could have been better.

He gathered up his books and notebook, set his cassette recorder carefully on top of the stack, and headed for class.

At the break, Bailey lingered in the cafeteria, looking for her. The warning bell finally rang and he drained his coffee cup, making a face at the watery brew, before he went back out the door and crossed the quad to a nearby building.

It was a good thing Bailey had taped the introduction to his Spanish class. He hadn't been concentrating; instead he'd thought about the mysterious Maureen. It was undoubtedly the worst time in his life for anything other than a casual friendship, and he told himself that he wasn't looking for anything more than that. If he saw Maureen again, and if she was receptive, he could at least be friendly. No harm in that.

While Bailey was walking down the hall, he happened to glance through the window in the closed door of another classroom. Light gold hair drew his attention and he stopped to get a better look.

There was Maureen, wearing horn-rimmed glasses as she stood in front of a roomful of students. She was obviously teaching the class. Bailey watched her, thinking back over their conversation. No, she hadn't actually said she was a student. She hadn't said much, at all. He made note of her room number and hurried back to his own class as the final bell sounded.

"We start promptly after the break each night, Mr. McGuire," his teacher, a young man with a serious expression, said as Bailey slid into his seat.

"Yes, sir. I'll remember that."

The teacher eyed Bailey's grin with obvious suspicion, then turned to the blackboard, chalk poised.

When the last of her students had filed from the room, Maureen packed her briefcase and switched off the light, shutting the door behind her. She walked down the hall and out into the darkening night. A bulky shape stepped into the circle of light from an outdoor lamp and she caught her breath, steps faltering, before she recognized the man from the cafeteria. She released the breath she had dragged in.

"Hello, again." Her voice was strained.

Two more people came out the door and brushed past her, hurrying toward the parking lot. Maureen turned as if to follow them, and Bailey fell into step beside her. She was surprised he had bothered to wait; she had certainly offered no encouragement.

"You didn't say you were a teacher," he scolded gently as he looked down at her. The shadows brought his cheekbones into sharp relief and shaded his mouth below his mustache. She couldn't see if he was smiling.

"I didn't say I wasn't."

She kept moving and he stayed beside her. "No, you didn't, not exactly."

Maureen couldn't help but wonder about him. Was he an aging model, an aspiring actor or a more ordinary man? Though ordinary was hardly the right word.

"How's your easy A going so far?" she asked to break the silence. "Mr. Howard is no pushover."

Bailey sighed. "I suppose my bad luck is holding and Spanish is one of your subjects." He didn't sound the least bit embarrassed.

"Daytime, this quarter."

They walked from the shadows into another pool of light and again that bold grin flashed across his face. "My bad luck."

She couldn't imagine him as a student, sitting quietly in front of her as she taught. "What do you do days?" she asked, stopping at the entrance to reserved parking.

He reached into his pocket and pulled out a card. Maureen took it, careful not to let her fingers touch his, and then held it up, reading the black printing. "McGuire Electrical." She glanced up. "Is that you?"

He nodded.

"I'm impressed."

"It's a small business," he said, "but it's growing."

Maureen extended the card.

"Keep it. You never know when you might have a problem I could help you with."

When he made no move to take back the card, she tucked it into her purse, then met his steady gaze.

"Thanks," she said, remembering his earlier invitation. Would he ask again? Could she withstand the almost compulsive attraction she felt toward him?

"I'll walk you to your car," Bailey said.

A shiver of response to his nearness whispered through her, as she glanced around. There were still people everywhere. "It's not necessary. I'm parked in the first row."

"That's okay." His tone was firm, as he cupped a hand beneath her elbow.

Maureen felt the heat of his touch all the way up her arm. When she stopped at her car she tried a cool smile, but his expression was thoughtful, his brows a dark line as he shifted his books to his other side. "I'll say good night, then." He held out his hand. "Nice meeting you."

The sudden formality was a bit of a shock. Maureen slid her hand into his automatically and his strong fingers curled around hers. His skin was hard, calloused, warm. She smothered a gasp. Bailey had an air about him that was both exciting and terribly scary.

She wiggled her fingers and he released her hand. "Good night," she echoed.

Suddenly he leaned forward, and she took a hasty step back. His face came closer. Sheer panic made her speechless, eyes widened.

As she froze, Bailey reached past her and opened the driver's door. "You should keep your car locked."

Maureen went limp, cheeks hot. She was glad it was too dark for him to see her blush. She would die if he realized what she had thought he was going to do. What on earth was wrong with her?

Deciding to take offense at his bossy tone, she said, "It's perfectly safe." She tossed her briefcase onto the seat and slid behind the wheel. When he shut the door she locked it, feeling safer, then lifted her hand and waved.

Bailey waited until she had started the motor, before he tossed off a casual salute and turned toward the other parking lot. Maureen resisted the urge to sit for a few moments and get a grip on her jangled nerves, instead backing up carefully to join the line of cars exiting the lot. It had been a long day and all she wanted to do was to go home, slip into a comfortable robe and forget all about Bailey McGuire as she fed her cat and put her feet up.

Perhaps it was because of her birthday that she suddenly felt so tired. Right now a cup of herbal tea was a much more comfortable prospect than time spent in the company of a devastating male whose smile made her feel like she was having an early hot flash. At least that was what she told herself as she drove the few miles home, glad she had insisted to her friends that she absolutely didn't want a fuss on this birthday. For a milestone event, it was one she could have cheerfully done without.

Turning her car into the lot that ran behind the apartment complex, Maureen parked in her assigned slot. She walked through the breezeway of the building that contained her condo, shivering in the cool spring air. Nights in the Puget Sound area wouldn't really be warm for a couple more months, and her lightweight coat was thin. When she had left home earlier the sun had been shining, and that always fooled her into thinking it would still be warm later.

Maureen stopped at the entrance next to hers and rang the bell. After a long moment the door opened a crack, revealing one brown eye below tight white curls. In the background, voices from a television could be heard arguing. "Just a moment, dear."

The door shut quickly and its safety chain was released before the opening widened to reveal a tiny old woman who greeted Maureen with a smile of enthusiasm on her lined face.

"Come in, come in. I'm glad to see you."

Maureen bent down to give her a hug. "Hello, Mrs. Bondini. I'm home from class. Is everything okay with you?"

She entered the cluttered living room of her neighbor's unit, its floor plan the opposite of her own. While Maureen's only close relative was a married brother in California, Mrs. Bondini had a large family. Numerous pictures and keepsakes covered the walls and rested on the end tables and the top of the television. Maureen had examined and heard about each photograph. Because of the wealth of possessions covering every surface, this apartment seemed much smaller than her own, which Maureen kept ruthlessly neat.

"I'm fine, dear." Mrs. Bondini plumped a needlepoint pillow. "Do sit down."

Maureen had gotten into the habit of checking on her elderly friend almost every day. Mrs. Bondini lived alone and appreciated the attention. In return, she fed Maureen's cat and watered her plants whenever Maureen, who liked to travel, was away. It was a comfortable arrangement.

Mrs. Bondini waited until Maureen sat down on a dark red velvet love seat. "I know what day this is, and I have a little something for you." The old woman's face creased into several hundred wrinkles as her smile widened. "I won't keep you long. I know you probably have work to do."

Turning down an offer of herbal tea, Maureen said apologetically, "I do have to prepare tomorrow's lesson." That was actually almost done and wouldn't take long to finish up, but the idea of snuggling into her robe and putting her feet up was a powerful lure.

"I understand, dear. Besides, one of my favorite shows is starting soon. That nice young detective was left in the worst situation last week. I can't wait to see how he gets out of it." She picked up the remote control and turned off the sound on her television, then moved slowly to a low table where a gaily wrapped package sat like a colorful butterfly. Maureen watched her carefully, trying to gauge how much Mrs. Bondini's arthritis was bothering her.

Above them a bright yellow canary in a cage warbled a few musical notes. "Quiet, Frankie." Mrs. Bondini barely glanced at the bird before she handed the present to Maureen.

She unwrapped the small box and opened it, revealing a pair of beautifully worked silver earrings.

"They're lovely." Maureen rose and crossed to a mirror with an ornately gilded frame, pushing back her hair to remove her pearls and fasten the filigreed hoops in their place.

"I knew they would suit you," Mrs. Bondini said when Maureen turned around, earrings swaying gently. "I'm too old for dangles now, but they're pretty on you. We got them in Arizona when the mister and I vacationed there."

"I love them." Maureen thanked her, bending to kiss the dry cheek and give her thin shoulders a gentle hug. As Maureen straightened, the grandfather clock began to chime the hour and the canary joined in with a series of chirps.

"Any interesting men in your class tonight?" Mrs. Bondini asked as Maureen crossed to the door. Her smile faded with disappointment as Maureen shook her head.

If she mentioned Bailey McGuire, she'd be there for another half hour, answering questions, and her friend would miss her television show. No point in getting her hopes up. Bailey might be handsome and charming, but too much about him set off alarm bells when it came to Maureen's instinct for self preservation.

"You just have to try harder," Mrs. Bondini scolded, wagging a finger at her. Maureen's single state was a subject the elderly woman had mentioned more than once.

"I will. Have you been remembering to take your medicine?" No harm in a change of subject.

Mrs. Bondini gave an exaggerated sigh. "Yes, Mother," she said in a teasing voice. "Don't think I can't see what you're doing, distracting me like that."

"I'm just trying to make sure you take good care of yourself," Maureen said, bidding her neighbor good night and thanking her again for the earrings. As soon as she turned the key to release the lock on her own front door, Mrs. Bondini's shut behind her.

Maureen was barely inside when Max, her Siamese cat, greeted her by twining his lean body around her ankles, crying pitifully. Maureen bent down to scratch his head.

There was usually something satisfying about coming home and having Max greet her, knowing her apartment would be just the way she had left it and being able to do exactly what she wanted. Tonight, though, Max's feline greeting didn't warm her as it usually did. Maureen felt like Mrs. Bondini was her contemporary, not her elder. They were both set in their ways, both living alone.

Maureen sighed and went to put the kettle on. They even drank the same brand of herbal tea.

She fed Max as she always did, poured the tea and wandered into the bedroom to change out of her work clothes while it steeped. The bedroom, too, was just as she had left it, bed neatly made, a solitary pair of feminine slippers peeking out from under the edge of the spread, closet door shut on the wardrobe of female clothing. The crossword-puzzle book she had left on the nightstand was still there, not a single word she hadn't written herself filling the squares. The pencil she had left next to it hadn't been carried off, the lamp was still on low. Tonight the scene didn't give her the satisfaction she had previously managed to convince herself it did.

"It must be because it's my birthday," she said to Max, who had followed her into the room and jumped onto the bed. "I'm just restless."

He stared at her, blinking slowly. The deep rumble of a purr rose from his throat as he sat down and began to wash one dark paw.

Maureen glanced into the mirror and found herself searching for new lines around her eyes. "This is ridiculous," she muttered. "I'm happy, I'm content. I don't need a Bailey McGuire to add excitement to my life." She didn't want anything to do with a man like him, a man so appealing that he overrode her common sense. It wasn't that he scared her, she insisted to her reflected image, he just made her uncomfortable.

The litany didn't help a bit. Neither did the strand of white hair she noticed springing out from the golden ones above her right ear.

Over the next week Maureen did her best to forget about Bailey. She only saw him once, from a distance, talking to two pretty young coeds. He had obviously forgotten all about her, for which she breathed a sigh of relief. Then she studiously ignored the wave of unexpected regret that rose up and slapped her. He was undoubtedly a perfectly nice man, the best-looking one she'd met in ages, and she was probably once again being way too cautious. And now he'd lost interest.

Maureen told herself she was glad, having no time in her well-ordered life for someone like him, an electrician who took basket-weaving classes for easy grades. A wickedly handsome devil who made her heart palpitate.

A dinner date with a colleague who almost put her to sleep describing a paper he was doing on "The Political Parallels Between Humans in a Democratic Society and Colonizing Insects," and several visits with Mrs. Bondini convinced Maureen that she had to do something, though, before she sank out of sight in the well-ordered boredom of her humdrum existence. Maybe it was the advent of another decade of her life that made it so difficult for Maureen to keep telling herself that she had everything she wanted.

It wasn't an excessive fear of involvement that made her cautious, she told herself sternly, but a healthy sense of independence. The last thing she needed was a relationship that began with good intentions and ended in heartache. But for once the brisk reminder didn't bring with it the usual reassurance. Instead she felt a strange emptiness, a restless discontent.

Later that week Maureen slept through the alarm, something she *never* did. She had to hurry from the time her feet first hit the floor that morning, running errands after her day classes and stopping at home for a quick supper, then realizing suddenly, as she ate, that she was going to be late for the evening session if she didn't run.

There wasn't time to stop at the cafeteria for coffee; then one of her students kept her talking about the current assignment right through the break. Maureen felt almost motherly toward her students, no matter what their age, and she made a point to give them as much time and encouragement as they needed.

When class was finally over, she was still rushing automatically as she tossed pencils and paper into her briefcase and clicked it shut. Too bad the campus cafeteria closed at the same time evening classes ended. She'd never been able to understand the reason behind that bit of scheduling.

So what was the point in hurrying now? With a determined sigh, she willed herself to slow down, walking sedately as she took a last check around the classroom and shut the door behind her.

Whirling around in the hallway, Maureen almost collided with a familiar figure who looked every bit as good as she remembered. In a split second she took in the details of his red plaid shirt and snug, faded jeans, blue this time instead of gray. He looked like a sexy lumberjack. One with wide shoulders.

"Hi," Bailey said, steadying the disposable cup that she had almost knocked from his hand. "I didn't see you in the cafeteria earlier, so I brought you this."

Maureen was so surprised that she automatically reached to take the cup from his hand. "Thank you. But how did you get it? The cafeteria's closed now."

Bailey's golden-brown eyes danced. "My class got out early."

"Oh." Maureen's mind went blank as she stared up at him. "Well, thank you again," she repeated, feeling about as clever as Mrs. Bondini's canary. She popped the lid and took a long drink of the weak, lukewarm brew. "Ah, that tastes good."

"You must have been desperate. I've tasted the coffee here."

Their gazes met in the shared joke. Maureen felt a little of her tension slip away. "I *was* desperate. I didn't have time for a cup after supper."

The flash of Bailey's grin was intensely masculine as they began walking toward the parking lot. "It must have been one of those days."

"How could you tell?" she asked. Before she realized what was happening, Maureen found herself returning his smile as they made their way down the path across the quad.

"I've had one or two days like that myself."

As Maureen called good night to someone she knew, Bailey watched her. He wasn't sure why he'd bothered to bring her coffee, after she'd expressed such a total lack of enthusiasm toward him before. There were other women around, but none of them interested him. He shifted his books, content to saunter along beside her while she finished the coffee.

Every cell in Maureen's body was alert to his masculine presence. Now that he had sought her out again, she could hardly remember why she had discouraged him in the first place. It was unlike her to have a case of maidenly vapors just because a man was attractive. Even one as compelling as Bailey. The scent of his cologne drifted her way and she put her concerns on hold. After all, she was only talking to the man, not walking down the aisle with him. She was in no danger of becoming involved; if he asked for a date she could always refuse. She relaxed a little more.

"How's your class going?" she asked to break the silence as they neared her car.

Bailey leaned against the fender, setting his books carefully on the hood. "My class is what I wanted to talk to you about," he said, surprising her. "I don't seem to have much of a knack for Spanish."

"Some people find foreign languages more difficult than others do," she replied diplomatically.

"I've been studying as much as I've had time to, but my life has become impossible lately." Bailey didn't elaborate, even when she gazed at him expectantly. His thick

brows were bunched, his expression serious. "I got behind and now it's hard to catch up. I was wondering..."
He paused, his honey-brown stare considering.

Maureen waited for him to continue. "Wondering what?" she prompted when he remained silent. If he kept looking at her like he was now, she knew she would have a hard time saying no to another invitation.

"I was wondering if, since you teach Spanish yourself, you would have the time to help me with it?" he finished. "I'd pay you, of course."

His question wasn't what she had expected. "You mean *tutor* you?"

His lips quirked into a grin. "Yeah, that's what I meant. It would be a big help, and I'd really appreciate it." When she didn't speak, he asked, "Is there some rule against it?"

Maureen shook her head, stunned. "But why don't you ask Mr. Howard for help?"

"He's already told the class that he doesn't have any extra time this quarter. His wife's recovering from surgery and he has three small children."

Maureen opened her briefcase and began to dig around inside. "I have a list of qualified tutors in here somewhere," she muttered. "You could call one of them." She found what she was looking for and pulled it out. "They're all second-year Spanish students." There was no way she could tutor Bailey, even if she did have the time. She was attracted to him and didn't want to wind up embarrassing them both.

For a moment his eyes bored into hers, making her feel like a heel, then his fingers closed on the paper. "Thanks," he said softly.

Maureen felt bad. She shrugged. "I'm really sorry, but I don't have the time, with evening classes of my own as well as a full daytime schedule.'' For a moment, she wished she could find a few hours for him. Strictly business, no lustful thoughts allowed.

Before she could say anything more, he glanced at his watch. ''No problem. I understand, and thanks for the names.'' He folded the list and put it in his pocket.

Maureen forced a smile, about to say good night.

''Let's stop somewhere for a drink.''

His sudden invitation came as a surprise. Again, as he smiled, that sizzling attraction flared between them, melting Maureen's resistance. She remembered thinking that she had become too cautious. Collecting her wits without giving herself time for second thoughts, she obeyed a momentary impulse to throw caution to the wind. ''Sure.''

Bailey's eyes crinkled and an elusive dimple dented his cheek. ''Great,'' he said. ''Let's go.''

Maureen followed in her car, wondering with a shake of her head if she had truly lost her mind, as Bailey led her to a bar close to campus. Its interior was dark and cozy, booths and tables clustered around a circular fire pit topped with a gigantic copper hood. Bailey took her arm lightly as he escorted her to a small table along the wall and held out her chair.

''What do you do when you aren't teaching?'' he asked after they'd given their order to a waitress in a miniskirt and sequined vest.

Maureen frowned while she took a peanut from the bowl on the table and concentrated on cracking its shell. ''Good question,'' she muttered.

''I beg your pardon?''

''Ever feel like you've lost touch with what you want? That you're drifting?'' She realized that she must sound terribly discontented and shook her head, smiling ruefully. "Scratch that. I've been in a strange mood lately. I just had a birthday, and I'm not handling it well."

Across from her, Bailey watched as she began to peel the dry skins from the two peanuts she had shelled.

"I passed the big four-oh a few months back," he volunteered. "Takes some getting used to."

"Then you know what I mean."

God, yes, he knew. But not for any of the reasons she might have. He felt out of control, not because he was drifting, but because someone else was disrupting the order he'd managed to regain in his life. For a moment frustration threatened to overtake him. Then the waitress brought their drinks and he took a long swallow of his beer.

"So?" he asked, "What do you do when you're not drifting?"

They both smiled.

"I like to ride bikes," Maureen offered. "And to hike and read. I enjoy music, plays, movies." It sounded deadly dull, even to her. Bailey was probably into windsurfing or skydiving. He had the body of a much younger man, but she had been rather pleasantly surprised to discover that he wasn't.

"What about you?" she asked, sipping her wine spritzer. Would they have anything in common?

"I played softball for a while," he said, licking a bit of foam from the corner of his mouth. He would much rather listen to her talk, but that was hardly fair. "And I love to fish in the Sound when I can find the time." He thought of the luxury of getting away by himself. "I used to run, but I haven't for a while."

"Too busy?"

Another couple sat at the table next to them. Bailey glanced up before returning his attention to Maureen.

"Yeah, the business takes some time." That and other things, he thought.

She nodded knowingly. "Ah, yes. The electrical business. Have you had it long?"

"Five years. Before that I worked for a different outfit."

Maureen finished her spritzer and set the glass back down. Instead of offering her another, Bailey surprised her by glancing at his watch and then draining his schooner.

"Now that I finally have you away from the campus, I wish I had more time," he said, his gaze warming her in a way that made her want to throw caution to the wind and wish he had, too. "But unfortunately I promised the sitter I'd be home by eleven. She has school tomorrow and I hate to keep her out late."

"Sitter?" Maureen echoed, stunned. "As in *baby-sitter*? Bailey, are you married?"

Chapter Two

When Bailey didn't answer right away, Maureen repeated her question. "Are you married?"

"No," he said, pushing his chair back, "but I do have to get going. Come on, I'll explain while we walk."

For a moment Maureen hesitated. Then she rose and preceded him to the door. "This better be good," she muttered, sure she had made a big mistake in coming with him.

Bailey held the door open for her and she stepped onto the sidewalk. It was a mild evening.

"So?" She hardly gave him time to get outside.

"No, I'm not married," he said, tucking her arm through his. "Not anymore."

Maureen was trying to ignore the warmth of his hard body where her arm was pressed against him and revise the image she'd had of him as a carefree bachelor. "But you obviously have a child."

"Children. Shawn is nine and Melissa just turned seven. I'm a single parent." Bailey's tone was matter-of-fact; he wasn't looking for sympathy.

Maureen gave it anyway. "It must be tough," she said, turning to him when they reached her car. "Running a business, going to school." Despite herself, she was impressed. The only ones she was responsible for were herself and her cat, and sometimes that seemed like too much.

"Boy Scouts, Blue Birds, PTA meetings." Bailey took up the chant where she left off. "It's a good thing I work for myself. I don't see how women do it, holding down a job and raising kids alone." He rubbed the side of his neck, and for a moment he looked tired. "How do they take time off work, spread themselves around like they must have to, and not fall apart?"

Maureen thought about it. "I don't know," she said finally. "But I can understand that it must be very difficult."

"No children of your own?" Bailey asked. When she shook her head, he asked, "Ever married?"

"Once." Maureen had been alone for nearly ten years, and since the divorce she had tried hard to forget about the whole devastating experience. "We married in college. It didn't work out, and we split up." Despite herself, she shivered at the memory of just how badly it had ended, her ex-husband betraying and then deserting her during one of the blackest periods of her life. "He took a job out of town a few months later and I haven't seen or heard of him since. Not that I wanted to."

"It's probably the best way," Bailey said, watching her closely. "No ex-spouses cluttering up your life." He must have read something on her face. "I'm sorry," he added quietly. "I'm sure there was more to it than that."

Maureen shook her head. It was not the kind of thing one shared with a relative stranger. *Especially* not an appealing one.

For a moment Bailey's expression seemed regretful. "I hope we'll be able to talk some more, but right now I have to go. Anyway, I'll see you at school, okay? The cafeteria before class?"

Thrusting aside unhappy memories, Maureen returned his smile. Bailey still looked more like the prime player in a sexy fantasy than a family man, a single parent. A man who had responsibilities with a capital R. She wondered how long he had been divorced and why he had the children, but it was too late to ask. He was holding the driver's door of her car open. It was probably just as well she didn't know, since she had no intention of getting involved with him.

"Okay," Maureen said, sliding in. Seeing him one more time wouldn't hurt. "Thanks for the drink."

For a moment Bailey's eyes locked onto hers. He lifted his hand and lightly brushed his thumb across her lower lip. "It makes me sad that you've been hurt," he said, voice low. "Good night." He shut her door carefully before turning away.

Maureen sat and watched his receding figure, tall and broad-shouldered, before starting her car. She felt the tingle of his unexpected caress half the way home.

"Why do you have to go back to school, Daddy? You're grown-up."

Bailey was buttoning his shirt while his daughter, Melissa, sat on his bed, watching him. She thought the idea of him taking classes was funny.

"I'm not going back to school because I have to, princess. I want to learn some more things. We never stop learning."

Melissa frowned with seven-year-old concentration, her brown eyes watching him with undivided attention. "Mommy doesn't go to school."

Bailey thought about his ex-wife, Angela, who had returned to town unexpectedly three weeks before. She had called and then stopped by that same day to see the children after a three-year absence. When Bailey had asked how long she was going to be around, she had been maddeningly vague, but her very presence made him watchful. The children hadn't fully adjusted to her sudden departure and now they were trying to cope with her return.

"Mommy doesn't think she needs to learn anything else," Bailey answered shortly, smoothing Melissa's long, dark hair. "She knows it all." Instantly he felt guilty. No matter what his feelings were about Angela, he shouldn't bad-mouth her to her daughter.

Melissa giggled, hugging him around the waist. "You're funny, Daddy."

Bailey returned her hug. Angela's defection had been hard on all of them, even harder to take than her drinking before she left. "That's right," he agreed. "Daddy was only making a joke. Your mother doesn't really know everything."

"I know that. She doesn't know what I like to eat, or my favorite color, and she didn't even remember who Rainbow is."

Rainbow was Melissa's number-one doll, which Bailey had given her several Christmases ago.

"She said that's why she came back from O O—"

"Oahu," Bailey supplied.

"Oahu. To learn all about us."

Bailey had to bite his tongue. If Angela hadn't walked out on him three years ago, leaving him with a business to run and two small children to raise, she wouldn't have to learn all about them now. She could have gotten control of the drinking and stayed to face her responsibilities. Instead she had taken off with a man she met in a bar. Why the hell did she have to come back? And why now?

Bailey ran a brush through his hair, thinking about Maureen, as he had frequently over the past two days. He would see her again tonight, and maybe they could make plans to meet away from campus. He glanced in the mirror on the closet door one last time. Usually he paid little attention to his appearance, but tonight he had thrust aside the worn sweatshirt he'd grabbed first. Making a good impression wouldn't hurt.

"You look nice."

For a moment he had forgotten all about his daughter, still perched on the bed. "Thank you, honey."

The doorbell sounded and he said, "The sitter is here. Would you let her in?"

"Shawn will get it," Melissa replied. But she slid to the floor and hurried from the room. She liked the girl who stayed with them two evenings a week while Bailey attended his class. He'd only had time to take one class a quarter, but perhaps someday he would have enough credits for an engineering degree. If not, his business would keep him busy enough. That and his two children.

Digger barked from the living room. Shawn shouted for the basset hound to get down off the couch. Bailey smiled to himself as he left the bedroom. Some things never changed; they were to be cherished in the midst of a hectic life-style.

"Hello, Jennifer," he greeted the sitter.

"Hi, Mr. McGuire." She dumped a pile of books onto the couch.

"Lots of homework tonight?" he asked.

Jennifer nodded, flipping back her straight hair. It was handy having a sitter who lived two doors down. Jennifer's older sister had sat before she outgrew the job, and by the time Jennifer was too old to be interested, Shawn would probably be able to watch Melissa himself.

Bailey kissed his daughter and gave Shawn a hug that the boy accepted awkwardly. At nine he thought outward shows of affection weren't manly. Bailey grinned at his red face. Shawn also had a crush on Jennifer, a fact that Bailey did his best to ignore.

"Be good, and don't give Jennifer a hard time," Bailey told them both as he scooped up his own books. "And don't forget to wash the supper dishes. I'll see you in the morning."

At the college Bailey glanced at the round wall clock, as he slid into a chair in the crowded cafeteria. He was early. Maureen probably wouldn't be there for a few more minutes.

While he waited he studied the other people settled at different tables. Some were reading, some were clustered in groups talking. The age span was as varied as any cross section of people anywhere. Bailey watched a young girl who looked as if she should be in high school. She was writing determinedly. The faster she wrote, the faster she chewed her gum. A tall boy stopped at her table, but she pointed to her paper and waved him away.

Bailey knew he should be studying himself instead of wasting time, but before he could open his book, Maureen sat down across from him. "Been here long?" she asked as she popped the lid from her coffee.

"A few minutes. I guess I was eager to see you again." He watched with amusement as her pale cheeks turned pink. Before she could form a reply, he spoke again. "I hope it wasn't too much of a shock to find out that I have children."

Maureen blinked and looked away. Could he read her mind? Actually, it *had* been a shock. She had pictured him as being a single man and had yet to accept the idea that he led a more complicated life than she had imagined.

"Have you always had custody?" she asked, dodging his question.

"Yes."

For a moment his expression was grim. It made Maureen wonder about him. Had Bailey been one of those men who expected his wife to raise the children while he followed more manly pursuits such as running his business? Somehow, when she really considered the idea, it was easy to picture him as a devoted parent. The image brought a momentary stab of pain that she did her best to ignore. In Bailey there was a basic kindness beneath the more obvious masculine charm. Maureen would bet he was a good father. But she reminded herself she had certainly been fooled before.

She was about to ask more, when a young woman dashed up to the table. "Bailey!" she exclaimed.

He glanced up and a warm smile lit his face. "Cathy! How have you been?"

Her blond ponytail fairly bounced with enthusiasm as she answered him. She was wearing shorts and a knit shirt and she carried a tennis racket in a case. Her taut legs were deeply tanned above her white athletic shoes, and her whole body radiated postadolescent youth and energy. Next to her, Maureen felt a thousand years old.

"Are you playing Jack-and-Jill softball this year?" the girl asked Bailey.

He shook his head regretfully. "No time, with night school." He turned to Maureen, who was embarrassed to be caught staring. "This is Cathy. We were on the same softball team last year. Maureen, a friend of mine."

The two women exchanged nods. Cathy's eyes were a brilliant blue in a California-pretty face. Maureen knew men usually went for younger women. The thought was an unsettling one.

"Gotta go," Cathy was saying. "I have an aerobics class at the health club."

It figured, Maureen thought, returning Cathy's radiant smile as she said goodbye. She watched Bailey watch the younger girl as she walked briskly away.

Then he turned back to Maureen, a bemused smile on his face. "All that bubbling makes me feel old," he said with an exaggerated sigh.

Startled, Maureen burst into laughter.

"How about Saturday night?" he asked. "West Texas is doing a concert at the Coliseum in Seattle. Would you go with me?"

"West who?" Maureen had never heard of the group he mentioned.

"West Texas. Don't tell me you aren't familiar with their music. They won a Country Music Award for best new group last year, and their first album got a Grammy."

"Oh." Obviously their taste in music wasn't remotely similar. Perhaps she shouldn't have dismissed diverse interests so blithely. "A country-and-western group."

"You don't like country music?" He looked disappointed.

Maureen shook her head. "Sorry. All those whining fiddles and lyrics about cheating and lost love depress me." Songs about cheating struck too close to home.

Bailey's dark eyes began to gleam. "Sounds like you haven't listened lately. There's a lot more to country music than that."

Maureen shrugged. "I'll take your word for it."

He patted her arm on the table. Again a little sizzle of awareness lingered where he'd touched. "I can't let such a big chunk of your education be neglected. And you can't possibly condemn a whole section of our heritage without giving it a fair chance."

Maureen leaned back and watched him through narrowed eyes, knowing she was playing with fire. "I can't?"

"No ma'am. It's un-American."

"What do you suggest?" she asked, barely containing her laughter. Lord, he could sure be persuasive when he wanted.

Bailey snapped his fingers. "I have a great idea. See, I have these tickets. You could go to a concert with me and listen to this terrific country group, before you make a final decision." He waited expectantly.

Maureen pretended to consider carefully, knowing she'd already made her decision. "That might be a wise idea," she mused. "I'll think it over."

She rose from her chair, tugging her arm loose from Bailey's warm grip.

"Maureen!" he exclaimed, rising with her.

She chuckled, and feeling reckless, relented. "I'd like to go with you." Even if the music gave her a headache, she suspected that spending an evening with him would never be dull.

Early Saturday evening Maureen stood in front of her closet trying to decide just what one wore to a country-music concert and dinner after. Since she didn't have a fringed skirt and cowboy boots, she was about to choose between slacks and a cotton sweater or a simple dress, when the ringing of the telephone interrupted.

Maureen gave Max a pat as she reached for the receiver. A deep rumbling purr rolled from his chest.

"Hello?"

"Hi, Maureen. It's me."

The husky sound of Bailey's voice made her shiver in reaction. Cradling the receiver, she sat down on the bed, one hand absently stroking Max's soft fur. "Hi."

"I hate to do this," Bailey said, "but it looks like I'm going to have to cancel for tonight. Melissa has a fever and I don't want to be out of touch, in case it gets worse. It can happen quickly with kids."

Disappointment made Maureen's fingers curl into Max's fur, until he meowed a protest and jumped off the bed. "I understand," she said. She had psyched herself for this night, and now she felt let down. "You can't leave a sick child."

"Thanks for being so nice about it," Bailey replied, picturing her face. "I'm unhappy as hell that it had to be tonight. I was really looking forward to this." He'd been thinking about sitting next to her in the dark, with the music drifting around them while he held her hand. And after... He couldn't let himself think about that now. About possibly kissing her. Melissa needed him.

"I was looking forward to this evening, too." Maureen's voice skipped over his nerve endings.

Bailey hoped that she was telling the truth. "Well, look, you can have the tickets if you still want to go. No point in wasting them."

There was silence on the other end of the line. "No, thanks anyway," she said. "I have some school papers I should go over before Monday. I think I'll do that tonight."

There wasn't much else to say. "I'm really sorry about this last-minute cancellation. I hope you'll let me make it up to you."

"That might be arranged," Maureen replied, a teasing note in her voice. "But the main thing is to get your daughter well. I hope it's nothing serious."

Bailey would have liked to keep her talking for a few more moments, but he heard Melissa call him from her bedroom. She probably wanted more juice. "Well, I had better let you go," he said reluctantly. "At least I'll see you Tuesday before class, won't I?"

Maureen agreed and they said goodbye. Bailey replaced the receiver slowly and got up. He would see what Melissa wanted, then call Randy, his helper at work, to see if he could use the concert tickets.

And he wouldn't see Maureen until Tuesday night. Thinking about the way her mouth moved when she talked, Bailey tacked a smile on his face and entered his daughter's room.

"I'm sorry, Daddy," she said when he sat beside her.

He lay his hand on her forehead. Still hot. "Don't worry, princess," he soothed. "Maureen understood. She said she hopes you feel better soon."

Melissa's big eyes stared up at him. "Is she nice?"

He smoothed her hair away from her face. "Very nice."

"Is she pretty?"

Bailey thought a minute. "Her hair is the same color as Sleeping Beauty in your book, kind of a pale gold. She's almost as pretty as you."

Melissa giggled. "Does she like little girls?"

"I'm sure she does." Melissa had asked him an endless stream of questions about Maureen since he had told her and Shawn that he had a date that evening. Shawn exhibited total disinterest, but Bailey noticed that his son paid close attention to his replies to Melissa's questions. Bailey couldn't blame the children for their curiosity. It was natural for them to be insecure after what they had been through with the divorce, and Bailey hadn't dated much since then. There hadn't been a lot of time, and he hadn't been very interested. Until Maureen.

"Does she have kids of her own?" Melissa persisted.

He stood up. "You asked me that before and I told you, no. Remember?"

She nodded, face flushed with fever, eyes bright.

"Now," he said, keeping his voice light, "how about some more pineapple juice?"

Maureen picked up a book she had been dying to find the time to read, then tossed it down again. She glanced at the television listings without interest, thought of the papers she could be correcting, and restlessly walked to the kitchen to peer into the refrigerator. Usually she didn't mind her own company, but tonight nothing tempted her.

She couldn't settle into anything. She wondered how Bailey's daughter was feeling, tempted to call just so she could hear his voice again. No, he was probably busy. She stuck her hands into the pockets of the jeans she had been wearing when he called to cancel, telling herself that if she had any sense she'd be glad he couldn't go.

She needed to eat, but wasn't hungry. The evening stretched before her with boring predictability. There were several friends she could call, but she wasn't in the mood. It was Bailey's company she had been looking forward to. With a tingle of warm reaction, she wondered if he would have kissed her tonight. She pictured his face, eyes narrowed, hard mouth quirked with laughter. She thought of that face descending closer, dark eyes drifting shut as his arms tightened around her.

With a groan of disappointment, Maureen collapsed into a chair, doing her best to banish the racy images that plagued her consciousness. What had gotten into her? She was about to pick her book back up when a light tap sounded at the door.

Bailey? Had he somehow gotten away for a few minutes?

She glanced down at her faded college sweatshirt and worn jeans, then crossed the room and peered through the peephole. One brown eye was looking back at her. Mrs. Bondini.

Maureen yanked open the door, glad for the interruption. "Come in. Is everything okay?"

Mrs. Bondini glanced pointedly at Maureen's clothes. "I thought you had a date," she said, walking slowly into the living room and extending a covered plate. "I made cookies, and I thought you might like a few for your young man."

Maureen thanked her and took the plate, peeking under the napkin. "Chocolate chip!" she exclaimed. "My favorite, as you well know." She picked one up and bit into it. "Sit down, can you stay?"

"What about your date? Those cookies are for him." Mrs. Bondini grabbed back the plate and went into Maureen's kitchen with the ease of long friendship. Setting them on the counter, she turned around, eyes bright with expectation.

Maureen followed, her, munching the rest of her cookie. "Want some tea? He cancelled."

Mrs. Bondini looked horrified. "Cancelled," she echoed. "Whatever for?"

Maureen filled the kettle and put it on the burner. "His daughter is sick. He has two children."

The older woman's eyes lit up. "He's a widower?"

"Divorced."

"Why doesn't his wife have the children?"

Maureen opened the cupboard and got out two mugs. "I don't know."

Mrs. Bondini moved out of her way. "Things have changed so," she muttered, shaking her head. "Families splitting up, fathers raising children." She pursed her lips. "Women of mature years living alone, when they should be happily married."

Maureen winced at the description, then stifled a grin as she got out the tea bags and sweetener. She had heard it all before. "It's a mixed-up world, all right," she agreed solemnly.

"Humph!" There was annoyance in the exclamation. Then the wrinkled face brightened. "Hmm, two children," she mused. "He needs a wife, a helpmate." She glanced at Maureen. "Maybe it's better, after all. You like children, don't you?"

"Please," Maureen implored her, ignoring the flash of pain as she wagged a finger. "Don't marry us off. I haven't even been out with Bailey, not really. He's just a friend." If she had any sense, she would make sure that's all he ever was.

Mrs. Bondini tossed her head and stalked to the living room to settle into her favorite chair. "Don't worry," she said over her stooped shoulder. "I won't give advice where it isn't appreciated."

Behind her, Maureen rolled her eyes and got out a tea tray.

"Is your television working?" Mrs. Bondini called from the other room. "Mine has funny lines across it, and my favorite show is about to start."

"I already told you," Bailey enunciated with exaggerated patience into the telephone receiver the next day. "She had a fever last night. She's still pale and I don't want you taking her."

"I'll keep her inside," his ex-wife said. "I promise. We'll just go to lunch and I'll bring the children back here to my motel room. Please, Bailey. Melissa will be just fine." Her voice had taken on a wheedling tone that Bailey despised. He remembered it too well from all the times she had made excuses because she had drunk the day away and forgotten everything else.

"No," he said. "You can't take them today. Melissa needs her rest, and Shawn and I are working on a science project for school tomorrow."

Angela hated not getting her own way. "You're just being selfish," she cried. "You want to keep them from me, so they'll forget all about their mother who loves them." Her voice ended on a sob.

Bailey clenched his teeth and motioned at Shawn, who had just come into the kitchen, to leave again. Shawn frowned and departed.

"You don't need my help for that. It wasn't me who kept you away from them for three years with no contact," Bailey ground out. "That was your own doing." He raked his fingers through his hair impatiently. He didn't want to be drawn into another argument. "I have to go. Shawn needs my help."

"Wait!" Angela wailed. "When can I see them?"

"Call tomorrow after work, and I'll see how Melissa's feeling." Without listening to her reply, he hung up. Then he took two deep breaths and vowed again not to let her get to him.

Shawn stuck his head through the kitchen door. "Done yet?"

"Yeah." Bailey curved his lips into a smile. "Let me check on your sister, and then we'll get started."

He went into his bedroom, where Melissa was tucked into the queen-size bed watching a nature show on his television. Bailey made sure she had the remote control.

"Remember," he said, feeling her forehead, which was much cooler, "as soon as this program is over you turn off the set and take a nap."

"Okay, Daddy."

"I'll be in the kitchen with Shawn." He stepped over Digger, who was collapsed on the carpet, and pulled the door almost shut behind him. He was glad it had only been a mild virus, but he still deplored the timing, thinking of Maureen and the evening with her that he had missed.

He and Shawn were almost done with the wiring on the science project when a knock sounded at the kitchen door. Bailey looked up to see Angela's face peering in through the window. Damn. Didn't she ever listen?

"Your mother's here," he told Shawn, who was concentrating on splicing two wires as Bailey had shown him. Shawn's head went up and he raced to the door.

"Mom! Come in!" He pulled it open and Angela stepped into the room, her gray eyes meeting Bailey's over Shawn's head. The expression on her beautiful face was smug. See, she seemed to be saying, my children still love me, even if you don't.

Angela began to unbutton the suede jacket she wore over faultlessly tailored cream slacks and a jade silk blouse that turned her red-blond hair, a shade brighter than her son's, to liquid fire.

"Don't bother," Bailey said in a cold voice. "You aren't staying."

"Da-ad!" Shawn's gaze went from one to the other.

Bailey moved closer to his son and put a hand on his shoulder. "I told your mom, when she called, that Melissa was sick and we were busy," he explained, looking into Shawn's confused face. "I set aside this afternoon to help you with your project."

"I'll only check on Melissa and take Shawn out for a quick ice-cream sundae," Angela interjected breathlessly. "I promise to have him back in a half hour."

Bailey knew all about her promises, but he could see that Shawn was becoming more upset by the minute. Now was not the time to try to explain anything, not with Angela interrupting with tempting offers.

"All right," Bailey relented. "But if Melissa's asleep, please don't wake her."

Angela gave him a wounded look as she crossed the kitchen. "You don't have to tell me how to act around my own children," she chided.

As she left the room, Bailey's fists tightened with frustration, threatening to snap in two the thick carpenter's pencil he had been holding. "Get your jacket," he told his son. When Shawn didn't move, Bailey forced a smile. "It's okay," he said. Shawn rewarded him with a wide grin.

Two hours later Bailey looked at the kitchen clock again and decided that first thing in the morning he would call his lawyer and find out what his rights were concerning Angela and the kids. He had wanted to call Maureen but kept putting it off, thinking that the moment he got her on the phone Shawn and his mother would return.

They still weren't back and Bailey was growing impatient.

As he reached for the receiver, deciding to chance it, he heard a car door slam. Moments later the front door burst open.

"Dad! Dad! Look what Mom bought me."

Bailey went into the living room, almost tripping over Digger, who was racing down the hall to see what the commotion was. Shawn had a model kit that he'd been saving his allowance toward for two months now.

"It's the bomber I wanted," he said, holding up the box so the picture of the old plane was facing Bailey. "Isn't it neat?"

"I thought you were going to buy that yourself." Bailey could hardly keep the annoyance from his voice.

"But now I don't have to," Shawn explained. "It would have taken me another three weeks to get the money, and now I don't have to wait."

Again Bailey's eyes flashed to Angela, whose mouth curved into a kittenish smirk. She had done it deliberately.

"I want to give Melissa her present," she said, brushing past him. "Then I'll go."

"Hold it!" Bailey grabbed her arm. "You told me you'd be back in half an hour."

She shrugged. "Shawn wanted to go to the toy store at the mall."

Bailey doubted seriously that it had been Shawn's idea. "Why are you here?" he demanded in a low voice, darting a glance at his son, who was immersed in the instructions to the model. "What do you want?"

Chapter Three

Angela's mouth thinned. "I want to see my kids. I've missed them, okay?" She wrenched free and moved quickly toward Melissa's room. Bailey was about to follow her, to head her off before she woke Melissa up, when the phone rang. Groaning with frustration, he glanced at Shawn, who was still oblivious.

Bailey hurried into the kitchen, muttering an oath.

"Hello," he snarled.

On the other end of the phone, Maureen raised her eyebrows and stared at the receiver. She had been right about not disturbing Bailey at home.

"I'm sorry," she said hesitantly. "I guess I've called at a bad time."

"No, no," he said. "It's okay." But his voice was still edged with annoyance.

"I just wondered how your little girl is feeling." Maureen was embarrassed. She should have obeyed her instinct and not bothered him.

"Melissa's much better. Thanks for asking."

There was a silence as Maureen tried to think of something else to say. Then Bailey muttered a low curse. "Can I call you back?"

"Sure," she said quickly. "I have to go, anyway. My cat wants out." Max rarely deigned to go outside, but Bailey didn't need to know that.

"Okay, bye," he said hanging up before she had time to reply.

Cheeks burning, Maureen returned to the papers she had been grading, trying to keep him out of her thoughts.

While she sat and stared blankly at the paragraphs written in mostly fractured French, Bailey was hurrying down the hall to his bedroom.

"I'm not a baby," Melissa wailed again. "I like big-girl dolls."

When he rushed into the room, Angela was holding a chubby baby doll in a cradle and staring at their daughter, who sat up in Bailey's bed with her arms folded across her candy-striped nightgown, a mutinous expression on her face. It was all Bailey could do not to burst into laughter at the scene. He controlled himself, knowing that Melissa's tender feelings would be hurt more than ever if he laughed.

Both of the females in the room turned to stare at him.

"How have you been raising my daughter?" Angela demanded.

"Daddy, tell her I'm too old for baby dolls," Melissa pleaded at the same time.

"*I* know, honey," he said in a soothing voice.

Angela shot him a venomous look. She stuffed the offending doll under one arm and bent over Melissa, kissing the air by her cheek. "I'll call you later, baby."

"I'm *not* a baby."

Rolling her eyes, Angela left the room. After sending Melissa a reassuring wink, Bailey followed his ex-wife down the hall.

"If you're going to be in town long, we'll need to set up some kind of schedule," he said firmly. "This dropping in whenever you feel like it is too disruptive."

To his surprise, Angela whirled and grabbed his arm. "I've come back to stay, sweetheart. I'm not drinking anymore, and I want to come home."

Bailey froze, staring. Her words had taken him completely by surprise. Before he could speak, Shawn called him from the living room.

"Dad, Digger just puked on the rug."

Bailey pushed by Angela. "Now is not the time to discuss this. I think the best thing would be for you to leave."

Angela's eyes filled with tears. Before she could reply, Shawn called again from the living room.

"Please," Bailey grated, glancing back at her. "Unless you'd rather stay and clean up after the dog."

Angela hurried past him, slamming the front door behind her without saying goodbye to Shawn.

It was hours later and the kids were finally settled into bed when Bailey was able to give a thought to Maureen and his offer to call her back. He glanced at the clock and groaned, wondering if she turned in early on Sunday nights. Then he went into the kitchen and stared at the phone. He hated not being able to explain things in person, and he wished that he could just go over and see her for a few moments. He thought of calling Jennifer to stay with the children, but then he remembered the time. She had school tomorrow, too.

Frustrated, Bailey flipped off the kitchen light. His attempt at smoothing things over with Maureen would just have to keep until he could watch her face and try to read her expression, not plead his case over an impersonal telephone. Remembering the glimpse of wariness he had seen in her eyes he suspected she had been hurt before, and badly. He wanted to make sure she understood him.

As Bailey waited for Digger to make a last circuit of the backyard before settling in for the night, he let his racing thoughts return to Angela and her startling announcement. The idea of taking her back chilled him. When he had been struggling to keep family and business afloat, and doing neither with any level of competence while he got used to coping without a wife, he would have given anything to hear that she wanted to come home. Now her announcement only made him furious. How dare she drop back into their lives like a disruptive virus? Did she really expect him to seriously consider taking her back after three years of total silence?

Knowing Angela, she probably did. But it was way too late for them. Bailey would treat her with the consideration she deserved as the kids' mother, but that was it. Even before she had left, he knew that whatever love he had once felt for her was gone, killed by her drinking and their bitter arguments. Maybe she had sensed his feelings; perhaps that knowledge had added to her inability to deal with the everyday responsibilities of their life. Bailey was quite sure that *he* wasn't entirely blameless, either, but he had never considered walking out, as some men might. As Angela herself had.

When she took off he had stayed and done his best to reassure their children, who were shattered almost beyond bearing by their mother's desertion. And now, when they finally seemed to be recovering, she was here again to stir them up, undermining him and making him furious.

What would Angela do, when she realized that she could no longer have him back? That she couldn't erase her mistakes with a tearful apology and make everything okay? Bailey's knuckles turned white on the doorknob as he locked up after Digger's return. The hell with her reaction. He was way past caring.

Bailey swore under his breath as he followed the dog quietly to Shawn's room. Digger looked up at him and snuffled before he nosed his way into the bedroom and settled with a soft thump on the carpet, where he slept every night by Shawn's bed. With a heart full of love, Bailey stared at his sleeping son for a timeless moment before shutting the door gently and moving on to Melissa's room.

He bent over her bed, studying her long lashes and rounded cheeks in the light from the hallway. While Bailey watched, she murmured in her sleep and opened her eyes.

"'Night, princess," he whispered, pressing a kiss to her forehead, grateful that her skin was no longer hot with fever.

"'Night, Daddy," she echoed, already halfway back to dreamland.

For a moment Bailey watched her, then he tiptoed out, taking care to shut the door softly behind him.

No way, he thought. Angela had a right to visit the children as long as she accepted his rules, but he wouldn't let her disrupt the life he had built with them. He was in charge now.

* * *

Maureen was returning from a brisk walk early Monday evening, panting lightly and too warm in the baggy sweats that had seemed just right when she left the apartment three-quarters of an hour before. As she crossed the street she glanced up at her front door and saw Bailey waiting on the steps.

She ran a hand across her perspiring forehead, licked her dry lips and groaned softly. From the looks of his crisp shirt and familiar faded jeans, if *he* had worked up a sweat that day he'd taken the time to shower it away.

"Hi," she called, noticing his serious expression. She was about to ask anxiously about his daughter, when his face was transformed by an answering grin.

"Hi, yourself," he said as she joined him at her doorstep, digging into a pocket for her house key. "I hope you don't mind that I just stopped by. I took the kids to my sister's for supper and she had rented a movie, something from Walt Disney, I think. So I took a chance and sneaked over."

He sounded slightly breathless. Maureen wondered if he could possibly be unsure of himself. Did men who looked like Bailey ever question their welcome?

"I've been walking," she explained unnecessarily.

"So I gathered. I was about to leave when I spotted you coming down the street. I really need to talk to you."

She opened the door to her apartment, glad she kept it neat. "Come in."

"Thanks." Bailey stopped inside the doorway, squatting down to extend a hand to Max, who had been coming to meet her when he noticed Bailey and froze.

"I'm afraid he takes a while to warm up to strangers," Maureen said, as Max walked over to Bailey and butted against his extended hand.

"Usually," she added with a wry grin as Max began to purr. Apparently the man's lethal charm extended to animals.

Bailey scratched behind the cat's ears before straightening. "This is nice," he said, glancing around. "A far cry from my house."

Maureen wondered if his home was shabby or just cluttered. She pictured muddy footprints across her own beige carpeting and grape-juice stains on the couch. Then she reminded herself that those things were only a small part of raising children, a consideration that the rewards of having a family completely overshadowed. Muddy footprints would be a small price to pay for the unconditional love one shared with a child. Not to mention the child's father. She looked at Bailey as longing curled within her.

"Thanks," she managed. "I'm glad you like it. Want some juice?"

"Sure," he said, "if it isn't too much trouble."

"No trouble. Come on out to the kitchen." She opened the door of the fridge and grabbed a bottle of grapefruit juice, as Bailey settled onto a rattan bar stool at one end of the counter.

"I'm sorry about last night," she said, handing him a full glass. "I called at a bad time." She pulled the ponytail holder from her hair and tried to smooth the damp strands with her fingers.

"No," he corrected, watching her hands move restlessly. "Well, I guess you did, but it wasn't your fault. My ex-wife had come by, and I wasn't in the best of moods. I'm sorry I took it out on you."

"She's still around, then." Maureen hoped he would say more about her. Like how he felt, and how long they had been divorced.

"Actually, she's back," Bailey said in a grim tone. "She took off three years ago, without so much as a 'see you,' and she popped up a few weeks ago, just when I thought the kids were finally used to her being gone."

Maureen didn't know what to say. "That must be hard on all of you."

He took a long swallow of juice. "It's Shawn and Melissa that I worry about."

She was dying to ask more questions, but didn't. Obviously talking about the situation didn't improve his mood. Maybe that was good, at least from Maureen's point of view. When he remained silent, she cast about for something else to say. "I'm glad you came by," was the best she could do.

His grin flashed as she sipped at her juice and wished she didn't look like she had just run twenty miles.

"I'm sorry I didn't call you back," he said. "But I wanted to explain in person. I hate trying to talk about things like that on the phone, and I didn't want to wait until tomorrow night." His dark eyes pinned hers.

Maureen smiled, waiting.

For a moment he kept staring, then he dropped his gaze to the juice glass he was absently rotating in a circle on the counter. Maureen took advantage of the lull to grab a towel and blot her neck and face.

"You probably want a shower," he said, rising.

"No! I mean, do you have to leave already?"

Their gazes met in silent communication. Bailey relaxed, sitting back down. "I have a few more minutes, but I need to get back to my sister's before the movie's over."

Maureen took the stool next to him, turning to study his profile before he shifted. It was noble, dependable. He was a complex man, capable of both great tenderness and powerful determination. Then he turned to look full at her once again, and something heated arced between them. She swallowed, shifting her own gaze away from the sudden blaze in his eyes. Neither of them spoke.

After a long moment, Bailey broke the silence. "Damned if I know what she's up to," he began abruptly, rubbing his neck as if his ex-wife made it ache. "But I'm not tolerating much more from her. The kids are already stirred up."

Maureen remained silent, trying to look understanding. She was dying to ask how he felt about this woman, the mother of his children. As she studied his thick lashes, the high curve of his cheek, the hard line of his jaw, her fingers itched to touch his mustache. Was it soft or bristly? How could any woman leave him without regrets? Maybe that was why this Angela was back. Because she had regrets.

While Maureen watched him, Bailey's expression hardened, his eyes chilling over. Their coldness made Maureen want to shiver. Bailey would be a dangerous man when crossed.

"I love my kids." His voice was edged with resolve.

"Of course you do." Without thinking, she leaned closer, stroking his hard forearm. It was hot beneath her touch, the dark hairs springy.

"I don't want to see them hurt anymore," he said firmly. Then he stood and jammed his hands into his pockets as he paced restlessly across her small kitchen.

"I shouldn't be talking so much," he continued, stopping across the counter from her. "My life must seem pretty hectic to you. But I wanted to say..." His voice trailed off as he stared into her eyes.

"Aw, hell," he said softly, reaching out a hand to cup her chin. His fingers were gentle. "I might not have the right, and you'd probably be smart to run like the devil, but I haven't been so interested in anyone for a very long time. Maybe never.'' He flashed that devastating, dimpled grin. "Perhaps I can persuade you to overlook all the baggage I seem to come with, and..." Once again his voice trailed away, as he stared at her mouth.

It was all Maureen could do to keep from moistening her lips with her tongue. Where was all her caution now? Instead she croaked, "And what?"

Bailey tore his gaze from her mouth. "Be patient," he said, releasing her chin.

Maureen let out the breath she had been holding, ignoring the little burst of disappointment deep inside her. "Any chance for a reconciliation?" she asked.

He frowned. "Oh, you mean Angela." Maureen felt herself tense until he shook his head. "No."

She relaxed slowly, reaching for his hand. "Friends?" she asked softly as he enfolded her fingers in a warm grip. To her surprise, instead of shaking her hand to seal the bargain, he pulled lightly. When she leaned forward, he bent his head and touched his lips gently to hers. A spark of heat seared her mouth, as his mustache tickled her sensitive skin.

"Damn," he muttered thickly. "I knew I was kidding myself." With that he released her hand and moved quickly around the end of the counter. "Come here," he commanded in a low voice, standing before her.

Heart thumping like a drum, Maureen slid off the bar stool into his waiting arms.

Like a wary animal scenting danger, Bailey studied her from beneath lowered lids for a timeless moment. Then he leaned toward her. Maureen's eyes fluttered shut. His mouth was warm, smooth as velvet, settling over hers like a sigh. Her whole being turned to liquid as he kissed her, her mouth clinging to his, needy. His arms tightened and she slid her hands around his waist as her breasts settled against the hard wall of his chest, tingling sensations radiating through her like electric shocks.

Bailey lifted his mouth and she moaned, bereft, her eyes shut tight. His warm breath drifted over her face, then his mouth took hers again. The kiss was rougher, hotter, one of his big hands sliding to her hips to pull her against him. A tremor shook him and he deepened the kiss, stroking her tongue with his own, tasting, teasing.

Swamped by sensation, Maureen returned his caresses, enjoying the feel of him. Bailey's hands moved restlessly, glided up, across her shoulders and back down to her waist, as Maureen hung on tight, giving and taking with mindless hunger.

Finally, as reason was making its last appeal to Maureen's befuddled senses, Bailey pulled away and buried his face against her neck, shuddering as he dragged in long gulps of air.

"You're so sweet," he murmured, voice thick, as his hands smoothed down her back and settled at her waist.

She eased away from him, aware once again of her dampened, rumpled state. Sanity returned, and with it, embarrassment. How had she lost control so quickly, after years of discipline that had never been this sorely tempted by rising desire?

He crooked a finger beneath her chin, urging her to meet his gaze. When she did his thumb brushed her mouth.

"You're a very special woman," he said.

She opened her mouth but wasn't sure what to say. She shrugged lightly, cheeks warming.

"I have to go." His voice was edged with regret. "There never seems to be enough time. That's one thing I haven't gotten used to." His hands gripped her shoulders for a moment and then released them. "I want to see you again, take you out on a real date."

"Sure," Maureen said, surprised. She had been wondering if perhaps the return of his ex-wife had something to do with his not asking her again. Had thought that maybe he still cared about Angela more than he wanted to admit, even to himself.

Bailey grinned. "Good. How do you feel about pizza and the new suspense movie that's playing out at the mall tomorrow night? Naw, we have classes. The next night? Six o'clock? That will give me time to pick Melissa up from Brownies first." He arched a brow as he gazed down at Maureen.

"Perfect. I have a weakness for scary movies." She returned his smile.

Curling an arm around her waist, he moved toward the front door. "After Angela left, when I first thought about dating again I felt like I was back in high school."

"I know what you mean," Maureen agreed. "If you think about it, dating is a rather bizarre social custom."

Bailey grinned down at her. "As long as you don't mind participating in this 'bizarre custom' with me. I'm glad I came over."

"I am, too," she echoed.

He dropped a kiss onto her nose. "See you tomorrow night." Then he was gone, bounding down the front steps. At the street he turned to wave. Maureen returned the salute, smiling despite herself. Part of her wished he had stayed, but her sensible side heaved a sigh of relief that he'd left, taking temptation with him. At least for now.

Thank goodness Mrs. Bondini was at bingo.

After sharing a spicy, gooey pan pizza at a small Italian restaurant Maureen had never been to before, she and

Bailey went to the multiscreen theatre complex and prepared to watch the show, with cold drinks and a bucket of popcorn. As the lights went down, Bailey wedged the container between his leg and the side of his seat, and squeezed her hand. His presence next to her in the dark and the tempting scent of his cologne were heady distractions, and she had to concentrate hard on the movie.

Bailey set the popcorn, which Maureen hadn't touched, on the floor and slid his arm along the seat behind her. She felt him looking at her, but suddenly self-conscious, didn't turn her head. After a few moments, he returned his attention to the screen.

To her disappointment, the movie relied more on bloodcurdling special effects than well-plotted suspense, but even that wasn't enough to dim the evening's sparkle. Bailey's arm pressed her shoulder absently whenever the soundtrack foreshadowed an especially gruesome event on the screen before them. At one such incident, Maureen had squeezed her eyes shut. When she opened them cautiously she was surprised to see Bailey peering at her.

"Too much blood?" he whispered, leaning close. His breath bathed her cheek as his lips all but nuzzled her ear.

"Weak stomach," she admitted. "I thought this movie was something different." She suppressed the shiver his nearness brought.

"Me, too. Want to leave?" In the dimness his eyes looked black.

She nodded. "Do you mind?"

He shook his head and stood, quickly escorting her from the theatre. In the lobby they dumped their cups and the remainder of the popcorn in the trash container by the door. Instead of taking her hand, Bailey put his arm around her shoulders.

"Sorry about the movie," he said as they walked to his car. "I thought it was a thriller, not special effects run amok."

Maureen was warm all down the side that brushed against his hard body. "Teenagers seem to enjoy all that gore," she said as he unlocked her door.

"Yes, and I'm not sure why."

Maureen slid into the car, waiting until he had joined her. "Neither am I. All that blood . . ."

"It's not really blood, you know," he teased. "Red food coloring."

"And I suppose the maggots were only grains of rice."

Bailey's grin and the gleam in his eye were doing things to her pulse rate. He shrugged, fastening his seat belt. "I'd rather think they were." He put the key into the ignition and turned to her. "Remember the old days before bucket seats and seat belts, when the girl snuggled next to her date in the car?"

Maureen stared into his lean face. "Mm-hm."

His finger traced a line down her cheek. Then he turned. "I would have liked that better," he said softly, starting the engine.

Music from the radio swirled around them as Maureen absorbed what he had said. She would have preferred it, too.

When they got back to her apartment, Bailey took her keys and opened the door, as she waited breathlessly beside him. The evening spent in his company had made her more aware than ever of the strong physical attraction between them.

"It's late," he commented, "so I won't stay."

He was assuming she would have invited him in. Well, perhaps she would have. But his sitter probably needed to get home. School tomorrow. Maureen stared into his dark eyes, thinking that at the moment it was difficult to think of him as a parent.

Bailey was studying her face in the glow from the porch light.

"I had a nice time," she said.

To Maureen's surprise, he took her elbow and urged her into the open doorway. Reaching around her, he clicked off the switch, plunging the entry into relative darkness. Then he rested his hands on her shoulders, his thumbs braced beneath her chin. "So did I." His voice was deep, his gaze intent.

Sudden heat washed over her as she remembered the way his kiss had made her feel. Maureen lifted her face to meet his descending mouth. Bailey's hands shifted to frame her jaw, holding her still as he gently pressed his lips to hers. The tenderness of the kiss was her undoing. As she relaxed against him, she heard his breath catch. His arms went around her and his lips shifted against hers. What had begun as a simple good night became a sensual feast. Her mouth opened beneath his, and the heat ignited her senses. His tongue searched deftly, stroking hers, withdrawing, then plunging again. His arms tightened. For a timeless moment Maureen forgot where they were, as everything but Bailey faded. He groaned, then ended the scorching kiss.

Maureen made a sound of longing as his lips drifted to her cheek and then to her throat, stringing tiny kisses along her sensitized skin.

He sucked in a breath, then set her away from him. "I didn't mean to start this," he murmured, gazing down at her in the faint glow from a living-room lamp she'd left on. "But when I kiss you, I can't seem to stop."

Maureen ducked her head, unable to speak.

He sighed and touched her hair. "I know it's too soon," he said, "and I won't push you. I'd better leave."

"Good night," she managed to murmur.

He echoed her words, voice husky, then tucked her inside, pulling the door shut behind him. Maureen leaned against the closed panel until she heard his car pull away. Only then did she notice Max rubbing determinedly against her leg.

Picking up the cat and absently stroking his soft fur, she wandered into the kitchen to look out the window. Street lamps, the glow from other windows and an occasional pair of headlights brightened the dark scene below. Maureen stared until Max squirmed to get down. Then she moved to the counter and stood in front of the bleached wood cabinet, trying to remember what she had been going to do. Giving up, she went into the living room and sank down onto the couch, cuddling a throw pillow in her arms. Max immediately jumped up and curled into a large, fluffy lump in her lap.

"This is getting complicated," she told him, bemused.

Max merely stared, unblinking.

With a dreamy smile, Maureen remembered the way Bailey's arms had felt around her, the heated caress of his mouth and the warm approval in his dark eyes. It would be easy to forget all her carefully developed defenses and allow herself to be swept away by feelings alone. It would be easy at the time, but she knew herself well enough to realize that for her the aftermath would be devastating.

Since her divorce she had become extremely careful about relationships. Control was important to her, and perhaps subconsciously she had made sure she was in no danger of losing it. Losing control, caring too much, could bring endless heartache and wrenching loneliness. She had learned that lesson the hard way.

Perhaps Bailey was different. But what made him so special? Just because he came with a ready-made family to love, a family to replace what had been snatched away from her under the cruelest of circumstances, was no reason for her to abandon good sense. Who could say if the two of them would have anything in common besides fondness for pizza and a sizzling mutual attraction? Not much on which to build a relationship.

"If I were smart," Maureen told Max, waking him, "I'd run the other way, and fast." A sense of dread touched her with an icy finger. If she wasn't careful, she could end up badly hurt again. The possibility was one she was beginning to realize she had been avoiding, telling herself instead it was only a desire to be independent that had kept her alone.

Maureen released a trembling sigh. "Why don't I want to do the smart thing?"

Max didn't bother to reply.

Then next weekend Bailey spent all of Saturday with his children, taking them to the zoo and lunch, stopping at a huge toy store to browse on the way home. On Sunday Angela picked them up, and Bailey arranged to collect them later at her motel.

With the whole day facing him, he looked out at the lawn that needed to be mowed, thought about the paperwork he had brought home and not touched, and shifted restlessly.

He reached for the phone, punching out a series of numbers. Then he swore when it rang and rang.

Returning Digger's soulful stare, Bailey grabbed his car keys. "I need a break," he said to the dog, who followed him outside, wagging his tail with apparent approval as Bailey left him in the fenced backyard.

Slapping the steering wheel to the beat of the car radio, Bailey drove to Maureen's. Perhaps she was close by, somewhere in the neighborhood. He had the idea of persuading her to join him for a walk along the beach and a late lunch. The sun was breaking through the clouds and the wind had slowed to a playful breeze.

When Bailey pulled around the back of her building, he saw Maureen walking toward her car carrying a bucket of soapy water. She glanced up and a smile broke across her face.

"You're just in time," she said when he shut off the motor and joined her. "Four hands work faster than two." She glanced at his jeans, T-shirt and worn tennis shoes. "You're even dressed for it."

Bailey was almost too busy admiring her slim hips and long legs in her own tight jeans to reply. "What's in it for me?" he asked in a teasing voice as she set down the bucket and stood facing him, hands braced against her narrow waist. His question obviously surprised her.

"What do you want?" she demanded, then blushed deeply.

Bailey's grin widened. "Your mind works in fascinating patterns."

Maureen shook her head. "Maybe we should begin again."

Stepping closer, Bailey allowed his fingers to touch the silken strands of her hair, pulled back with a band and falling straight to her shoulders. "Actually what I had in mind was picking up some food and heading down to the water, maybe walking on the beach if the sun stays out."

Maureen glanced over at his dusty car. "Let's wash them both," she suggested. "Then we'll see."

He picked up the coiled hose that lay on the ground and glanced around for an outside faucet.

"Over there," Maureen pointed.

Moments later, she finished soaping the hood of her car and reached for the hose. Bailey was crouched on the other side, scrubbing the whitewalls. Moving quietly, she gave in to temptation, took aim and squeezed the trigger on the nozzle.

"Hey!" Bailey exclaimed, jumping out of the way as the icy spray overshot the car's hood.

"Oh, sorry," Maureen exclaimed, releasing the trigger and trying not to grin.

Scowling fiercely, Bailey began to circle the coupe, watching her intently. In his hand he held a dripping sponge.

Maureen giggled, trying to hide her smile behind her free hand. "I said I was sorry."

"Not good enough." He stopped, eyeing the hose.

Maureen began to back away. "Stop or I'll shoot," she threatened.

Bailey kept coming. The nozzle slipped out of her hand and she grabbed for it, trying to point the hose at Bailey.

With a shout, he charged. Screaming, she dropped it and ran, darting around his car. She glanced back. Bailey tossed the sponge into the bucket as he passed, then slowed to stalk her.

"I'm unarmed," Maureen exclaimed, laughing.

"Like hell you are." His voice was a low growl, his eyes gleamed darkly and his mouth below the buccaneer's mustache curved into a devilish grin.

Maureen feinted one way and then ran the other. Bailey dashed after her. She shrieked as his big hands caught her waist from behind. Turning her around, he pushed her lightly against the side of his car.

"Gotcha."

They were both breathing hard. Maureen trembled in reaction to their game, as Bailey glanced up at the building. "I wonder if anyone's watching," he murmured.

"Who cares?" she said boldly.

"I don't." His head descended. He pressed against her. Maureen's arms slid around his neck and she welcomed his kiss. For a moment their mouths melded hotly. His heart thudded against her breast. Awakening passion coiled low in her belly and she could feel the shuddering response of his hard body as he moved even closer.

Maureen moaned. Bailey lifted his mouth and swore under his breath. He stepped back, glancing around as he raised an unsteady hand to touch her cheek. For a moment they just looked at each other. Finally Maureen's breathing began to slow.

"I'm not going to apologize," Bailey said in a low voice.

Maureen shook her head, unable to speak. Whatever he saw in her eyes made him smile crookedly. "Let's finish the cars," he said after a moment.

She managed to smile brightly. "Good idea."

"This time *I* man the hose," Bailey said firmly, walking away. "It's not that I don't trust you, but..." He let his voice trail off as he picked up the nozzle.

"Revenge is petty," Maureen reminded him, staying on the other side of his car.

"Don't worry. The sooner we're done, the sooner we eat. Right?"

She returned his smile, relieved that they had recaptured the light mood. "Right."

When both cars were washed, they bought deli sandwiches and cans of cold pop, taking an impromptu picnic to the beach to watch the gulls and the waves. Sitting side by side on a blanket taken from Bailey's trunk, their backs against a log, they finished the food and talked lazily of unimportant things.

When Bailey rose regretfully and extended a hand Maureen was sorely tempted to invite him back to her apartment, but she knew he had to pick up his children. At her front door he left her with a quick kiss, and an unreadable expression on his hard face. Maureen's feelings were hopelessly confused.

Despite her earlier concern that she wouldn't be able to concentrate around him, she spent two evenings that week, after he was finished with Little League turnout, helping him study for his Spanish midterm. After each session they shared a heated embrace, but Bailey was careful to leave before things could get out of hand. His sense of timing was becoming a real sore point with Maureen, who found herself fantasizing about more than passionate kisses.

The next evening she saw him after class. His dark brows were pulled into a frown that barely faded when he answered her greeting. Concerned by his obvious black mood, she invited him over to share the rhubarb pie that Mrs. Bondini had brought her.

"Maybe I'd better not," he said, refusing to meet Maureen's gaze. Then before she could ask why, he changed his mind abruptly. "Okay, sure. Why not?"

Maureen peered at him anxiously. Why not, indeed? There were lines of tension around his mouth, and his eyes seemed shadowed.

"Is everything okay?"

"Yeah," he said. "Just fine." His lips stretched into a smile that didn't reach his eyes as they walked to the parking lot.

Maureen began wondering as Bailey followed her home, if he was starting to regret their friendship. Did his hesitation, his bad mood, have something to do with shifting feelings toward her? The thought made Maureen's insides tighten. Maybe he wasn't sure what to say to her, she thought anxiously.

But wait a minute. Why would he feel differently? They'd been getting along well, becoming closer. She was probably just being paranoid, her self-confidence going the way of her cool independence and her common sense, both seriously weakened since Bailey's entrance into her life. If Maureen wasn't careful, next she'd be doodling his name in the margins of her school papers.

At her apartment Bailey followed her silently to the kitchen, dropping into a chair and stretching his long legs beneath the table, then bending to scratch behind Max's ears. Maureen watched him closely as she made tea and dished up the pie. He definitely seemed preoccupied with something.

Tired of being ignored, Maureen thrust out her chin as she set the plates on the table with a bang.

"Thanks," Bailey said absently, glancing up and flashing her another empty smile.

Maureen wanted to scream. Instead she sat down and began poking at her dessert with her fork. Across from her, Bailey studied his as if trying to recall what it was.

"Still worried about Spanish?" she asked, sipping her tea. Her voice sounded shaky, even to her. She cleared her throat. Talk to me, she begged silently, watching him.

He seemed to come back from a long way off, blinking as he focused on her face. "I'm sorry," he said after a moment, turning his attention to his plate. "I guess I have a lot on my mind."

Maureen's stiff smile turned into a frown of concern as she studied his bent head, dark hair shining richly in the light. "Is it the children? Is something wrong with one of them?" She knew how much they meant to him.

Bailey sighed and pushed his plate away. To her surprise, there was a shadow in his eyes. She abandoned her selfish concerns as he raked a hand over his face, leaned back and gazed out the window. A nerve flickered in his cheek.

"I found out what Angela's up to," he muttered grimly, just as Maureen was beginning to think he'd forgotten about her presence altogether. His fingers curled into a fist on the table, knuckles white.

Maureen leaned forward, really worried now. "What?"

His expression was angry as he stared into her face. "She wants to take the kids. My ex-wife is suing me for full custody."

Chapter Four

"Oh, Bailey, I'm sorry. Could Angela win custody?"

He was grateful for Maureen's concern. For a moment he simply sat and stared, absorbing the tenderness that showed so plainly on her beautiful face. Her blue eyes had darkened beneath the anxious frown that pinched the smooth skin of her forehead. To Bailey her interest was like a balm, soothing and sweet.

"She won't win if I have anything to say about it. And not without a fight."

Bailey's harsh tone made Maureen catch her breath, hoping that he'd never have cause to turn his anger against her. His expression was formidable, strong jaw knotted, eyes narrowed. Without thinking, she touched his hand. Immediately his face cleared, as he glanced down.

"Enough about my problems," he said, raising a bite of pie to his mouth. "We can't let this luscious dessert go to waste. Did you bake it?"

"No, my neighbor did, the same sweet lady who delights in nagging me mercilessly about my single state." Realizing what she had just said, Maureen felt the heat climb into her cheeks. Bailey would think she was looking for a husband!

Instead, he just chuckled. "I know what you mean. My buddies' wives act as if I'm fouling up the whole procreational system by not remarrying." He covered her hand with his own on the kitchen table. "We single folk have to stick together."

Maureen couldn't resist a response to the gleam in his eyes. "Sounds like a terrific idea to me." Sticking around Bailey was no hardship.

He finished his pie and emitted a gusty sigh. "As usual," he said with a wry grin as he glanced at the sturdy watch on his tanned wrist, "I'd better get home." He drained his coffee cup and scraped back his chair.

Maureen rose quickly, awareness of him flooding her senses. In the short time she had known Bailey, he had become important to her. When they were together it was easy to forget the risks, to forget how painful emotional involvement could be.

"Thanks for listening," Bailey said, wrapping his arms around her and pulling her close to his big body. "I promise that next time I'll be in a better mood."

Before Maureen could tell him not to worry about it, he had released her and was speaking again. "I'm taking the kids to the Seattle Center Friday afternoon for a showing of local Native American art. Want to come with us?"

It wasn't the first time he had suggested that Maureen meet his children, but she had been reluctant to do so. As long as she didn't know Shawn and Melissa, it was easier to remain detached. This time though, the decision not to meet them wasn't hers to make.

"Sorry, I have a staff meeting at four on Friday. One I can't miss."

"Another time, then," Bailey said, looking disappointed.

"Sure." Maureen's gaze flicked away from his direct one. He hadn't said anything yet, but he was bound to notice her apparent lack of enthusiasm soon. Bailey's children were obviously the most important part of his life, a part it would be natural for him to want to share with a woman he liked. And he seemed to like Maureen. If he was interested only in a brief encounter would he be so insistent that she meet his children?

Bailey walked with her toward the front door, watching the telltale color bloom on her sculpted cheeks. Should he push it or let it slide? Was Maureen one of those people who just didn't like children, or was something else bothering her? Not one to avoid anything just because it was difficult, he decided to forge ahead.

"Are you always going to be busy when my kids are involved, or has this all just been coincidence?" He reached out to lace his fingers with hers. "They're important to me, and so are you. I want you to get to know them, that's all." His gaze searched hers. "Is it so difficult?"

He waited while she bent to pat Max, who had followed them into the room. The sleek Siamese butted his head against her hand, purring. Then to Bailey's relief she straightened, her blue eyes searching his.

"I haven't been around many children in the past few years," she said. "Oh, I know my share, but not well, I guess. The thought of meeting yours, and wanting to make a good impression, intimidates me."

Bailey let out the breath he hadn't realized he'd been holding. "Is that all? I was beginning to think perhaps you didn't like kids."

Maureen answered his smile with a sad one of her own. "I'm sure that yours are very special," she said after a slight hesitation. How could she explain that she was *afraid* to meet them? Afraid they might steal her heart, as he was doing. The memory of other wrenching losses, one the star of a dozen memories, one a nameless heartache, intruded briefly. She struggled to overcome the tears that threatened.

Bailey would never understand the kind of cowardice that held her in its frozen embrace. When threatened he would fight, not run. The danger of losing custody of his children would only make him love them more, hold them tighter. If he lost, he would survive. Maureen wasn't so sure any more that she could. As she cast about for something else to say, Bailey spoke again.

"Don't worry about Shawn and Melissa, okay? When the time is right, they'll adore you. They're good kids." His hand went to the doorknob. "Thanks again for the pie and the company."

Maureen ached to reassure him about his custody worries, but couldn't think what to say. "Anytime. I'm a good listener."

Bailey's smile flashed. "Yes, you are." He dropped a kiss onto her nose. "Angela might not even file. Her attention span isn't that long, and she's been gone for quite a while without contact. That won't work in her favor."

The mantel clock pinged the hour softly and he glanced at its round face. "There I go getting sidetracked when I should be sending the sitter home right now." Bailey settled his hands on Maureen's shoulders. "Thanks, again," he said softly. "My life is usually busy, but not this hectic. It will smooth out again soon, one way or the other." For a moment his expression was grim, and Maureen knew what he meant.

"It will work out," she told him.

"It has to."

Their eyes met in wordless understanding. Then she raised her mouth to his, distracting him with great success.

Bailey was good at working casual meetings with Maureen into his schedule. They almost always got together during the break in evening classes, and unless Maureen had to confer with a student, they saw each other afterward, too. Bailey often stopped by her apartment, always calling first.

Over coffee or a plate of Mrs. Bondini's cookies, they had lively discussions about all the things they seemed to disagree on, books, art and music. Their tastes were almost universally dissimilar, but Maureen enjoyed their talks nearly as much as she did watching Bailey's eyes light up with enthusiasm, or the way his mouth moved, or the gestures his strong hands made when he was trying to prove a point. Bailey's interests, though different from hers, were easily as varied, and now that she knew him better, he didn't remind her of her former husband, at all.

"I never realized that anything so lovely could be made from glass," Maureen told Bailey one afternoon as they left a gallery in Everett. Several artists from the world-famous Pilchuck School, which was located only a few miles away, were showing there. "The colors and patterns take my breath away."

Bailey took her hand as they crossed the street to his car. They'd managed to steal a couple of hours, he from work and she after her last class. "I'm glad you went with me," he said, holding her car door wide. "Perhaps we'll make it to the open house the school puts on every summer. I've been told the grounds are beautiful, and we could take a picnic."

The thought occurred to Maureen that it sounded like the ideal kind of outing to share with his children, but she didn't say anything. He hadn't suggested again that she meet them; the pressure she felt was of her own making.

"How did Shawn do on the science project you helped him with?" she asked as Bailey started the car and pulled away from the curb. She wished they had time for an early meal together, but knew that he had to go back to work.

Bailey glanced at her and smiled, his expression sending a warm response dancing across her nerve endings. "Shawn got an A-minus," he said proudly. "And he said he guessed it would be okay if I wanted to help him again sometime."

Maureen managed an appreciative chuckle, envying Bailey the closeness he shared with his children. During her marriage she'd had an unplanned pregnancy that ended in a miscarriage. Shortly after that she and her husband had gone through a bitter divorce. Even now Maureen often wondered what her life would have been like if the child had lived.

Banishing the painful memories, she distracted herself by studying Bailey, seated beside her. His strong, tanned arms were bare and smooth beneath the short sleeves of his striped shirt, hands resting on the wheel. Below his flat stomach the long muscles of his thigh, encased in worn jeans, flexed smoothly as he shifted his foot from accelerator to brake and back again. When Maureen returned her attention to his face, Bailey's dark eyes met hers. "I wish I didn't have to go back to work right away," he said. "If it wasn't for the PTA meeting at school this evening I could put in a few hours then, instead."

"I understand," Maureen said, placing her hand in his when he extended it. "But I do wish we had more time."

Bailey's heated gaze touched her mouth for an instant. "Me, too." His voice had taken on a husky tone and his grip on her hand tightened for a moment before he released it. "Brownies and Boy Scouts are over for the summer, but baseball starts next week. I hope you can make it to some of Shawn's games."

His words brought back the memory of another little boy who'd loved baseball. "Sounds like I'll have to go to the ballpark if I want to see anything of you at all," Maureen said in a deliberately teasing voice.

Bailey's expression, as he drew up in front of her apartment, was as potent as a kiss. "I'd find the time for you, no matter what," he said as he reached for her. Right before he leaned close, Maureen saw Mrs. Bondini coming down the street, a big smile on her lined face.

"Nice young man," Mrs. Bondini remarked after Maureen had introduced them and Bailey had driven away. "You can always tell a man by his eyes, and your Bailey has friendly eyes."

"He's not 'my Bailey,' " Maureen felt compelled to protest. "Our relationship is very casual."

"If you say so, dear," Mrs. Bondini said over her shoulder as she unlocked her front door and went inside. "I'll see you later."

Maureen handed her the grocery sack she'd carried up the steps, feeling hopelessly flustered. As she went into her own apartment, bending absently to scratch Max's head when he came to greet her, she muttered, "I hope I'm not getting in too deep."

Max's expression when he returned her worried gaze was indifferent to her dilemma. "Meow," he said.

* * *

"Come on, Melissa," Bailey urged from the living room. "We have several errands to run and we don't have all day."

It was Saturday and he was taking both kids to the mall. They had to pick out a birthday present for Melissa to take to a party that afternoon, and get a new batting glove for Shawn, who had practice. Bailey had hoped to see Maureen that evening, but she was busy with a wedding shower for one of the other teachers. The shower was definitely a ladies-only event.

It was just as well that she was busy. Jennifer, Bailey's usual sitter, was going on a date and he hated to leave the children with a stranger. Maureen had promised to call him when she got home, and this time he would have to be content with that.

Melissa emerged from her room carrying her favorite doll. "I thought she was getting a cold," Bailey remarked. "Perhaps you should leave her home."

"She has cabin fever," Melissa told him, tucking the doll under her arm. "She needs to get out." Melissa's words were a direct quote from what Bailey had told her a few days before, when Jennifer had come over for an hour so he could run to Maureen's. He couldn't help but smile at Melissa's explanation.

"Just don't leave her anywhere," he said. "I'd hate for Rainbow to get lost."

Beside him, Shawn gave a disgusted snort as he shoved his arms into a dark blue windbreaker. Bailey glanced down at his son. "Did you put Digger out and visit the bathroom?"

Shawn rolled his eyes. "Yeah, Dad."

"Good," Bailey said. "Then I guess we're all set."

"What if Mom calls while we're gone?" Shawn asked.

Bailey did his best to hide his annoyance. Angela hadn't contacted the children for over a week. "Then she'll have to call back."

When they got to the mall it was crowded with couples, knots of teenagers and women pushing strollers. "Stay close," Bailey said. "I don't want to spend time searching for you."

"Can we go in there?" Melissa asked, pointing at a toy store.

"I thought you wanted to get Heather a stuffed animal for her collection? They have more of them at that card shop next to the big shoe store."

"Oh, yeah," Melissa agreed. "Let's go there."

Shawn groaned. "I want to look at posters in the music store."

"After the errands are done," Bailey said firmly. "Why don't you go to the sporting-goods shop and find a batting glove? We'll meet you there."

Shawn brightened at the idea of not having to go with them to pick out a stuffed animal. "Okay." He looked in the direction that Bailey pointed, then began walking that way.

"Shawn," Bailey called after him, "wait for us there."

Shawn waved to indicate that he had heard.

They were all coming out of a department store where Bailey had bought both children some much-needed spring clothes, when he glanced around and saw Maureen headed right for them, her slim figure striking in a short purple skirt and lavender blouse, long legs grabbing his attention before he forced it back to her face. Her expression was preoccupied and she hadn't seen him. For a moment Bailey hesitated, then he realized he was being foolish. Perhaps an accidental meeting was the best way to break the ice between her and his children.

Maureen looked around when she heard a familiar voice call her name. When she saw Bailey, a smile curved her mouth. Then she noticed the children with him. They were staring curiously. The girl had Bailey's coloring, but the boy's hair was lighter and his eyes were blue or perhaps hazel.

"Hi," Bailey said when Maureen stopped before them. "Running errands?"

Maureen held up the bag she carried. "Wedding-shower gift for tonight," she explained, then smiled down at the children. The boy's eyes were hazel and right now they looked distinctly hostile. Maureen's smile faltered, then widened purposefully as Bailey introduced them.

"This is my daughter, Melissa," he said, resting his hands briefly on the little girl's shoulders.

Melissa's smile was sweet but shy and she didn't answer Maureen's greeting, only stared with big brown eyes so like her father's.

"And this is my son, Shawn. He's nine."

"I'm seven," Melissa burst out, drawing Maureen's attention away from Shawn's reluctant hello.

"You look older." Maureen's gaze darted to Bailey and she saw the quick flair of approval in his dark eyes. She was trying to think of something else to say, when Bailey turned to look around them.

"How about about an ice-cream cone? We're ready for a break, I think."

The children's eager acceptance all but drowned out Maureen's murmur of consent. "Good idea," she told him as Shawn and Melissa hurried ahead of them.

"I'm sorry," Bailey said. "I know that Shawn isn't being very friendly, but this whole thing has been hard on him."

"That's okay," Maureen interjected quickly. "I'm sure that they're both very nice, but I'm not terribly at ease with children."

Bailey resisted the urge to catch her hand in his. "Have you ever wanted children of your own?"

A frown crossed her face and he regretted the probing question. "I'm sorry," he said hastily, shaking his head. "You don't need to answer. That's too personal."

She paused, facing him. "Don't apologize. I've wondered what it would be like to have a family of my own, but now it's almost too late."

Bailey couldn't resist a glance at her willowy figure as he tried to picture her heavy with child. The image refused to come, but the idea made him feel strangely warm.

"What about you?" she asked, surprising him. "Do you want more children someday?"

It was something he hadn't thought about, but now he did, glancing ahead to make sure that his kids were waiting for them at the ice-cream booth. They were, Shawn gesturing impatiently.

"I don't think so," Bailey replied, remembering how difficult things had been when Angela first left him. "With a son and a daughter already, I can't see myself starting all over again."

Maureen's expression revealed nothing of her reaction to his reply, leaving him to wonder if she agreed or not. Her answer hadn't really given him much of a clue as to how she felt, either. Only that she had thought about it at some time. Probably if Maureen did ever remarry, it would be to some scholarly type who shared her interests and perhaps her profession. They would teach and travel together, with no need for children to disrupt their lives. For some reason, the thought made Bailey's mood plummet.

"Come on," he urged, taking a proprietary hold on her elbow. "Let's not keep them waiting."

When the four of them sat at one of the white metal tables with their ice-cream cones, Maureen's instincts as a teacher seemed to take over and she saw, with great relief, that both children were warming to her, neither content to let the other take the limelight for too long as she questioned them about school and their other interests.

When Melissa told Maureen about the story her teacher was reading aloud to them, Shawn finally interrupted with a detailed description of the science project he and Bailey had done together. When Melissa told Maureen about Digger, their dog, Shawn broke in eagerly to announce that he wanted a kitten.

Bailey said he didn't think they needed any more animals, and Shawn scowled. He took a bite out of his ice cream, almost knocking it from the cone.

"Do you have a pet?" Melissa asked Maureen, effectively diverting the conversation away from potentially dangerous ground.

Maureen smiled at Bailey over his daughter's head of straight, dark hair.

"Watch out," he cautioned Maureen. "Your cone's about to drip."

Catching the dribble with her tongue, Maureen turned her attention back to Melissa, doing her best to ignore the way Bailey's eyes had darkened while he watched her. "I have a cat named Max," she said. "He's a Siamese, with a tan body and black legs, ears and tail. Have you seen cats like him before?"

Melissa nodded.

"Where did you get him?" Shawn asked.

"How old is he?" Melissa hugged her doll, who had already been introduced to Maureen, tight in her arms. "I'd like a kitty, too."

Bailey reached forward with his napkin to wipe her chin. "Eat your ice cream, princess, and don't pepper Maureen with questions. It's melting and we have to get going."

"I want to look for a poster." Shawn was frowning again.

Bailey glanced at his watch. "Next time."

"I didn't mean to keep you," Maureen apologized after she had swallowed the last bite from her small cone. She'd forgotten all about being nervous, as she and the children talked.

Bailey dabbed at her chin with his napkin. "You didn't keep us. We were done with our errands, but now we had better think about going."

Melissa started to protest until he reminded her about the birthday party. Shawn jammed the rest of his cone into his mouth, earning a frown from his father as he crunched it noisily.

Maureen rose to drop her napkin into the trash receptacle near the front of the shop. While she was away from the table, Bailey took the opportunity to ask the children if it was okay for him to invite her over to share the barbecue they'd planned for the next afternoon.

"Oh, yes!" Melissa exclaimed, jumping up and clapping her hands together.

"If you want," Shawn said with a total lack of enthusiasm, but at least he had stopped frowning. "Is Mom coming?"

"Not this time." Bailey mopped at Melissa's sticky fingers and reminded Shawn to wipe his hands and face as they left the table. Catching up to Maureen, who was waiting out front, he glanced again at both children.

"Ask her," Melissa urged in a stage whisper.

Maureen's brows rose questioningly. "Ask me what?"

"Would you like to come over tomorrow?" Bailey asked. "We're cooking hamburgers on the grill. My sister and her family will be there, and my helper from work might come by with a date."

Maureen hesitated, surprised by the burst of warmth she felt at the invitation. Wouldn't her relationship with Bailey only grow more complicated if she got to know his family? Was she ready for that?

Telling herself that there was really no way to refuse gracefully, she glanced at Melissa, who wore an expectant smile on the face that was a small, feminine version of Bailey's. All Maureen had planned to do was to spend a quiet day at home, cleaning the apartment and then curling up with a best-seller she had just bought.

"It sounds like fun," she said finally, giving in to temptation as she returned Melissa's smile. "What can I bring?"

"Just yourself," Bailey answered.

"Ice cream!" Melissa shouted at the same time.

"Good idea," Maureen said before Bailey could scold his daughter. "I'll buy some right here and put it in my freezer."

"That isn't necessary," Bailey said.

"But I want to." She remembered the flavor both kids had chosen for their cones. "Chocolate-chip-mint, okay?"

The next afternoon Maureen applied light makeup, studying the effect in the full-length mirror attached to the back of her bedroom door. Bailey had said to come by around four, after offering to drive over and pick her up, which Maureen had refused to let him do. He had enough to think about, and she could certainly find the way to his house herself.

"Do you think these pants are too dressy?" she asked Max, who was curled on the corner of her bed washing his front paws.

Max ignored her, turning his attention to his other foot as she looked again into the mirror. She had donned royal blue slacks and a coordinating striped knit top in red, white and blue, but now she wondered about the slacks. Perhaps she should wear jeans, instead. Maureen looked over her shoulder at her back view in the mirror. At least her hips and bottom were still trim, thanks to the walking she did and a healthy diet. Bailey's body was certainly in good shape, and he probably wouldn't find a woman who had let her figure go very appealing.

Maureen remembered the young tennis player who had stopped to talk to him in the college cafeteria. *She* had certainly been in terrific form, Maureen remembered with a rueful grimace.

Muttering to herself, she stripped off the slacks and pulled on her jeans, sucking in a breath as she zipped them. They were much snugger than the slacks, but she felt younger and more casual in the narrow-legged denim. Deciding to wear them with the striped top and white flat-soled sandals, she put the blue slacks back onto their padded hanger and replaced them with the other pairs grouped together in her neatly organized closet.

Opening her jewelry case, Maureen selected casual red hoops for her pierced ears and then, after a moment's indecision, added a light spray of her favorite floral scent to her throat and wrists. If she got stung by a bee it would be no one's fault but her own, she thought, remembering the magazine article she had read claiming that bees were attracted to bright colors and perfume. She qualified on both counts.

Wouldn't it be nice if Bailey were attracted to her, also? Or was she taking chances there, too, of getting stung?

Maureen pictured his children and sighed. Was she being foolhardy, deliberately opening herself up to the risk of being hurt as she got to know them better?

Maureen had worked hard to create a life for herself that was both orderly and satisfying. Predictable in a way, but not confining. Within reasonable limits, she could do whatever she wanted without asking anyone's permission or considering anyone else's feelings, and her time was her own. The only people she had to answer to were her superiors at the college. She had learned to appreciate what she had, trying not to dwell on all she had missed. After getting to know first Bailey and now his children, she might never be able to find contentment in her own life again.

For a panicky moment Maureen thought about calling Bailey and canceling for that afternoon. Then she remembered the way his lips felt when he kissed her, and reconsidered with a little shiver of reaction. Dangerous to her peace of mind, or not, Bailey was definitely worth her time.

Let the future sort itself out, she thought briskly as she gathered up her purse, sunglasses and the container of ice cream from the freezer. Today all she needed to do was to meet some of Bailey's family and see his kids again. And do her best not to fall head over heels for all of them.

"If you really want to help, you could cut up some carrot and celery sticks," Bailey's sister, Janice, told Maureen as they stood together in Bailey's kitchen.

Wallpaper sprinkled with flowers coordinated with the blue curtains that framed the window above an almond double sink. School artwork covered the front of the fridge and a plaster handprint painted orange hung next to a calendar scattered with penciled-in notations.

"I meant to do the raw vegetables this morning, but I got sidetracked." Janice glanced down at the youngest of her three children, a little girl who stayed by her side and clung with sticky fingers to the tail of her plaid shirt.

"I'd be glad to." Maureen took a bunch of carrots from the grocery bag and began to peel them, grateful for something to do. Everyone she had met so far was friendly enough, but she still felt out of place.

Bailey had spent a few minutes showing her around. The house, was small and cozy in a neighborhood thick with children, dogs and bicycles. Then he led her outside to the neatly fenced backyard, where he introduced everyone to her. The shorthaired dog that had come over to investigate was named Digger, and it wasn't hard to guess why, as Maureen noticed several holes by the fence. Then Bailey had been called away to confer with his brother-in-law about the coals for the barbecue. After a few moments Maureen had followed Janice back into the house.

"I'm going to see if Ashley will play outside with the other kids," Janice said, scooping up her little girl as she left the kitchen.

Smiling at Ashley over her mother's shoulder, Maureen returned her attention to the carrots. She had peeled and cut up two more when the screen door opened again and Bailey walked in, looking devastatingly handsome in a red tank top, cutoff jeans and canvas shoes without socks. When she had first seen him, Maureen was doubly glad she'd decided against the blue slacks.

"Someone put you to work," he said, crossing the kitchen to take a can of beer from the fridge. "Want one?"

Maureen usually didn't drink, except for an occasional glass of wine, but the day had been unseasonably hot for the Northwest in springtime and a beer sounded tempting.

"Yes, please."

Bailey pulled the tab before setting it on the table next to her. Then he surprised her by leaning over and dropping a kiss onto her lips.

"Mmm," he murmured, nuzzling her ear as his mustache tickled lightly. "You smell terrific."

Maureen's pulse rate sped into overdrive as she absorbed his nearness. When he began to straighten, her hand curled around his neck, pulling him back before she even realized what she was doing. Unhesitatingly his mouth covered hers again. This time his hands cupped her face and his tongue parted her lips.

Maureen's senses began to spin as he took the kiss deeper. She dropped the carrot she'd been holding and splayed the fingers of her free hand against his chest. She could feel the insistent drumming of his heart.

After a timeless moment Bailey lifted his mouth from hers, his eyes dark and hot. "Don't stay in here by yourself," he urged. "Come back outside. I didn't expect you to work."

"I don't mind." Her voice sounded dreamy and preoccupied, even to her.

Bailey's thumb brushed her mouth before he picked her beer up and handed it to her. "Come on. The carrots will wait."

Walking on shaky legs, Maureen followed him into the backyard, admiring the width of his tanned shoulders. He pulled two lawn chairs together and waited until she sat down before joining her. Then he reached out and took her free hand, lacing his fingers with hers. Maureen returned his grin before swallowing a sip of her beer and turning her attention to the group of children who were swarming over the swing set that sat in one corner of the backyard. Digger ran back and forth, barking. Maureen saw that all three of Janice's offspring were playing with Melissa and Shawn.

"Sorry," Janice said to Maureen from where she stood talking to Bailey's assistant and his girlfriend. "I didn't mean to desert you."

Maureen smiled and shook her head. Before she could reply, Melissa came over to her. "Would you like to see my dolls?"

Understanding the significance of the offer as one of friendship, Maureen rose and excused herself to Bailey. Only Shawn's frown as she took Melissa's hand and followed her into the house marred the gesture.

In Melissa's pink-and-white bedroom, Maureen gazed at the ruffled bedspread scattered with pastel unicorns and at the ballerina prints on one wall. When she was introduced to several dolls, she listened attentively and did her best to make appropriate comments. Only when Melissa turned away to get another doll from the shelf did Maureen glance around and see Shawn standing in the doorway.

"We don't want you here," he said baldly. "Our parents are going to get back together, and you're only going to spoil everything."

Chapter Five

Before Maureen could find her voice and reply to Shawn's attack, Bailey appeared behind him in the doorway, one hand grabbing his son's shoulder. "Apologize to Maureen right now," he said in an angry voice. "We aren't rude to company here."

Shawn's hostile expression didn't change as he muttered, "I'm sorry."

As Maureen's wounded gaze shifted from him to Bailey, Shawn twisted away suddenly and ran into his own room, slamming the door behind him.

"What's the matter with Shawn?" Melissa asked, clutching her doll close as Bailey tried to get a grip on his temper. "What did he mean about Maureen spoiling things?"

Bailey glanced from Maureen's face, pinched with embarrassment, to his daughter's. "We'll talk about this later, princess. Right now I want to talk to Maureen, and then I'd better see about Shawn. Okay?''

After a moment, Melissa's head bobbed in agreement. "I'll go back outside and swing," she said in a resigned voice.

"Thank you," Bailey said, gratified that at least *she* wasn't making waves. Right now Shawn's behavior was enough to deal with. Bailey hadn't realized before how much of Angela's plans to rejoin the family Shawn had absorbed. Or perhaps she'd been busy engaging their son as an ally. Bailey wouldn't put it past her to use a child to her own advantage.

He pushed the bedroom door partially closed and put his arms around Maureen. "I'm sorry," he said, breathing in her scent, his body responding to her nearness. "Angela's been spending time with the kids, and it's clear now what she's been saying to them. I'll have a talk with Shawn. I don't want him to put any blame on you."

Maureen had been standing tensely in the circle of his arms. At his words, she relaxed a little.

"Maybe I should just leave."

"No!" Bailey exclaimed, hating to let her go. "Please don't. I'll talk to Shawn right now."

He leaned back to peer into her worried face. "I know things seem complicated," he said earnestly, "but be patient, okay? I'll get it all straightened out, I promise."

"I don't want to put any pressure on you. You have enough to deal with." Maureen moved away from him, toward the door.

"You're not putting pressure on me," Bailey protested. "I want you here." His hands circled her waist. "Please stay," he coaxed again.

Maureen studied his face. Something in Bailey urged him to take her back into his arms and kiss her again, but he overcame the temptation. When she nodded he released her wrist, and together they exited Melissa's room. Maureen turned toward the kitchen, while Bailey knocked on his son's closed bedroom door.

As she took a moment to compose herself before joining the others outside, Maureen blamed herself for pushing in where she wasn't wanted. She should have waited a while before seeing his children again. If she came around all the time, they would think she was an unwanted addition to their lives, pushed on them when they had no say. All she really wanted was to spend time with Bailey without laying herself open to heartache. She was no longer sure if that was even a possibility.

"There you are," Janice exclaimed as Maureen came into the kitchen. "Been getting to know Bailey's kids a little better?"

"I think that Shawn resents me," Maureen burst out, picking up another carrot to peel. "Perhaps I shouldn't have come."

Janice's eyes darkened with concern. "Don't take it personally," she said. "Angela's return has been especially hard on Shawn, but he'll adjust."

"He wants Bailey and Angela to get back together."

Janice patted Maureen's shoulder. "That will never happen. It's Bailey's place to elaborate, but take my word for it, okay?"

Maureen managed a nod before she turned her attention to the carrot she was gripping so tightly. "Thanks," she said before Janice again left the kitchen. From the little Bailey had told her about his ex-wife, she hoped that Janice was right, and not just for her own selfish reasons. Angela didn't sound right for Bailey or his children.

An hour later everyone had eaten his fill of grilled hamburgers, potato salad, cake and the ice cream that Maureen had brought. The kids were tired and dirty, and the adults were throwing out garbage and cleaning up the leftover food.

"I appreciate your help," Janice told Maureen when she brought the dirty ice-cream dishes to the sink where Janice was washing up. "I just want to get these dishes done before we go. Bailey has so little time, as it is." Suddenly she looked uncomfortable. "I didn't mean—"

"Don't worry about it," Maureen said. "I didn't take it that way."

Janice looked as if she meant to say more, but the screen door to the backyard swung open and Shawn came in, carrying a plastic garbage bag. For a second his gaze locked with Maureen's before he turned away, color flooding his cheeks. Janice caught Maureen's eye and shrugged as Shawn set the bag alongside one of empty pop and beer cans.

For a moment Maureen stood chewing on her lower lip. "Shawn," she said as he turned to go back outside, "would you show me that model you were talking about while we ate?"

He looked as if he wanted to refuse her request, but then he shrugged. "Sure. It's in my room."

As Maureen followed him from the kitchen she turned to see Janice give her a thumbs-up sign and an encouraging smile.

While Maureen was trying to smooth over the awkwardness with Shawn, Bailey was stacking lawn chairs outside and thinking over the unsatisfactory talk he'd had with his son. Bailey had been stunned to discover that his children believed there was a good chance he and Angela would get back together. Then, knowing his ex-wife as well as he did, Bailey realized it shouldn't have surprised him at all. Angela had obviously been telling the children just that when she was with them. Perhaps she had even managed to convince herself it was a possibility.

Bailey shook his head as he bent to pick up a plastic fork from beneath the picnic table. Even if he hadn't met Maureen, there would be no chance of a reconciliation with Angela, but now that Maureen was in the picture he knew for sure it wouldn't happen.

He straightened as warmth spread through his body at the thought of Maureen tucked into his arms, returning his kisses with the sweet response she had shown him. He was glad she had come today, but wished they had been able to find a few more private moments together. Most of all, he wished the scene with Shawn hadn't happened.

Realizing how long he had been standing there, Bailey went inside to see what Maureen was doing. Last time he'd noticed, she was carrying leftover food into the kitchen. He knew that she had felt a little shy at first, but then she had mingled with the others and even pitched in to help. Her skills in the kitchen weren't what Bailey was thinking about as he pulled open the screen door.

"Where's Maureen?" he asked Janice.

She looked uncomfortable, making Bailey instantly suspicious. "I think she's with Shawn."

Shawn! Bailey frowned, then made himself shake off the instant tension that gripped him. Perhaps Shawn had taken some of what Bailey told him to heart, and was giving Maureen the chance that Bailey suggested he do.

"I think I'll see what they're up to," he said in what he hoped was a casual tone. "Unless you want some help here?"

Janice shook her head. "I'm almost through, thanks, and Tim's helping." There was still worry in her eyes as she glanced from her husband back to Bailey. "Be patient," she implored as he left the room.

When Bailey stopped outside his son's partially open door, he could hear Maureen's voice clearly. She was telling Shawn about a trip she'd taken to Mexico to see one of the Mayan ruins that had been discovered on the Yucatán peninsula. When she stopped speaking there was a silence. Then Shawn, who was just beginning to take an interest in archeology, asked her a question about the Mayan culture.

Bailey listened for a few more minutes, satisfied that Shawn's earlier hostility, if not gone, was at least well hidden. Bailey was encouraged that Maureen was making an effort to get along with Shawn after the boy's rudeness. Despite her initial wariness Bailey thought she liked his children, and he couldn't help wonder why she had been so reluctant to meet them.

Deciding it was time to rescue her, he knocked softly on the door. "Shawn, are you in there? I'd like you to crush the cans for me and put the garbage out."

Shawn opened the door. "Yeah, okay." Then he glanced at Maureen, who was perched on the edge of his bed. "Uh, thanks for telling me about Chichén Itzá. Maybe I'll go there myself someday."

Maureen rose, smiling at Bailey before she turned her gaze on his son. "I hope you do. I think you'd really enjoy it. And you're doing a great job on your model."

Shawn ducked his head. "Thanks."

When he disappeared through the doorway to the kitchen, Bailey raised an eyebrow at Maureen. "Sounds like you two have formed a truce."

She shrugged. "Of sorts, I guess. He's an intelligent boy."

"Yes, and curious about everything. Sometimes I can hardly keep up with him." Bailey slid an arm around her shoulder and pulled her close, breathing in her scent. "Can you stick around for a while? Janice and Tim and their brood are leaving, and Shawn and Melissa will be watching one of their favorite television shows in half an hour."

"And what do you propose we do?" Maureen asked in a teasing voice.

Bailey made a point of thinking hard for a moment. "I guess watching that James Bond movie on the TV in my bedroom is out, so we could always have a cup of coffee in the kitchen and finish off the two pieces of Janice's chocolate cake that I managed to hide before she wrapped up the leftovers."

"You devil!" Maureen exclaimed, laughing. "I'd never turn down a second piece of chocolate cake." Sliding her arm around his waist, she exchanged a brief hug with him before he let his arm drop from her shoulders and preceded her back into the kitchen, glad she had decided to stay.

They'd finished the cake and were having a second cup of coffee when Melissa came into the kitchen and climbed onto Bailey's lap.

"Whatcha talking about?" She looked at Maureen and then up into her dad's face.

For a moment Maureen's gaze met his as she tried not to laugh. They couldn't very well tell a seven-year-old that her father had just made an imaginative, teasing remark about other uses for a kitchen table besides sitting at it drinking coffee.

To Maureen's amusement, Bailey's face went a dusky red beneath his tan.

"Your dad was describing a way to exercise," Maureen told Melissa. "To keep in shape."

Bailey's eyes narrowed as he flashed her a distinctly piratical grin and twirled one end of his mustache. "Is that what I was doing?" he asked in a soft growl.

The sensual promise in his tone and expression made shivers of anticipation run up Maureen's spine. For a selfish moment she wished that she and Bailey were alone.

"Unless I misunderstood." She batted her eyelashes for effect.

"Daddy used to work out at a club," Melissa volunteered before Bailey could respond. "It gave him muscles." She wrapped her fingers around his upper arm and he flexed it obligingly as she giggled.

"Your dad is still in pretty good shape," Maureen said, eyeing his broad shoulders beneath the red tank top.

Bailey's dark eyes locked with hers over the top of his daughter's head. "You're not so bad yourself."

Aware of the increasing tension in the room, Maureen decided it was time to change the subject. "Is your show over?" she asked Melissa.

"Oh, I forgot. It was just a commercial." Melissa scrambled down and left in a rush.

Bailey glanced at his watch. "Baths and bed in fifteen minutes." His expression was alive with promise.

Maureen bit her tongue on the naughty reply that came to mind. "Can I help?"

"You can wash my back." Again he gave her a roguish grin as his heated gaze raked over her. Was he hinting that he was ready to take their relationship further?

"I thought we were talking about the children," Maureen replied. She wasn't sure how she felt about getting closer. She was growing to care for Bailey, and his touch shredded her control. They would be good together, she was sure, but a relationship with him would not be a casual thing she could walk away from without scars.

And what of the children? What would it cost her to walk away from them? The thought raised complex emotions she wasn't ready to deal with.

As Maureen finished her coffee, the silence in the kitchen was offset by the sound of the television. When it ended abruptly, Bailey excused himself to supervise bedtime activities.

"I should leave," Maureen said reluctantly.

He stopped behind her and put his hands on her shoulders. "Not yet. I'll be done with the kids in thirty minutes, and there are some magazines in the living room you could read while you're waiting."

Maureen thought of her neat empty apartment, Max napping on the couch. "Sure."

Bailey's range of interests was wide, she realized as she looked over the stack of periodicals she'd found on an end table. Everything from *National Geographic* to *The Weekend Bicyclist* was there. While she glanced at a copy of *Modern Parenting* she listened to the sound of voices from the other end of the house, Bailey's deep and patient, Melissa's pleading for another story, Shawn's asking to stay up later, both answering Bailey's questions about the next week's activities. Was Shawn's uniform clean for the game on Tuesday? Did Melissa remember that Bailey was picking her up from school early Monday for a dentist appointment?

When at last silence fell and Bailey came down the hallway, Maureen stood to tell him she really did have to go. Surely the man wanted a little time alone to collect his wits and relax before he faced another busy week.

She was pleased when he came over and put his arms around her.

"I'm glad you waited," he said softly. And before Maureen could protest, he lowered his head.

The first touch of Maureen's mouth fed a need in Bailey that had been growing steadily all afternoon. Their lips fused, their bodies brushing against each other. When she made a sound back in her throat and tightened her fingers in his hair, he loosened another notch on his control and plunged his tongue deeper into her mouth, savoring her taste and the dark pleasure he took in their shared passion. She crowded closer, her tongue stroking his.

Groaning, Bailey finally tore his mouth from hers and was stringing kisses down her jaw and into the curve of her throat when Digger flopped down by their feet and began to scratch energetically, reminding Bailey that this was neither the time nor the place to test the strength of his willpower. Gently his hands cupped Maureen's shoulders as he buried his face into her sweet-smelling hair and did his best to quiet his shallow breathing and runaway pulse.

Maureen sighed shakily and locked her hands together behind his head, easing away from his aroused body. She should have remembered where they were and not let herself be seduced by his potent kisses and enticing touch.

Bailey straightened, running a hand over his hair where it had fallen across his forehead. "I almost forgot where we were," he said in a deep voice. "You could probably make me forget my name, if you tried."

His eyes glowed with dark fire as he raised one of Maureen's hands to his mouth and kissed the knuckles. A shiver traveled up her arm and burst somewhere deep within her. When she felt the tip of Bailey's tongue touch the sensitive skin between her fingers, she moaned and leaned closer.

Bailey immediately released her hand and stepped back, shaking his head. "Damn," he said.

"It's time I left." Maureen couldn't stand being so close to him without being able to kiss and hold him the way she wanted to. She knew she would have to do some hard thinking, and soon. In the meantime, she picked up her purse and turned to thank him for inviting her to the barbecue.

Later that night, as Maureen tossed and turned, remembering the way Bailey had kissed her good night before he let her slip into her car and drive herself home, Maureen admitted to herself that Bailey McGuire had stormed past her defenses.

Picturing herself as a part of his life was still impossible. She didn't have the courage. Tears filled her eyes, overflowing to run down her cheeks unnoticed as she tried to deal with painful memories. Loving could be such a terrible risk.

For once Maureen didn't shut out memories of the small brother she had practically raised while their parents pursued busy careers. Her throat burned and she swallowed painfully, reaching to the nightstand for a tissue as a kaleidoscope of images filled her head. Tony laughing, the sun shining on his white-blond hair, Tony throwing his chubby arms around her neck for a kiss, blue eyes full of mischief. Tony's sweet, childish voice telling Maureen he loved her best of all.

Her older brother had been in a world of his own, filled with high school and sports and girls, but Tony was like her own child. Maureen loved him more than anyone else in her life.

When she lost him, she thought her heart had been broken beyond repair. Years later, carrying her own child,

Maureen had begun to heal. When she miscarried, she had learned a painful lesson. She wasn't meant to know a mother's love without paying a terrible price. It was easier not to love at all.

Blowing her nose and wiping her eyes, Maureen began resolutely to go over in her mind the lesson plan for the next day's French 1 class. Beside her on the bed Max shifted and began to purr, as her fingers stroked his head.

Then the memory of the hug Melissa had given her, smelling of soap and lilac shampoo, made Maureen smile tenderly in the dark. The little girl had looked like a doll in her pink-checkered bathrobe and bunny slippers, her cheek as soft as a flower petal when it rubbed against Maureen's. Who could resist such a charmer?

With a sigh, Maureen flopped over and punched her pillow into a semicomfortable mound, willing sleep to come. Her last conscious thought was of Melissa's smiling brown eyes.

Melissa's smiling eyes were the last things on Maureen's mind the next time she saw Bailey. He was standing outside the campus bookstore talking to a petite brunette with a knockout figure and a ready laugh. Maureen faltered to a stop when she saw Bailey reach out and squeeze the woman's shoulder as they both smiled. The jagged blade of jealousy that stabbed through Maureen was as surprising as it was painful. She had a strong urge to rush over and scratch the brunette's eyes out.

Instead Maureen took a deep breath and changed direction, pushing through the door of the administration building to see if there were any messages in her box. Her hands were shaking as she stopped in the office, trying to remember what it was she meant to do. Seeing the pigeonhole teachers' boxes, she checked hers, but it was empty except for a notice reminding her not to park in the instructor's lot without a special decal on her car window.

Maureen stuffed the notice into her briefcase and went down the hall toward the ladies' lounge, hoping for a moment of privacy. Her mind still carried the picture of Bailey and the grinning brunette.

Good, the lounge was deserted. Maureen threw herself into a vinyl-covered chair in front of the mirror and sighed deeply as she opened her purse to find a lip gloss and a comb. Her reflection stared back at her, pale and mussed, eyes dark with emotion.

"Stop that," she muttered to her image. "You're jumping to all kinds of conclusions, and you have no real reason to feel so possessive." She glanced around, feeling like an idiot for talking out loud to herself. She ripped the comb through her blond hair and repaired her makeup with a hand that shook, then rose on unsteady legs. Bailey had asked her to meet him in the cafeteria. If he hadn't forgotten, he should already be there.

"I can't stand waiting around without doing anything," Bailey told the woman who was sitting across from him as he resisted the urge to look for Maureen. "I wish that Angela would do something if she's going to, and get it over with."

"You said she might just change her mind and go away," his companion reminded him. "If she does, that would be easier than a court fight."

Bailey frowned at her logic, and she put a comforting hand on his wrist.

"Patience," she continued with an encouraging smile. "Even though I don't imagine you're used to just waiting for anything."

He smiled back at her. She was right. They couldn't counterattack until Angela did something first.

"I don't like feeling helpless. I'd rather be doing something. Running her out of town on a rail." He was half serious. Angela was a thorn in his side and sometimes he did wish he could make her leave town.

"I understand, but I don't think that's quite legal."

Before Bailey could reply, he glanced up to see Maureen coming toward them. With a rush of pleasure, he stood up.

Maureen couldn't help but raise her eyebrows questioningly as her glance strayed from Bailey to his companion at the round table. It was the same woman she'd seen him with earlier and she was even prettier up close, although she appeared to be several years older than Maureen would have first guessed.

"Am I interrupting?" She hesitated as Bailey pulled a chair out for her.

"No," he said. "I wanted you to meet Susan Brown, my attorney." He turned and introduced Maureen to the woman she'd been having black thoughts about for twenty minutes.

"I'm glad to finally meet you," Susan said warmly. "Bailey's mentioned you before."

Maureen sat down, her gaze sliding to him and then back to Susan. "He has?"

"I've mentioned Susan to you, also," he chided.

"Yes, you've mentioned your lawyer, but not by name. I didn't even realize you were a woman," she said to Susan, who smiled, revealing dimples. "Do the two of you need to talk about something private?" Maureen felt a little better, but wasn't totally reassured. Susan was very attractive.

"I ran into Bailey quite by accident," Susan said. "My husband teaches an accounting course evenings and I came by to bring him some papers he'd left at home."

"Tom Brown's your husband?"

Susan nodded.

Maureen wasn't the least bit unhappy to discover that Susan was married to a handsome, well-liked member of the teaching staff. Her own feelings of jealousy were finally ebbing.

Susan drained her coffee cup. "It was good seeing you again, Bailey. Remember what I said about being patient." She turned to Maureen and extended her hand. "Nice to meet you."

Maureen's smile came easily. "You, too."

After Susan left, Bailey, who had risen, leaned over Maureen and gazed intently into her eyes. "Are PDA's with teachers frowned on here?" he asked in a teasing voice.

"PDA's?" Maureen echoed, reacting with pleasure to his dark attractiveness as she always did.

He leaned closer and whispered, "Public displays of affection," in his hypnotic voice as his mustache caressed her cheek.

Pulling away, Maureen couldn't resist a chuckle. "Yes, I imagine they are. But hold the thought, okay?"

Bailey's eyes darkened as he sat back down. "You bet."

Flustered by the intensity of his stare, Maureen sought to change the subject. "How are things going with your case?"

Instantly his expression of intense male interest changed to one of somber determination. "We can't do much until Angela makes her move." He smashed his fist into the flat of his other hand. "I wish to hell I knew what she's waiting for."

Maureen was almost sorry she had brought the subject up. "Is Susan hopeful?"

Bailey leaned forward, lacing his fingers together. "As much as she dares, given the background. She thinks there wouldn't be any reason the judge won't leave the children with me, but you can never be sure when a mother is involved."

"I thought attitudes were changing," Maureen ventured.

"To a big extent they are, but you can't count on what a particular judge will decide. Susan's told me she's seen some pretty unbelievable rulings in custody cases." Jaw set, he pushed away his coffee cup. "If you're finished, we had better get going."

Maureen glanced at her watch. She'd forgotten all about the time and the class she was supposed to be teaching in five minutes. Picking up her briefcase and purse, she preceded Bailey from the cafeteria. When they got outside, he squeezed her shoulder.

"Thanks for taking an interest," he said quietly. "It helps a lot."

Maureen glanced up at him, smiling briefly. "I wish I could do more."

For a moment a crazy, impulsive idea danced through Bailey's head. There was something she could do that would undoubtedly influence his case. She could marry him.

Stunned by the direction of his thoughts, Bailey sobered instantly. No way would he consider, even for a moment, using Maureen to strengthen his position.

He left her at her classroom door, still musing over the idea of being married to her. Somehow he couldn't picture Maureen in an apron, stirring up a cake mix as she helped Shawn with his homework and listened to Melissa's latest adventure with Rainbow, Saturday-morning cartoons blaring in the background. But he definitely *could* picture her curled up in his bed, wearing nothing but a sheet and a smile.

"See you later," Maureen called, shattering the mental image that was making his blood pressure soar.

"Uh, yeah." He gave her a guilty grin and hurried to his Spanish class as the warning bell rang.

After they were done for the evening, Bailey walked Maureen to her car and then, whistling tunelessly, was almost to his own when Angela's voice came at him, riveting his wandering attention.

"We need to talk."

"What the hell are you doing here?" Bailey hadn't even noticed her in the shadows, leaning against his car. Was she trying to spy on him? Collecting evidence?

"Tsk, tsk. Guilty conscience?"

Angela's smug tone made him angry. "I don't have anything to be guilty about."

She stared toward where he'd left Maureen. "Girlfriend?" she asked lightly.

"None of your business." If his answer fueled her suspicions, Bailey was too incensed to care. What right did she have? Impatiently he pulled out his keys.

Angela immediately stepped forward and put a detaining hand on his arm. "I'm sorry, baby. I wasn't checking up on you, honest."

Bailey tensed at her wheedling tone. And was that whiskey he smelled on her breath?

Before he could ask what she wanted, Angela moved closer, flipping her red hair back in a calculated gesture Bailey remembered well, and gazed into his eyes. "I missed you." She moistened her full lips and leaned forward. "Let me show you how much."

He felt nothing as he moved carefully around her. "Cut it out, Angela. What do you want, anyway?"

He could see signs of an inner struggle on her face before she managed to smile softly and lay one hand against his cheek. Wary, he jerked away.

"You loved me once," she said in a low voice. "You ... wanted me."

Bailey felt pity war with the distaste inside him. Then he steeled himself against her wiles. She would be furious that he was no longer interested.

Angela reached out again to touch his face. Bailey pushed her hand away.

"It's late and I'm tired," he said, choosing his words carefully. "Yes, I did love you once, but it's way too late for that now."

Angela licked her lips. "You could want me again. We could start over."

Until she got bored? Until her drinking once again began to affect the kids? The little patience he'd been trying to show Angela evaporated. "Is there a reason for all this?"

Something in his tone must have gotten through to her. The trembling smile faded and her eyes narrowed. "You won't even give me a chance, will you?"

Her voice had risen, and Bailey glanced around. Luckily they were relatively alone in their section of the parking lot.

"Why should I?" He was getting angry, too. She'd had more than enough chances, and he was way past letting her get to him again.

For a moment he thought Angela was going to cry. Then her chin went up, face twisted with sudden fury.

"I'll make you pay for this," she raged. Before Bailey could speak, she whirled away and jumped into the car he hadn't noticed before. "You'll be sorry."

While he watched, she gunned the engine and slammed the gear shift into reverse, screeching from the lot as several people turned to stare. Shaking his head, Bailey climbed into his own car, cursing over the futility of their conversation. He felt shaken by the whole unpleasant incident.

When he followed Angela's path from the parking lot, he found himself turning in the direction of Maureen's house even though they had agreed earlier not to meet after class that evening. Somehow, after such a distasteful reminder of his unfortunate marriage, he found himself wanting to hold Maureen in his arms and be reminded that the contact between a man and a woman could be sweet and uncomplicated. He needed to touch base with someone who cared for him, and it didn't matter how casual, how temporary that caring was.

Moments later he was on Maureen's front step, ringing the bell. When she opened the door, her slim form already wrapped into a thin burgundy robe, she took one look into his face and held out her arms. He stepped into her embrace with a deep sigh, kicking the door shut behind him as he gave himself up to her womanly warmth and comfort.

"What's happened?" Maureen asked as she held him close, her hands stroking his back.

Bailey lifted his head and looked into her concerned blue eyes. Something within him broke loose, sweeping away the careful control he'd tried so hard to maintain with her.

"I need you." His voice sounded raw to his own ears.

For a long moment Maureen studied his expression, then she smiled. "You've come to the right place," she said softly, and pulled his head down to hers.

Chapter Six

It was clear to Maureen that something major had happened to upset Bailey's usually unshakable equilibrium. It was equally clear that now was not the time for talking. He would tell her when he was ready, but in the meantime his lips closed over hers, drowning her in passion and need.

Her own desire for him had been growing within her, and at the heat and ardor of his kiss, her hunger burst into life. When he groaned, his tongue seeking entrance to the dark welcome of her mouth, she yielded without hesitation. Her senses were swimming, her control swamped by his raw greed.

It was achingly clear that Bailey was no longer holding himself back. His hands stroked her trembling body relentlessly, leaving a path of fire as they caressed her. His mouth left hers to scatter kisses over her closed eyes and down her cheek before he nuzzled the sensitive skin below her ear, his mustache a silken brush, the touch of his tongue increasing her already rapid pulse.

Maureen speared her fingers through his soft hair and urged his mouth back to hers. When he lifted his head, his golden-brown eyes blazed before his thick lashes swept downward and his mouth burned across hers. The kiss was hotter, rougher, and her response was as fiery as his own. Her legs were shaking as her body melted against his hard frame.

For a moment Bailey's arms tightened around her and then he loosened his hold. Maureen almost moaned aloud when he tore his lips from hers. Her eyes, which had drifted shut, flew open. Was he going to pull away again?

"Come with me to your bedroom." His voice was urgent. "Let me love you."

Maureen's answer was to fuse her mouth with his. There was no question of stopping. With Bailey it was dangerously easy to be swept away, beyond rational thought or the fears that usually made control a necessity. They were both caught up in the passion that flared around them with the heat of a runaway forest fire. He needed her, and she wanted him desperately. For now that was enough.

At last Maureen released him, taking his hand in hers as their eyes locked for a long moment. She turned to lead him down the hall, and when he hesitated she wanted to scream with frustration. He'd brought her his passion and ignited her own. Surely he couldn't have second thoughts now?

Her fingers tightened as she searched his face, almost fearful of what she might see there. Had he changed his mind? Had she done something?

"I'm not prepared," Bailey confessed, surprising her.

Maureen stiffened beside him. She hadn't given a thought to protection and it made her feel especially cherished that he had. Closing her eyes, she tried to think. It was her safest time. At this place in her cycle and at her age, surely there was no risk.

"It's okay," she told him with certainty. "That's taken care of."

Bailey let out the breath he'd been holding, relieved. He would have stopped if he'd had to, but it would have been difficult, almost impossible. Now he smiled down at her, thinking that she was the most beautiful woman he'd ever seen. Her cheeks were flushed with passion, her eyes wide and dreamy, her mouth swollen from his kisses.

He'd wanted her almost since they had first met, and now she was about to become his. He reached a hand out slowly, trailing his fingers down the softness of her cheek before he cupped her chin. Her tiny moan of response shattered the restraint he'd been hanging onto so desperately.

"Are you sure?" Bailey's fingers trembled against the warmth of her skin.

Maureen returned his smile with one brimming with womanly secrets. "I'm sure. Come with me."

Inside her bedroom, lit only by the soft glow of a bedside lamp, Bailey took a minute to glance around while he sought to regain the control he needed to love her as slowly, as completely as she deserved. He wanted to give her more pleasure than she had ever known, more delight than she had imagined two people could share.

It wasn't only to forget the unpleasant scene with Angela that he was here. It was because he'd realized how special Maureen was, and how much he needed her on so many more levels than just the physical. He wanted to be part of her and to make her part of him. He wanted to share himself and be accepted and cared for, and he wanted to give the same support and caring to her. He needed to be close to her, and he was grateful that she seemed to understand.

When he had studied the neatly feminine room, done in pale gray and powder blue, long enough to regain a measure of his control, Bailey returned his attention to Maureen's face. "This is pretty," he told her. "I've pictured you in a room like this."

"I'm glad you like it."

He could see that her bloom of womanly confidence was beginning to waver, replaced by an uncertainty that was both endearing and painful for him to see.

Bailey framed her oval face with his hands, trying to still their trembling. "I've wanted you for what seems like forever," he confessed. "You can't know how often I've thought of holding you, loving you. I can hardly believe it's about to happen."

"I was beginning to think you didn't want me this way," Maureen admitted as she watched his intent expression, glad to be able to finally share her fears with him after all the times he had pulled back. "You have such self-control."

He shook his head, eyes burning with desire. "Not with you, not now. But it wasn't you that made me hold back. It was everything else. And you don't know the pain and sleepless nights it cost me. But I want you so much, and now the waiting is over." His voice roughened over those last words.

Before Maureen could speak, he swept her up, into his arms, making her feel delicate and precious. Holding her against his wildly thudding heart, he crossed to her bed and braced himself on one knee as he laid her down tenderly. Then he leaned over her, his smile full of promise as he bent to kiss her deeply. His fingers began to undo the knotted sash at her waist.

When it came loose, he peeled aside the edges of the satin robe to reveal the matching gown with its narrow straps and deep, wrapped bodice. Maureen trembled beneath his hands. The tightening of his features told her more clearly than words that he was pleased with what he found.

"Breathtaking," Bailey finally murmured as he leaned over her to touch his tongue to one tightly beaded nipple through the sheer burgundy fabric.

Maureen gasped as sensation exploded deep within her. Arching into him, she bunched the fabric of his shirt in her hands and dragged it free from his jeans. Bailey levered himself away, to aid her efforts. When she succeeded, he leaned forward again and drew her breast deeper into his mouth as she burrowed against the hot, bare skin of his back and sides.

Bailey pulled away from her and fumbled with his buttons. When his shirt hung completely open he slipped the narrow straps of her gown off her shoulders and paused to look at her.

"Your breasts are exquisite," he breathed, bracing himself on one elbow. First his hand and then his mouth returned to one and then the other, lingering at the puckered tips, his lower body crushing her into the bed as his arousal nestled against her intimately.

Maureen's head was flung back, pressing into the mattress. Her blood was on fire, her body alive with sensations. Bailey's hands wandered over her, leaving a burning trail his lips and tongue only heightened as he explored and tormented her.

She'd dreamed of him like this, and the reality made the dream pale by comparison. He was by turns gentle, urgent, tender, demanding. Everything she had ever wanted in a lover, and more.

Bailey shrugged out of his clothes while Maureen watched. Then he came back to her, drawing one knee between her thighs, urging them apart. His eyes bored into hers as he settled himself intimately. His breathing was shallow and his face suffused with passion, but his eyes held more than Maureen could possibly read as he gazed at her and smiled.

"Take me into you," he whispered. "Let me love you completely."

Eyes wide, she did as he asked, wrapping her legs around him as he poised over her. Impatient to know his total possession, she grasped his hips as he thrust deeply, filling her. The rhythm of their movements perfectly matched, they soared together. Deep within Maureen the tension twisted tighter and tighter. Finally it exploded, flinging her higher than she had ever been. Dimly she heard Bailey groan her name as, with a last mighty surge, he followed her into the sun.

It was several moments later when Bailey, who had been lying with his arm around Maureen's shoulders as she curled next to him, pulled her close and dropped a tender kiss onto her lips. "You're wonderful," he said in a low voice.

She looked deep into his darkened eyes, hypnotized by the intensity she saw there. "You're pretty special yourself." She was limp and satiated, totally content to lie within his arms, but she knew without asking that he wouldn't be able to stay the night. Even as the thought struck her that he would have to leave, he pulled himself to a sitting position and glared at the clock radio on her nightstand.

"Damn," Bailey said. "I didn't even think about the time. Good thing Janice is watching the kids instead of the sitter, but I suppose I'd better give her a call." His lips quirked into a smile. "Sorry, honey. You don't mind if I use your phone, do you?"

Maureen shook her head, wishing for an instant that he had no one to consider but the two of them. "Help yourself."

After he'd spoken to his sister he slid back down beneath the covers and gathered Maureen close, dropping a kiss onto the tangle of her hair. "I wish I could stay," he said, echoing her own thoughts. "Sometimes I wish life were simpler."

"Me, too. But at least you came to me." She could feel the heat in her cheeks as she averted her gaze and ran a hand across the dark pelt on his chest. The soft curls wound themselves around her fingers as if trying to keep her hand there.

"I'm glad you didn't turn me away." Bailey's voice was slightly hoarse.

"Me, too."

Again he glanced at the clock, then he flipped aside the covers and sat up. "I hate leaving."

He reached for his scattered clothing and began to dress, as Maureen stuck a pillow against the headboard and pulled the sheet back up. Boldly she watched him, admiring the masculine grace of his movements and the beautiful shape of his lean body.

When Bailey was finished except for his shoes he sat back down on the edge of the bed and wrapped his hands around her upper arms, pulling her close. When the sheet slid down, he followed its path with his eyes before shaking his head ruefully.

"God, I wish I could stay." His gaze locked with hers. "Once wasn't enough, you know. I'm still hungry for you."

Before Maureen could utter a reply, he covered her mouth in a burning kiss, his tongue caressing hers with heated strokes. When he finally lifted his head, leaving her wanting more, he took her hand and pressed it to the fly of his jeans.

"See? I warned you." Her fingers curled against the bulge in the worn denim. He groaned at the sweet pressure, then stood. "I'd best get out of here before I decide to throw all this damned responsibility away and love you again."

After staring intently for a moment he turned toward the door. Maureen took the opportunity to slip from the bed and scoop up the robe he'd stripped from her not that long ago. As he left the room she put it on and followed him through the apartment. At the front door he stopped, then drew her into his arms. His eyes bore a hidden message as his fingers traced a pattern across her mouth and down her throat.

"What happened before I came here shouldn't have upset me," he said, surprising her. "Angela waylaid me at my car." His arms settled around her waist. "It had nothing to do with you and me, but it made me realize how lucky I am to know you, and I needed to share the closeness I feel with you." He paused and took in a breath. "Do you understand?"

"I think so." Really, she didn't. All she knew was that he was trying to tell her that Angela hadn't driven him into her arms. Maureen couldn't help but wonder if he really knew for sure. "If you want to talk about anything, ever, I'll be happy to listen," she added. She couldn't seem to stop herself from getting in deeper.

"Thanks." His smile was intimate as he studied her face. "Do you have any plans for this weekend?"

"No." Sometimes it was difficult to keep up with his leapfrogging subject changes.

"Good. You do now. I'll persuade Janice to take the kids and we'll go somewhere, perhaps the peninsula, okay? The weatherman's promising a warm, sunny weekend." He paused, kissing her tenderly. "Would you stay overnight with me?"

The thought of spending a whole night with him made Maureen's insides flutter helplessly. He aroused needs she hadn't dealt with in a long time.

"I'd like that." Suddenly she felt shy around him. She needed time to herself, to sort out everything that had happened.

Bailey's smile was like sunshine. "Great. But now I gotta go," he said with regret. "I'll see you later."

As Maureen stood in the doorway he left without looking back.

The weatherman's prediction had come true. The sky was so blue it looked like an artificial backdrop and the sun flashed against a thousand facets on the water as the Edmonds-Kingston ferry plowed across Puget Sound. Maureen leaned against the railing, Bailey's arm hooked possessively around her waist, and watched the fishing boats as the breeze lifted her hair.

"Are you glad we came?" Bailey's voice was deep as he murmured into her ear.

Maureen leaned away so she could look directly into his brown eyes. "Absolutely. Even if it was pouring down rain and cold, I'd still be glad."

"Even if we had to spend the entire weekend indoors?" The teasing note in Bailey's voice bespoke the new, easy intimacy that had sprung up between them. With him Maureen felt totally relaxed, determined to take each day as it came and to enjoy it to the fullest. Whenever a note of her usual caution inserted itself into her head she banished it quickly. Now was not the time for methodical introspection or groundless fears.

Deliberately she considered his question. "Well, I guess I wouldn't mind. But I'm really looking forward to walking along the water and getting some sun. It's been a long winter."

Bailey shared her lighthearted mood. "If the weather turns bad we could play cards, I guess. Or maybe they've got one of those closed circuit hookups on the television. I'm sure we wouldn't get bored."

Maureen hit him playfully. "I certainly hope not."

In front of them loomed the ferry landing at the small town of Kingston, surrounded by rocky beaches and waterfront homes.

"Guess we'd better go to the car." Bailey took his arm from around Maureen's waist and gripped her hand in his, as a gull circled overhead, crying plaintively. Together they descended the stairs to the car deck below.

The drive to the Port Ludlow resort was a short one. After they had checked in and unpacked their luggage in an attractive room with a private balcony and a charming view of the water, Bailey suggested they have lunch in the dining room and then go exploring.

Maureen, who hadn't shared a motel room with a man since her marriage, was still trying to overcome the embarrassment she'd felt when Bailey had opened the door to their room and deposited both bags on the bench at the foot of the solitary queen-size bed. Before he made the reservation, he had offered to book two rooms. Her halting reply that two rooms weren't necessary had drawn a tender smile from Bailey and a warm, soul-stirring kiss.

"Hungry?" he asked now, as they walked down the hill to the lodge.

Maureen's gaze flashed to his, not sure how to take the seemingly innocent question. His smile was warm below the dark mustache, and if there was a light in his eyes that made her heart beat faster, she chose not to acknowledge it at the moment.

"Starved. Must be the sea air."

Bailey's smile widened and he gave her shoulders a squeeze, enjoying the feel of her closeness before he let his attention wander down her body. "I love that outfit," he said of the gently clinging turquoise knit top and the white split skirt that ended just above her knees. Below its hem her legs were slim and shapely, her feet dainty in bright pink canvas sandals. Her eyes were shielded from him by pink-framed sunglasses and her lips curved seductively, tinted with a pearly gloss. As they entered the foyer with its beach-and-sea decor and mounted the steps to the restaurant, pride swelled within him. She had to be the loveliest woman there, to his eyes the loveliest in the Northwest.

Maureen slipped the sunglasses from her face as he spoke to the hostess, who acknowledged his request for a table with a much warmer than necessary smile. For once Maureen didn't feel the least bit threatened by the younger woman's almost dewy appeal. Bailey, resplendent in navy polo shirt and khaki slacks, wanted to be with her this weekend, and that was all that mattered. She glanced at him, admiring his gleaming hair and sun-darkened complexion before she turned to follow the hostess. The light touch of his hand on her back brought a flushed response to her cheeks as she walked through the half-full dining room to sit at a round table overlooking the crowded marina.

"Enjoy your lunch." If the expression of regret Maureen thought she saw on the younger woman's face was only a figment of her imagination, the admiring glance of a redhead at the next table was not. Bailey, intent on pushing in Maureen's chair, didn't even notice. For some reason, that pleased her immensely.

After a memorable meal of chowder and fresh seafood salad, they sat companionably enjoying their coffee.

"This is terrific," Bailey said expansively as he leaned back in his chair. "Just you and me, with no interruptions and no deadlines."

"I think you needed the break more than I did," Maureen said, enjoying his relaxed expression. "All I have to worry about is Max."

"Where is Max? Does he fend for himself while you're gone?"

Maureen chuckled as she took another sip of the delicious coffee, so different from what the campus cafeteria offered. "No, I think Max would feel quite abandoned if left to his own devices. My neighbor, Mrs. Bondini, is feeding him for me."

She had to give the elderly woman credit. When Maureen had explained that she was going away overnight, Mrs. Bondini hadn't raised her eyebrows or asked any awkward questions. She had only patted Maureen's arm, told her to have fun and said not to worry about the cat. No small accomplishment when Maureen knew her friend was fairly bursting with curiosity.

When Maureen and Bailey returned to their room to change after lunch, he asked if she would rather take advantage of the outdoor pool instead of walking along the beach, but she declined.

"I'm a sand-and-sea person," she said. "I love the beach." Boats had been going in and out of the marina during lunch, and she had seen other guests walking along the channel that was separated from a pitch-and-putt golf course by a ribbon of sand.

"We could try the pool later," Maureen suggested as she emerged from the bathroom where she'd changed into shorts and a T-shirt. "The sign said it's open till ten."

Bailey approached her, smiling. "We'll see." His hands slid down her bare arms to capture her wrists before he guided her hands to his shoulders. Automatically she circled his neck, the action pressing her breasts to his broad chest.

Bailey groaned deep in his throat, bending his head to capture her mouth with his. "There's another activity we could explore this afternoon," he murmured as his big hands caressed Maureen's waist beneath the hem of her T-shirt.

"And waste all that lovely sunshine?" Maureen had meant her comment to be joking, but instead her voice came out in a breathy sigh.

Bailey's eyes darkened until his golden-brown irises were as narrow as wedding bands. "Would it be a waste?" His voice was rough with intensity.

Maureen went still against him, sensing the urgency in his question. He needed reassurance; the realization moved her. It had been a long time since her opinion mattered so much to anyone, and she was tempted to savor the moment. Instead she smiled, determined to wipe the sudden tension from his face.

She cupped a hand against his cheek. "None of the time I spend with you is ever a waste," she said softly.

For a moment Bailey tilted his head back and closed his eyes, as if her words had given him intense pleasure. Then his gaze fastened on hers once again and he leaned closer. "Let's make some more memories," he murmured. "The beach will still be there in an hour."

Maureen lifted her face to his, parting her lips as he kissed her, joy at being with him flooding her heart and soul. She'd missed this kind of sharing, not just the physical but the emotional closeness, as well.

Without taking his lips from hers, Bailey bent and scooped her into his arms. Crossing to the wide bed, he settled her there gently and began to remove her clothes. When his fingers caught the hem of her T-shirt, she raised her arms and let him pull it free. When he leaned forward, hands braced on either side of her, to trail fiery kisses from her throat across her wispy bra to the waistband of her shorts, Maureen groaned and her grip on his shoulders tightened. When he smoothed away the rest of her clothing she hardly noticed, too caught up in what his mouth and hands were doing to her.

"This isn't fair," she murmured after a moment. "You're still dressed."

Bailey shrugged, sitting up on the bed. "I do feel a little warm." His eyes twinkled as he gazed down at her until she began to blush.

Thrusting aside her self-consciousness, she rose to her knees and began to undress him. Since she got distracted by each part of him she uncovered, pausing to investigate with curious fingers and inquisitive lips until his breath was rapid and shallow, it took quite a little time before he was as bare as she.

By then Bailey's control, not to mention his patience, was in shreds. Trying not to rush, he bore her down onto the spread and began to reacquaint himself with every square inch of her pale, satiny skin. When he got to the silvery blond thatch above her thighs, Maureen was already urging him to take her. Instead he made himself move slowly, tracing a finger through the soft down to gently explore the moist flesh below. At his first touch, she arched upward, moaning. Beads of perspiration broke out on Bailey's heated skin, his hand trembled and he ached with each beat of the pulsating hunger that echoed through him.

"Not yet," he rasped as her hands reached for him and she thrashed her head from side to side on the pillow. As she moaned again, he traced his fingers down her sensitive inner thighs and gently urged her knees further apart. When he leaned over her, one hand wandering back up toward her hip, her eyes flew open and their gazes clashed.

"No," she whispered. "I can't stand it."

"Yes. I have to." He set his lips against the part of her that burned the hottest, inhaling her spicy scent. Then he parted her with his tongue, tasting with gentle strokes. When she cried out, his hands curled around her hips to hold her still while he continued the sensual assault.

Every muscle in Maureen's body went rigid, and then she plunged, flesh quivering wildly. Before she could breathe, or think, or react at all, Bailey had shifted his body upward and slid into her. His complete possession sent her over the edge again. Buried deep inside her, he thrust once, twice, and then a third time, his body stiffening and the breath exploding from his lungs as he found his own thunderous release.

It was several moments before Maureen had the strength to speak or to raise her hand and stroke it down his back as he shifted to lie next to her, one powerful thigh flung across her legs as if to anchor her beneath him.

"That was worth . . . the delay," she gasped finally.

"Mmm." Bailey nuzzled his face into the warmth of her neck, his still-rapid breath tickling her sensitized skin. "I think you've killed me." His hand slid across her waist to pull her even closer.

"Then we're both in heaven," she murmured, one hand resting on his muscular buttock, enjoying the feel of it flexing as he moved his leg.

He turned her onto her side so she was looking directly into his eyes. "This is the closest to heaven I've ever been," he said, tone serious. "You're very special to me."

Maureen wasn't sure what to say. She'd tried to bury the devastation of her marriage beneath ten years of independence, but since she'd met Bailey, individual memories kept resurfacing, as if to remind her of the hazards of a serious relationship. Torn, she tried to smile.

"Thank you," she said. "You're special, too."

His smile widened into a grin. "The afternoon is going by without us, woman." He pulled her into a sitting position. "I think we'd better shower and hit the beach before we both decide that a nap is something we can't do without."

She straightened, responding to the challenge in his voice. "A nap!" she echoed scornfully. "I'll have you know that I don't take *naps*."

"Glad to hear it." Hauling her up with him, he shifted his grip to her hand and pulled her toward the shower. "Come on, let's see if we can resist temptation and actually get out of here this time."

Maureen couldn't help but chuckle at his high spirits as she followed him into the luxurious bathroom, unembarrassed by her own nudity, and waited while he adjusted the water.

After they thoroughly explored the beach, Bailey using his handkerchief to carry the shells Maureen found and both of them wading barefoot in the shockingly cold water, they changed and went to dinner. Disposing of a meal of grilled swordfish, rice and steamed baby vegetables, they took advantage of the mild weather and gentle breeze to stroll arm-in-arm through the marina, stopping every so often beneath the light from a string of lanterns to study an especially beautiful boat.

"Would you like a nightcap?" Bailey asked, breaking the silence that had settled comfortably over them as they left the dock and began to walk back up the hill past the main building to their room.

Maureen turned to study him under the glow of an outside lamp. What she wanted was to be in his arms again, but she was uncomfortable with such urgent need. "A glass of wine might be nice."

"Good idea." They turned and went through the carved double doors of the lobby, then down the carpeted stairs to the lounge below the restaurant where they'd eaten earlier. There they found a small table in the corner by the tall windows that framed the marina and its lights like a marvelous seaside photograph.

As soon as the waitress took their order, Maureen excused herself to freshen up. While she was gone, Bailey's mind drifted back over the pleasant way they'd spent the afternoon. Fresh hunger filled him at the memory of Maureen's open response to his lovemaking. He'd never felt such passion before, and she had stayed with him every step of the way to their mutual explosion. Shifting uncomfortably as his body responded to the vivid mental images of them tangled together, he forced himself to recall their lighter moments on the beach and at dinner as they had talked and laughed together with the ease that comes of long friendship or deep devotion.

His feelings for Maureen were quickly getting out of hand, but the last thing he wanted was to back off or even slow down. There was a rightness between them that he wondered if she felt as strongly as he did. Her sudden hesitance after they'd made love that afternoon made him wonder if he was seeing only what he wanted to see. How did she feel?

Before Bailey could torture himself with questions, the waitress brought their wine, and then Maureen slipped back into her chair. The dress she'd put on for dinner, some shimmery blue material with flowers worked into the weave and a wide belt that defined her slim waist, shone softly in the candlelight from their table centerpiece. Picking up her glass, she smiled into his eyes.

"To us," he said, watching her closely.

Her face seemed to glow as she returned the salute, whatever doubts she'd had earlier apparently banished, at least temporarily.

Across from him, Maureen decided to put aside her apprehension for the rest of the weekend and just enjoy being with him. There was no reason for her to believe that Bailey would hurt her. Just because one man had been overbearing, insensitive and ultimately cruel, didn't mean she couldn't have a relationship with someone who would be glad for the love she'd stored up over a long span of time. Someone who wouldn't take advantage of her feelings and betray her when she least expected it.

"Are you glad we came?" Bailey's deep voice scattered the unhappy memories.

She linked her fingers with his across the small table. "Yes, I am. It's really been perfect."

Bailey shifted his grip, then raised her hand to kiss her knuckles. "It can be even more perfect, if we let it," he said. "I can't imagine not having you somewhere in my life."

Maureen blinked in surprise at the way he had worded his statement. It sounded as if he meant for her to stay tucked into the odd corner, wherever he happened to find the room for her. She withdrew her hand, not sure just where in his life she wanted to be.

"Let's take things slowly," she said. "There's no rush."

Bailey sensed her withdrawal, wondering if she had just remembered his responsibilities and the court battle he faced. Surely she didn't think he was trying to use her somehow. For a moment he cast about for some way to ask without upsetting her further, but before he could think of anything, she finished her wine and stirred restlessly.

"Do you want to go?" he asked.

Maureen nodded, her expression unreadable. The joking remark Bailey was going to make about her impatience to get him back to the room died on his tongue. Somehow the new strain between them didn't encourage such teasing.

When they stepped outside, Maureen tilted her head back, pale hair shimmering, and gazed at the night sky.

"Oh, look," she gasped. "Isn't it spectacular?"

Above them the blackness was dotted with thousands of stars, some bright and others just tiny pinpoints of light.

"It's beautiful," Bailey agreed as they stood on the walkway for a moment, both studying nature's beauty. Then another couple came out the door and Bailey slipped his arm around Maureen's shoulders. Peace seemed to be restored, though he couldn't help but wonder at her earlier reaction.

When they got back to their room he thrust aside his dark thoughts and pulled her close, determined to banish any lingering strain between them. This time their lovemaking was leisurely and gentle, maddeningly thorough, only heating to an explosive crescendo at the end when restraint was finally shattered, their bodies wild for fulfillment. Afterward Bailey held her tightly, knowing how easy it would be to destroy the tentative closeness.

He drifted off to sleep almost immediately, but Maureen lay awake in the darkness, listening to the faint sounds of the water below through their open window. His earlier remark came back to her, about having her somewhere in his life.

Perhaps she'd overreacted. That was the kind of casual statement a man might make to a woman he was spending an intimate weekend with. What was he supposed to say? This is fun, but don't expect a lot of it?

Maureen grimaced in the darkness. She wanted to keep it casual, didn't she? Over the past ten years she had dated fairly frequently at first, allowing a couple of the relationships to progress toward intimacy. Then she had decided at some point that she wasn't meant to be half of a couple or to share a fulfilling love, and for a long time now she had only gone out with men who were no threat to her independence or her heart.

Then Bailey had come along, bursting into her life with an enthusiasm and attraction she'd all but convinced herself didn't exist. He made her feel things, physically and emotionally, that she didn't want to feel. Things she was afraid to feel.

Try as she might, she couldn't prevent the next thought from bursting into her consciousness. She could fall in love with a man such as Bailey. And then she would have to go through all the pain she'd managed so successfully to avoid for so long.

ACCEPT FOUR BRAND NEW

YOURS

We'd like to send you four free Silhouette novels, worth $11.80, to introduce you to the benefits of the Silhouette Reader Service™. We hope your free books will convince you to subscribe, but that's up to you. Accepting them places you under no obligation to buy anything, but we hope you'll want to continue your membership in the Reader Service.

So unless we hear from you, once a month we'll send you six additional Silhouette Special Edition® novels to read and enjoy. If you choose to keep them, you'll pay just $2.74* each—a saving of 21¢ off the cover price. And there is *no* charge for delivery. There are *no* hidden extras! You may cancel at any time, for any reason, just by sending us a note or a shipping statement marked ''cancel'' or by returning any shipment of books to us at our cost. Either way the free books and gifts are yours to keep!

ALSO FREE!
VICTORIAN PICTURE FRAME

This lovely Victorian pewter-finish miniature is perfect for displaying a treasured photograph—and it's yours *absolutely free*—when you accept our no-risk offer.

Perfect for a treasured Photograph

Plus a FREE mystery Gift! follow instructions at right.

WE EVEN PROVIDE FREE POSTAGE!

It costs you *nothing* to send for your free books — we've paid the postage on the attached reply card. And we'll pick up the postage on your shipment of free books and gifts, and also on any subsequent shipments of books, should you choose to become a subscriber. Unlike many book clubs, we charge *nothing* for postage and handling!

There was no "could" about it. She was half in love with him now. And racing toward possible destruction with the speed of a meteor plunging toward earth.

As Bailey continued to sleep beside her, Maureen did her best to convince herself that she was still in command of her emotions. Bailey didn't have the time in his busy life for a serious commitment, and neither did she. Thank goodness they'd taken precautions this weekend. Maureen's safe time was over and she didn't want to risk adding that kind of complication to an already complicated relationship. Satisfied that she had everything thought out, she snuggled close to the warm body next to her and drifted off. The last thing she was aware of before sleep claimed her was Bailey's arm curled possessively around her waist.

Chapter Seven

When Bailey picked his children up at Janice's late Sunday afternoon, Melissa threw herself into his arms.

"I missed you, Daddy! Did you have a good time?"

He had explained that he and Maureen were going away on a sort of short vacation, and promised that he would take Melissa and Shawn somewhere soon.

"We had a very nice time, thank you. What did you and Shawn do while I was gone?"

Melissa was holding onto his hand as she skipped alongside him. "We rented *Bambi* and had ice cream last night, and then this morning Aunt Janice fixed us blueberry pancakes and Uncle Tim let me help feed the rabbits and pet the horses."

Bailey followed her in the back door of the double-wide mobile home that sat on a five-acre tract south of Everett. A cat slipped out the door before he shut it behind him. Part of the reason Melissa and her brother liked going there so much was the pet population of dogs, cats and goats that Janice and her husband kept, as well as the horses and rabbits. Tim worked at a local aircraft-manufacturing plant, the county's largest employer, while Janice had taken a temporary detour from her career as a librarian to stay home and raise her three children.

They had helped Bailey out more times than he could remember, taking the children when his schedule became unmanageable, listening when he needed to let off steam, even filling in for him at school functions when he couldn't be in two places at once. In return Bailey had wired their barn and shop, and come to stay with their brood on occasion so they could get away by themselves.

Now Janice met him in the kitchen with an innocent expression on her face. "Nice weekend?"

Bailey felt his cheeks heat up as he tried without success to curb his wide grin. "Yeah," he said, feeling as transparent as a newly cleaned window. "The weather was nice, the accommodations were great—"

Janice's chuckle was enough to stop his discourse. "I take it the company lived up to expectations, too?"

The affection that Bailey and his sister had shared since they had gotten through adolescence and found they actually liked each other was enough to banish his discomfort.

"The company was everything I'd hoped it would be, and more," he admitted. "Thanks for watching the kids."

"No problem. They keep mine amused. Want to stay for supper?" She lifted the lid of a large pot on the stove and stirred something that smelled like homemade chili.

"No, thanks," Bailey said reluctantly. "I think we've taken up enough of your time." He'd planned on stopping for burgers on the way home. There was plenty to do before Monday morning hit again.

Realizing that Melissa was no longer in the kitchen with him, he asked, "Where's Shawn, anyway? Doesn't he know I'm here?"

For the first time in their conversation, Janice's gaze avoided his. "When he heard your car, I think he went out to the barn." She wiped her hands on her flowered apron. "He's been pretty quiet all weekend. Have you talked to him about Maureen and Angela?"

Bailey swore under his breath. "Not as much as I need to, I guess. He hasn't wanted to listen to anything I've had to say about Maureen, and when I try to tell him that his mother isn't going to be coming back to live with us, he leaves the room."

"Well, he's probably with the kittens. If you want to try to talk to him now, I'll keep Melissa busy in the house."

Bailey raked a hand through his hair and gave Janice a rueful smile. "No time like the present, I guess."

Bailey found Shawn in an empty stall, a kitten in his lap, another on his shoulder, and two more crawling around him in the straw as the indulgent mother cat looked on. When Bailey squatted down beside him, Shawn glanced up and then turned his attention back to the black-and-white kitten that was batting at his cheek while it clung to the fabric of Shawn's T-shirt and purred like a high-pitched motor.

"Hi." Shawn's voice was totally devoid of enthusiasm.

Bailey picked up one of the other kittens and set it on his thigh, where it immediately sank its claws into Bailey's leg, making him suck in his breath. "How was your weekend?" he asked Shawn, who had loosened the black-and-white kitten's hold and was rubbing its fuzzy coat against his cheek.

"Okay."

Shawn's attitude was rapidly getting to Bailey, but he held on to his patience, knowing that losing his temper would only make things worse.

"The resort at Port Ludlow is pretty nice," Bailey said in a casual tone, as he wiggled one finger for the kitten perched on his leg to play with. "I think you and Melissa would like it there. They have a great outdoor pool and a nice beach."

Shawn remained silent, stroking the kitten that was now burrowed into the bend of his elbow.

"Could we take this one home? Uncle Tim said he'd make a good mouser."

"We don't have mice."

"Then we could feed him cat food." Shawn scooped the kitten into his hands and dangled it over his head while the little animal stared down at him with bright blue eyes. Beside Bailey the mother cat washed her paw, while keeping track of her offspring. When one of the kittens wandered out of the stall in search of adventure, she picked it up by the nape of the neck and brought it back, dropping it with a thump and then licking its face as if to say she wasn't angry, just concerned.

"How do you think Digger would react to the kitten?" Bailey asked, searching for some way to bring Angela and Maureen into the conversation.

"He'd be jealous at first, but then he'd get used to it." Shawn looked at Bailey, his expression full of hope. "I'll take care of Ernie all by myself. You wouldn't even know he's around."

"Ernie?"

"That's the name of one of the kids on that TV show, 'Family and Friends.' I think it kinda suits him." Shawn flipped the kitten onto its back and began to tickle its white stomach. The kitten bit his finger.

"You know," Bailey said, trying to find the right words, "what you said about Digger being jealous but then getting used to the kitten makes me think of the way you feel about Maureen."

Shawn's eyes narrowed and he opened his mouth, then a thoughtful expression came over his face before he spoke. "How do you mean?" he asked after a moment.

Bailey watched the black-and-white kitten as it came over to wrestle with one of its litter mates. "You know I love you and Melissa, and that will never change," he said, feeling his way carefully. "But I also need the friendship of other adults, just like you have friends your own age." He glanced at Shawn, who looked mutinous.

"Maybe you feel jealous of my friends at first," Bailey continued, "just like Digger would feel about another animal, until he realized that you didn't love him any less."

"Maureen isn't just a friend," Shawn burst out suddenly. "She's your girlfriend. That's why you don't want Mom to come back."

Bailey studied the anxiety on his son's face, while trying to think of what to say. He knew now, without a doubt, who'd been filling Shawn's head with thoughts of one big reunited family.

"Maureen isn't the reason your mother and I aren't getting back together," he said, knowing he had to set Shawn straight without speaking ill of Angela.

"But Mom said—"

Bailey held up a detaining hand. "Mom can tell you how she feels, but now I'm telling you how I feel, okay?"

Shawn nodded. "Okay."

"I don't know how much you remember about the way things were before your mother left," Bailey began. Shawn had only been six then, hopelessly confused.

"I remember that you both yelled a lot," Shawn admitted. "I guess you weren't very happy."

Bailey was surprised at Shawn's admission. "No," he said, "we weren't. There were a lot of reasons, not all your mother's fault or mine. Sometimes people just can't live together."

"Mom said it was because of her drinking," Shawn said casually as he stroked his kitten, surprising Bailey again. "She said she doesn't drink anymore."

Bailey remembered the odor of whiskey on Angela's breath when she'd surprised him at the college parking lot. "It sounds like you and Mom have talked a lot," he said.

Shawn's eagerness tore at Bailey's heart. "We have. She said she's learned her lesson, that she didn't really want to leave, but she felt that she had to." He paused, frowning. "I really didn't understand that part," he said. "Why did she leave us for so long, if she didn't want to? Did someone make her go?"

Bailey was at a loss how to explain. "Maybe she thought it was the best thing to do at the time," he said finally. "And now she's changed, but I've changed, too. I don't have the feelings for her that I used to, feelings that are necessary between a husband and wife."

"Because of Maureen," Shawn said darkly.

Bailey bit off a curse, pushing the hair off his forehead. "No," he denied. "Not because of Maureen, even though I do like her a lot. You have to understand that my feelings toward your mother changed a long time ago. It's not Maureen's fault."

"But if you weren't seeing her, maybe you'd start loving Mom again," Shawn persisted.

Exasperated, Bailey set aside the kitten who'd gone to sleep on his thigh and stood up. "No, I wouldn't. I wish there was some way I could explain it so you could understand. Perhaps you just have to take my word for it, and accept the idea that your mom and I are divorced, and we're going to remain that way. If she stays here you can see her a lot, but we aren't all going to live together again. Sometimes grown-ups are suited to have a family and raise it, and sometimes it doesn't work out that way.''

Bailey thought about Angela possibly obtaining custody. There wasn't any way he could go into that now, he'd only confuse Shawn more than he had already. When Shawn kept comparing Maureen and Angela, Bailey wanted to tell him that Maureen probably had more love to give than Angela ever could. Neither childbirth nor motherhood seemed to have given his self-centered ex-wife any mothering instincts, but Bailey suspected that Maureen was holding back a wealth of untapped feelings. He just didn't understand why.

If the worst happened, and Angela did win custody of the children, Bailey would have to deal with it at the time. No point in borrowing trouble now.

Shawn rose, too, cradling Ernie against his chest. ''Aunt Janice said the kittens will be ready to live without their mom in another week. Can I tell her we want this one, before someone else gets him?''

Bailey looked into his son's eyes, wishing fiercely that there was some way he could protect Shawn from anything that might hurt him. At least this was one thing he could give the boy.

''Sure,'' he said, watching Shawn's mouth widen into a grin. ''As long as you feed him and change his litter box.''

''Oh boy! Wait till I tell Melissa.''

Before Bailey could say anything else, Shawn had raced outside toward the house, still holding the kitten. Any minute now, Melissa would be coming to demand that she, too, get a pet of her own.

Sighing, Bailey followed Shawn toward the mobile home, wishing that every problem was as easy to solve as this one had been.

Maureen's gaze kept drifting to the silent telephone in her apartment, as Mrs. Bondini told her all about what had gone on in the complex while Maureen had been away. For an old woman, her neighbor didn't miss much.

"Helen Jensen's dishwasher broke and flooded her kitchen yesterday morning. She said it took every towel she had to soak up the mess." Mrs. Bondini took a sip of her tea before continuing.

"That young fellow down at the other end, Mr. Baker, didn't get home until three-thirty this morning. My friend, Mabel Davis, said his wife yelled at him so loud she kept Mabel awake for an hour, and today she has a stiff neck from pressing her ear against the wall for such a long time."

Maureen couldn't help but laugh at the twinkle in Mrs. Bondini's brown eyes. "Are you making that up?"

"Would I do that? By the way, how was your weekend?"

Maureen had been trying to decide how much to reveal about her trip. Mrs. Bondini was a good friend, one not given to passing judgment on others, but she was of another, stricter generation.

"I had a nice time," Maureen said, trying not to blush as their gazes met. "The resort was beautiful and, of course, the weather was heavenly."

"And I take it from the way you keep eyeballing that phone that you and your Bailey got on well together?"

Maureen rose and began to pace the small living room.

"Yes," she said after a moment, "we did."

"Then what's the problem?"

Maureen spread her hands helplessly. "It's all so complicated."

"Tell me about it." Mrs. Bondini sat back and crossed her ankles.

Maureen was used to looking out for her elderly neighbor. This switch in roles was a new experience, but not one that Maureen minded. It was nice having someone mother her for a change. By the time she was done with her muddled explanation of how much she cared for Bailey and why she didn't want to get involved with him and his children, Mrs. Bondini looked thoroughly confused.

"Has he said anything about a permanent relationship yet?"

Maureen shook her head.

"Then it seems to me you have more of a problem worrying about his intentions than you do trying not to get hooked on him. Sounds like you already are."

Maureen sat back down with a thud. Trust her friend to cut through the fog. It was true. She already loved him. She liked his kids. It was too late to worry about being hurt. The only thing left to find out now was how much.

Before she could say anything, the phone rang. With an apologetic glance at her guest, Maureen picked up the receiver.

As soon as she said hello, an enthusiastic young man tried to interest her in buying a line of children's books.

"Thanks, anyway, but I don't have any children," she said.

"Oh," he replied. "I'm sorry." Perhaps he meant he was sorry he'd bothered her, or sorry he'd wasted his own time, but for some reason it seemed more likely to her that he was sorry she didn't have any children.

"Another salesman," she told Mrs. Bondini, shaking off the thoughts his words raised.

"Don't worry, dear. Bailey will call. You're just too special a person for him to let slip away." She rose and set aside her empty cup.

Maureen thanked her for the compliment, not sure if she wanted it to be true or not. Life had certainly been simpler before!

"Thanks again for feeding Max," Maureen said as she followed her neighbor to the front door.

"Oh, you're welcome. He's no trouble at all. See you later."

Maureen watched while Mrs. Bondini crossed to her own door, shutting it securely behind her. For a moment Maureen stood looking out onto the darkening street, thinking about Bailey and wondering what he was doing. Supervising homework and baths, no doubt, or reading bedtime stories. Wondering how much longer he would be able to keep his children.

Sighing, she closed the door, just as the phone began to ring again.

"Are you busy?" Bailey's familiar voice asked.

Smiling, she sat down, cradling the receiver to her ear. "No, not at all. How are the children?"

She could hear his quiet breathing on the other end before answered. "They're fine, both excited because they talked me into letting them bring home two of the kittens from Janice's house next week."

Maureen found herself wishing she could have been there to watch Shawn and Melissa's faces. Aloud she only said, "How will your dog like that?"

"He'll adjust." Digger and the kittens weren't what Bailey wanted to talk about, but now that Maureen was on the line he was finding it impossible to ask what the weekend had meant to her.

"I had a great time," he said instead.

"So did I! It was a perfect weekend."

Bailey could almost feel her warmth and softness curled up against him as she had been in their room. His physical reaction was immediate and predictable, and he had to stifle a groan.

"Perfect," he echoed.

There was a tiny silence and then Maureen said in a low voice, "I miss you."

If Bailey had been alone he would have dropped everything and gone to her. As it was, there was no way he could leave.

"Damn!" he growled in frustration. "I wish I could be there with you right now."

"Me, too. But I'll see you soon."

"Yeah, I guess that will have to do."

In a few more moments, they ended the conversation. After he had said goodbye and heard the click of her hanging up, Bailey sat holding the receiver, thinking about what she had admitted to him on the phone. God, he wished they were together so he could show her how she made him feel. Finally he forced himself to shake off his erotic thoughts and set down the receiver that he still gripped tightly. He picked up the television guide and flipped through it, but nothing caught his attention. After a few more restless moments, he picked up his Spanish text and opened it. Since he couldn't relax, he might as well try to work off some of his energy reviewing for the next quiz.

When Bailey realized he hadn't absorbed a word of what he'd been reading, he tossed the book aside, swearing under his breath. Digger, who had been napping nearby and snoring softly, got up and shook himself, then came over and put his head on Bailey's knee, staring up at him with droopy eyes.

"You wouldn't be so friendly if you knew what I'd agreed to," Bailey told Digger as he scratched the dog behind his ears. "After next week, I have a feeling your life will never be the same again."

Digger replied by slurping his wet tongue across Bailey's hand, while Bailey made a mental note to call his lawyer first thing the next morning and ask if she'd heard anything from Angela yet. How could he even think about the future, if he didn't know whether the kids would be with him or not? He felt as if his life was on hold, and the feeling wasn't a pleasant one. If Susan hadn't heard anything, it was probably time for another conversation with his ex-wife.

When Bailey spoke to Susan the next morning she told him that she hadn't heard from Angela's lawyer and suggested that Bailey leave things be for a little while longer. It was more difficult for him than taking action, but he finally agreed, knowing that Susan was right in saying that anything he did might provoke his ex-wife.

"I'll call you the minute I hear a thing," Susan promised. "And you let me know if she contacts you."

"I wish something would happen," Bailey said. "This waiting is driving me nuts."

"I know. But Angela hasn't even found a job yet, as far as we know. She's staying at a motel. I'm still hoping that she changes her mind. You said it was possible."

"With Angela anything's possible." Bailey let out a long breath. "Sorry I bothered you."

"No bother," Susan said quickly. "I'll talk to you later."

"Was that Mom on the phone?" Shawn asked as he came into the kitchen.

"No. Do you have your homework and your lunch?"

"Yeah. Can you give us a ride to school?"

Bailey glanced at the clock. "Sure. I'm almost ready to leave. See what your sister is doing, while I make myself a sandwich," It had been a long time since Angela had come by or even called the kids. What was she up to now?

Maureen looked up when Bailey pulled out the chair next to her in the crowded cafeteria, and her heart gave a happy lurch at the warmth of his smile. For a moment his eyes darkened as his gaze shifted to her mouth and back. "Consider yourself kissed hello," he said.

Maureen felt the color fill her cheeks. "It's not the same thing."

"No, it isn't," he agreed. "Maybe we can fix that later."

He was coming to her apartment for an hour after class to study Spanish. Although his pirate's smile was tempting, she reminded herself that he needed the help. He was intelligent and grasped the work quickly; unfortunately he just didn't have enough time to really master the subject on his own. He claimed that an hour of Maureen's tutoring was worth three of studying by himself. Since she liked to spend time with him no matter what they did, she wasn't inclined to argue.

"Any word from Angela?" she asked, finishing her coffee.

Bailey shook his head. "I wonder what she's playing at. After the argument we had in the parking lot last week I expected something big."

He'd elaborated about that a little more while they were at Port Ludlow, and now Maureen nodded. "You thought she would want to get back at you."

"I still do. And what better way than through the kids? But I talked to Susan this morning and she still hasn't heard a word."

Fifteen minutes later, while Bailey sat in class, he thought about how tense he had been lately, waiting for and wondering about Angela's next move, and how relieved he was each day when both children got off the school bus and came home. Did he really think she might just take them?

As common as that kind of thing was getting to be, deep down he really didn't believe she would disappear with them. Angela might be irresponsible and unpredictable, but he'd bet anything that she loved her children in her own way. She might leave them, knowing that Bailey would be there to take care of them, but she would never steal them from the only home they'd ever known. She wasn't that hard-hearted and, perhaps more to the point, she wouldn't be that eager to be a single parent on the run, totally responsible for the needs of two active, exhausting children. When she had found a job and rented a place more permanent than the motel, Bailey would need to really start worrying.

"I've been working!" Angela exclaimed as she swept into Bailey's living room, arms full of packages. "I just got my first paycheck today and I bought Melissa and Shawn each a little something."

"Oh boy," Melissa said, jumping up and down. She'd been sitting on the couch looking at library books when Angela rang the doorbell.

Bailey stood with one hand on the knob, wishing he could push her back outside and shut the door in her face.

"Where's Shawn?" Angela asked, acknowledging Bailey's presence for the first time. She wore a beautifully tailored gray suit and high heels. Her long red hair was swept into a knot in back and even her makeup was subdued. Bailey realized with a sinking heart that he was looking at Angela's version of a serious career woman.

"Shawn's at practice. Where are you working?"

Angela named the real-estate office she'd been at before. "They were glad to have me back."

"Did you tell them you wouldn't be staying?" he drawled, controlling the urge to reach out and shake her.

Angela's eyes widened in surprise. "Of course not. Why would I do that?"

Bailey glanced at Melissa, who was watching the two of them with great interest. "I know you, Angela. You've never stuck to anything in your life."

Her eyes filled with tears, a sight that might have moved him if he didn't know she could do it at will. Then, while he waited tensely, she tossed back her head and blinked several times, turning her attention to her daughter.

"Here, honey. See what Mommy bought you."

Bailey's heart warmed when Melissa looked at him for permission before taking the bag from Angela's outstretched hand. He nodded, smiling at her. When Melissa gave him a sweet smile of her own before returning her attention to her mother, he had to swallow the emotion that rose in his throat.

"Oh, thank you!" Melissa was looking at the set of Barbie luggage with an enraptured expression. "Can I go play with these now?" Again she sought Bailey's permission.

"Sure. Just until it's time to get ready for supper, though."

Melissa began to leave, then whirled toward her mother. "Thank you again," she said. "I love them."

After she'd left the room, Angela sat down on the couch, tossing Bailey a defiant glance. "When will Shawn be home?"

"Any minute. Care to wait?" He didn't try to keep the sarcasm from infiltrating his tone.

"Thank you."

She sat back and crossed her legs, giving Bailey a mocking smile when his attention was inadvertently drawn by the movement. It was all he could do not to make a blistering remark at her smug expression.

"How long are you planning to stay around?" he asked instead.

"Wouldn't you like to know?" The laughter in her voice set his teeth on edge. If she had any idea how furious she was making him, she'd never let up.

"It's your children who'd like to know," he replied coolly. "Or had you forgotten about them?"

Angela flushed, uncrossing her legs. "Of course not. They're the reason I'm staying. I put a deposit down on an apartment near here just this afternoon." A car door slammed and she turned to glance out the window. "Better get used to having me back in your life," she said as Shawn burst through the front door.

Bailey's muscles knotted with helpless frustration, his worst nightmare coming true, as he watched Angela hug their son and hand him a package.

"Neat!" Shawn said, holding up felt pens and a poster to color. "Thanks." He looked up guiltily, the anxious expression on his face tearing at Bailey's heart. How they put the kids in the middle!

Bailey forced himself to smile. "That's nice, Shawn. Do a good job and you can hang it in your room when it's done."

"Are you staying for supper?" Shawn asked his mother.

She glanced at Bailey, obviously waiting for him to say something.

"Sorry, son. Your mother has other plans tonight. Maybe she can take you and Melissa out sometime soon, if she calls first so we can plan on it." His gaze locked with Angela's as he defied her to contradict him. For a moment the air between them crackled with tension.

"That's right," she said finally as Bailey's shoulders sagged with relief. "I'll see you again soon." She kissed Shawn on the cheek and then called to Melissa, who came running out of her room to give Angela a hug.

"I'm packing my Barbie clothes for a trip," she said. "A short vacation," she added, "like Daddy and Maureen took last weekend."

The sudden silence in the room would have been funny under other circumstances, Bailey thought as he tried to keep his expression blank. Angela's attention had whipped from Melissa to him in less than a heartbeat, her eyes narrowed and her mouth a straight line.

"Is that the woman I saw you walk to her car at the college?"

He nodded. "Did you expect me to live like a monk?" As soon as the words were out, he regretted them. He didn't want to bring Maureen into it, and provoking Angela could be disastrous.

Her chin went up a fraction. "Of course not," she drawled. "*I* haven't."

If she expected the remark to wound him, she was bound for disappointment, he thought, experiencing not one iota of jealousy. With a flash of revelation he realized that if Maureen had said the same thing, his reaction would have been totally different.

Bailey crossed to the door, aware of both children watching him and their mother closely. "Thanks for coming by," he told Angela in a neutral tone. "Sorry you can't stay."

When he held the door open, her eyes flashed again, but then she bent to kiss Shawn and Melissa and tell them goodbye before brushing past Bailey.

"I'll be back," she said.

"We'll be here," Bailey replied, shutting the door behind her. When he turned, Shawn was staring at him.

"What is it?" Bailey asked.

"I guess you were right. You and Mom don't like each other very much, do you?"

Chapter Eight

Maureen read the directions that had come with the test kit sitting on her bathroom counter, then refolded the sheet carefully and tucked it back inside the box. She'd been putting off using the kit for almost a week, sure that her period would come.

Each day that Maureen was late she had told herself she would test herself; each day she reread the directions and then again put off taking the test. Just because she was as regular as a time clock didn't mean she could never be late without being pregnant. There had to be some other reason.

Maureen got up and turned on the shower taps, slipping off her robe and gown and testing the water with her hand before stepping into the tub and sliding the glass door shut behind her. As the warm spray relaxed her tense muscles, she glanced down at her flat stomach, then raised her arms and looked at her breasts, medium-sized, rather nicely rounded and showing no signs of age or surrender to the pull of gravity.

What would it be like to feel a baby moving inside her? What would it be like to hold that baby to her breast and nourish it? Maureen's lips curved upward at the image of herself with a fuzzy-haired infant. When the image expanded to reveal Bailey standing over the two of them with a tender smile on his face, the picture suddenly splintered into harsh reality.

Bailey didn't want any more children. He had told her so. In the several weeks since they had shared that wonderful time on the peninsula, he hadn't said anything to contradict his earlier statement. Bailey already had a family.

If Maureen was pregnant, she would be raising this child alone. The thought chilled her beneath the warm spray of the shower. Shivering, she turned off the water and grabbed a large bath towel from the rack.

As she wiped herself dry and threw on her clothes, she didn't glance at the pregnancy kit again. As long as she didn't know for sure, it was easy to tell herself she couldn't be pregnant. Easy to dismiss the what-if's that clamored for attention.

"You're the only family I need," she told Max, who was sitting outside the bathroom doorway.

When she bent to pet him, he arched into her hand, purring loudly. Then he padded toward the kitchen, looking over his shoulder to see if she was coming to fix his breakfast.

When she returned home late that afternoon, delayed by a staff meeting, Max was waiting on the couch where he had undoubtedly slept away most of the day. Maureen was tired, too, and stifled a yawn as she shut the door behind her. For once she wasn't looking forward to evening classes.

Was she tired because she hadn't slept well the night before, or because Bailey's child was growing inside her? Had her queasiness after breakfast been real or imagined? The pregnancy kit she had bought could be used at any time of day. A sudden urgency to know for sure before she saw Bailey again propelled her toward the bathroom, knees quaking.

Bailey sat at the round table he had begun to think of as his and Maureen's, watching his fellow students in the crowded cafeteria as he waited for her to join him. Since the two of them had spent some time on his Spanish, it had become more manageable. Maureen was a good teacher, patient but thorough. He couldn't help but notice how her students flocked around her, and the way she dealt with each of their individual concerns. She would make a good mother, he thought, wondering if she'd ever regretted not having children of her own.

Bailey had gotten a solid B in his midterm exam and hoped that he could maintain it in the final only a few weeks away. He had been planning to take another class summer quarter, but now, with Maureen taking a break from teaching until fall, he had lost his enthusiasm. Maybe he needed a break from classes, too.

Maureen always met him in the cafeteria before evening classes now, and they saw each other off-campus as often as their schedules permitted. The weekend before they had taken Bailey's children to the waterfront in Seattle, visiting the Aquarium and several import shops, and then stopping at the Seattle Center to ride the elevator to the observation deck at the top of the Space Needle before descending again to eat at the International Food Circus.

Bailey had been gratified to see the effort Maureen was making to get to know his children better. After hearing all about the new kittens, she had helped Melissa pick out a dinner of pizza and ice cream from the numerous booths at the Food Circus. Even Shawn hadn't been immune to Maureen's charm. The two of them had spent considerable time together discussing the colorful fish at the Aquarium, and then, at the adjoining gift shop, Shawn had helped her pick out a T-shirt for her brother's birthday.

Her brother Jason and his wife lived in San Diego, and Maureen had been there several times. On the ride home from Seattle she had described to Shawn and Melissa some of the things she had seen while visiting her older brother, including Sea World and the zoo.

Bailey and Maureen had also found several opportunities over the weeks to spend private time together at her apartment where they could be alone except for her cat, who was content to stay out of their way. There they had made passionate love, every time more satisfying that the time before as they each discovered what pleased the other. Bailey was beginning to see that he could never have enough of her. Even in the crowded cafeteria, the memory of Maureen pressed against him intimately made Bailey's body tighten with response.

If only Angela would make her move, so he could settle the question of the children's custody. Impatience made Bailey feel as if his hands were tied. His ex-wife was content to drop by every few days. Twice she had taken Shawn and Melissa to spend the weekend at the apartment she was furnishing, and both times Bailey's feelings had been pulled in two directions, his exasperation offset by the freedom to spend more time with Maureen.

While Bailey was waiting for Maureen at the cafeteria, she was pacing her apartment, wondering if she had done the right thing in calling in sick and having a substitute replace her in class that evening. Bailey would wonder what had happened. He would probably stop by on his way home to check on her, and the last thing she wanted was a showdown. She wasn't ready.

After she had double-checked the results of the home pregnancy test at least twice, Maureen had wandered into the bedroom and sat down on the edge of the bed, stunned. She hadn't really believed that pregnancy was a possibility. Now she kept telling herself that the test was wrong. How accurate could something that simple be?

Maureen wished she could put it out of her mind until she saw the doctor, but she couldn't. Bailey's face kept appearing before her, with his wide pirate's grin and dark, glowing eyes. Then, in her mind, his expression would change, features chilling, mouth thinning to a grim line as she told him the news.

Maureen surged to her feet, pacing. Her heart seemed to be pounding in double time. She blinked away tears of frustration. How was she going to break the news to Bailey? Could she even find the right words? Or the right time? She tried to think, but nothing came. At her sides, her hands curled into fists.

What would his response be? A half dozen possibilities crowded her thoughts, none of them good. Maybe she could just leave and not tell him. Ever. She could run away and change her name. He would never find out. The ridiculousness of her thoughts would have made her smile under different circumstances.

"Damn," she said out loud. "How can this be happening?" She bit her lip to stem the rising hysteria that threatened to bubble out and overwhelm her. Maybe it wasn't happening; maybe it was a bad dream and any moment now she would waken. Maureen tried, but it didn't work. This was no dream; this was real life.

She dragged in a deep breath, trying to calm herself. That proved easier said than done. While she paced, all kinds of things popped into her head. What would she do about work? She'd have to take a maternity leave. Would she be eligible? Maureen wouldn't be the first teacher to have a child while unmarried, but there would certainly be a lot of gossip. She hated to think that people she barely knew would be talking about her, exchanging bits of information about her private life. Speculating.

Her condo was roomy enough, so she wouldn't have to move unless she wanted to. The small spare bedroom could easily be converted to a nursery.

Telling herself not to think about a baby until she knew for sure was pointless. Deep inside she knew the test was right. She was forty years old, single, and expecting the child of a man who didn't want it.

Bailey had trouble concentrating in class as he watched the hands of the wall clock move slowly toward the time of the scheduled break. What had happened to Maureen? She hadn't made it to the cafeteria, and while he waited outside her classroom an older man finally showed up. All he could tell Bailey was that the assigned teacher had called in sick.

At least Maureen hadn't been in an accident on the way to the college, as he had feared, but Bailey couldn't imagine what might have come over her so suddenly that she hadn't been able to teach and hadn't known in time to tell him.

At the break he found a pay phone and called her apartment. The phone rang and rang, worrying Bailey all over again. What if Maureen was seriously ill? Lying on the floor, unconscious and alone? Making a sudden decision, he sprinted back to the classroom, told Mr. Howard that something had come up at home, got his next assignment and left.

In front of Maureen's door he started to ring the bell and then hesitated. This was crazy. She'd come down with the flu or a sudden cold, that was all. She probably didn't want visitors.

Bailey wasn't merely a visitor. He loved her. The realization didn't hit him like a thunderbolt, it sneaked up and insinuated itself so smoothly that he almost missed it.

He loved her.

For a moment his hand dropped to his side. Then with a bemused shake of his head, he reached up to ring the bell again. There was no way he could tell her how he felt until his life was in some kind of order, but he could still check to see if she needed anything.

After his finger pressed the button, he waited. Maybe she'd been at the drugstore when he'd called, getting medicine. She had to be back by now.

The doorbell caught Maureen by surprise and she glanced at her watch. It was too early for Bailey. Perhaps Mrs. Bondini had noticed that she hadn't gone to class. Maureen didn't feel like talking to anyone, but ignoring the bell would be rude if her neighbor knew she was there.

Maureen pulled the door open and then stood silent with surprise.

"I wanted to make sure you were all right," Bailey said, smiling at her with a warmth that made something curl tight inside her. "I called but there was no answer. Is it okay if I come in for a minute? I won't stay."

Maureen stepped aside. It hadn't occurred to her that he would cut class. "I'm sorry I didn't have a chance to call you," she said. "I hope you weren't worried."

His thick brows rose as she shut the front door. "Worried? Just because you didn't show up and I wasn't sure if you'd been in an accident, or what? Naw, I wasn't worried."

"I'm sorry. I didn't think." She'd been doing nothing *but* think.

Bailey's expression softened and he reached up a hand to stroke her cheek. "So what's wrong? Your nose isn't running, your eyes aren't glassy." His hand shifted. "You don't seem to be running a fever." He looked into her eyes. His own were glowing warmly. "In fact, you don't look sick. So what's the problem?"

Maureen couldn't tell him yet. Not until the doctor confirmed her condition. Then she would deal with how to break the news to Bailey. In the meantime, telling him, adding another burden to his full load of worry just to ease her own anxiety, wasn't the right thing to do at all. She had realized that when she began to calm down. Especially when it might not be true.

Maureen pressed one hand to her stomach. "Cramps," she said, the lie threatening to choke her. "I didn't decide to stay home until the last minute and it was too late to let you know." That much was true.

Bailey curled a protective arm around her shoulders, pulling her into the reassuring warmth of his body. "Here, sit down," he said, gently guiding her to the couch. The tenderness in his voice brought fresh tears to her eyes. "You shouldn't be on your feet. Can I fix you something, perhaps a cup of that herbal tea you like?"

Maureen allowed him to seat her and then shook her head as he hovered anxiously. "I think what I need the most is my heating pad and an early night." She peered into his face. "I'm sorry," she said again, sniffing.

Bailey felt an odd sense of foreboding settle on him like an icy hand, making him reluctant to leave. Maureen's skin was pale and she looked fragile as she sat huddled on the couch. She seemed almost ready to cry.

Still she clearly preferred being alone. Bailey wished he could climb into her bed and curl up behind her, massaging away the pain and letting his warmth seep into her to relax the muscles that were cramping. Most of all, he wished he could share his newly discovered feelings with her. But how would she take the news?

Frustrated, he straightened. "Sure I can't do anything before I go?"

The relief that crossed her face cut him like a knife. "No, thanks. But I appreciate your stopping by."

Bailey felt so helpless, as if there were a wall between them; a wall of something he couldn't see, but one that shut him out completely. Anguish twisted deep inside him. He couldn't put his finger on any reason he should feel that way. Everyone got sick occasionally.

"I'm sorry I worried you," Maureen said again, clearly impatient for him to leave. She started to rise.

"No, don't." He held her shoulder down with one hand. "I can see myself out. I hope you feel better soon."

A few minutes later Bailey was gone and Maureen was settled into her bed with a cup of tea, positive she wouldn't sleep that night. She had told him she was sure she'd be well enough to go to school the next morning. As he'd turned to leave, his wide shoulders filling the doorway, she'd almost stopped him, almost said the words that would have kept him with her.

The words that might have driven him away forever.

Now Maureen was glad she had remained silent. She put her empty cup aside and turned out the bedside lamp, expecting that she would toss and turn for hours as her conscience kept her awake. Lying down, she pulled the covers up to her chin. In moments she was asleep.

Maureen left the doctor's office the next day grateful she had gotten in so soon, but stunned by the news she thought she had already accepted. Her life was changed now, never to be the same. But how was she going to tell Bailey? What would he do? Would he offer to marry her? He had said he didn't want more children, but Bailey was an honorable man, and marriage was the honorable option. And he would feel trapped by that honor. Whatever affection he had for her would fade in the face of his obligation. Maureen shuddered at the idea of Bailey's resentment, perhaps even his eventual hatred.

And how did *she* feel about this? Maureen took a slow, deep breath, and then another. There were other options, she knew. Abortion, adoption. The doctor had mentioned both, but Maureen had shaken her head. For her, they weren't options. For her there was only one choice, to have this baby and to raise it.

Alone.

The responsibility was overwhelming. For a moment tears filled her eyes, but furiously she blinked them away. She wasn't young and this was her first child. There were tests that could be done later on, and then she might have an even more painful decision to make. The doctor had mentioned statistics that Maureen failed to take in, frightening conditions that were more common at her age.

She told herself not to think about that. There were too many other decisions for her to borrow trouble. A child was growing inside her, a child who would need her love, her care. A child she and Bailey had created together.

Maureen got into her car and started the engine, glad she didn't have to return to school until the next morning. Her knuckles turned white on the steering wheel and she made herself take a few deep breaths before backing out of the parking slot. Then a reluctant smile curved her lips as she turned onto the road.

A baby. As if it were yesterday, she could remember the way she'd felt when the doctor had told her and Bob, her husband at the time, that she was pregnant.

Even though the pregnancy had been unplanned, the news had filled her with excitement. With a thrill of expectation. Then she had turned to share the feeling with Bob. He'd been frowning, his eyes cold.

"Hell," he had said. "I thought we'd been more careful."

Maureen could still hear the relief in his voice when she had told him a month later that she had miscarried. The doctor said she could have other children, but Bob had refused to discuss it. When Maureen persisted, he'd told her about Shelly. No wonder he hadn't wanted a child with Maureen.

This time would be different. She didn't need anyone else. She would have her baby. Firmly she shoved aside the nagging doubts that rose to plague her. Bailey had already told her how *he* felt. It seemed that she had lost the man she loved to gain the child she now realized she had always wanted. Her fingers curled protectively across her stomach. Surely this child wouldn't be taken from her, too.

When she got back to the apartment complex, Maureen went straight to see Mrs. Bondini. She had thought about confiding in a friend at work or calling her brother, but quickly discarded both ideas. Jason would worry, and telling one of the other teachers would be putting an unfair burden of secrecy on her.

Mrs. Bondini opened the door wide. "Come in, dear. I haven't seen as much of you as I'd like to lately. Not that I expect you to keep exclusive company with an old lady," she continued as Maureen went past her to sit on the red velvet sofa. "At least when there are men like Bailey around to make your heart flutter."

He's done more than flutter my heart, Maureen thought to herself as she turned down an offer of tea and cookies. How would her dear old friend react to the news that Maureen was pregnant?

She was trying to figure out how to tell her, while Mrs. Bondini brought her up to date on the various activities of their fellow tenants. Maureen never could figure out how she knew so much about what was going on. Maureen also knew without a doubt that Mrs. Bondini's lips would be sealed unto death over anything of a confidential nature. She might like to gossip, but she was entirely trustworthy with secrets.

"There's a new tenant in 204," Mrs. Bondini said. "A retired secretary. Divorced, I think Margaret said."

Before she could continue, Maureen blurted out, "I'm pregnant."

There was silence while Mrs. Bondini stared at her, obviously struggling to assimilate the news. Then she rose to sit beside Maureen on the sofa.

"How are you feeling?" she asked, covering Maureen's hand with her own veined one.

"Fine. A little tired. A whole lot surprised."

"Have you been to the doctor?"

Maureen nodded.

"And everything's okay?"

"So far." Maureen had never mentioned her earlier miscarriage to her neighbor, but the doctor assured her that it wasn't that uncommon in a first pregnancy and probably had no bearing on this one.

"And how is Bailey taking it?" Mrs. Bondini asked.

Maureen shifted her gaze to the canary, Frankie, who was chirping quietly in the confines of his brass cage. "Bailey doesn't know. I just saw the doctor today."

"You *are* going to tell him." Mrs. Bondini's voice was firm with conviction.

"Am I?" Maureen asked rebelliously. "Do I really have the right to lay this on him when he has so many other things to worry about?" She had told her friend about Bailey's ex-wife and the threatened custody fight.

"Absolutely. He's the baby's father. He's a strong, caring man and he'll handle it."

"How do you know he's strong and caring?" Maureen was curious about the conviction in her neighbor's voice. She had only met Bailey once.

"I know because you wouldn't have become involved with someone who wasn't those things," Mrs. Bondini replied. Her words were immensely reassuring to Maureen, who began, for the first time since the doctor had told her the news, to wonder if everything just might work out. "It's his right and responsibility to know."

"I'm a modern woman," Maureen argued. "I don't need a man to rescue me."

"Rubbish." Mrs. Bondini made a sweeping gesture with her free hand. "You need the baby's father. Whether or not you marry, the man has a right to know he's helped create another life."

At least Mrs. Bondini wasn't lecturing her about birth control, or telling her that she had to get married. For an old lady, her outlook was surprisingly modern and practical.

"I take it that you want this baby?" Mrs. Bondini's voice was gentle, her expression kind.

"Very much," Maureen answered, knowing with absolute certainty that it was true. She did want this child, a child created in love, at least on her part.

"Then you must tell Bailey. I really think he'll want this child, too."

"He told me he *didn't* want more children," Maureen blurted, filled with sudden pain.

Mrs. Bondini shook her head dismissively. "I'll bet that was in the abstract. Probably one day when his son and daughter were straining his patience." She patted Maureen's hand. "All parents say that at one time or another, but they don't necessarily mean it. Give the man a chance."

Maureen rose reluctantly, knowing she needed to be alone to begin making some decisions. "Thanks for listening. I'll think about what you said."

"And call me if you need anything." Mrs. Bondini squeezed her arm as she followed Maureen to the door. "I mean it, dear. Anything at all. Even if it's just someone to listen."

Maureen gave her frail body a hug before she crossed to her own apartment. What she needed was a husband, she thought. Then she stiffened with shock as she entered her living room. Where had that idea come from? She didn't want to be married. She'd tried that once, with disastrous results. Besides, she enjoyed her independence, and she was perfectly capable of raising a child alone.

She was still wrestling with her thoughts, when the telephone rang.

"It's me," Bailey said after she'd answered. "I wondered if you were up to getting some dinner. Angela is going to take the kids for hamburgers and a movie."

Maureen glanced at her watch and then did some quick calculating. "Why don't you come here? I'll fix us something."

"I don't want you to go to any trouble," he said. "I can bring a pizza if you still don't feel well enough to go out."

He was so thoughtful.

"No, I'm much better. In fact, I feel like cooking up something in the kitchen. Really, I mean it." Maybe the preparations would take her mind off what she had to tell him.

Bailey's reply was hesitant. "Okay, if you're sure. But I didn't mean to make work for you."

"No problem." Maybe fate had arranged this meeting.

"What can I bring?"

"Wine," Maureen said, then remembered that she wouldn't be drinking. "That is, if you want some. I've sworn off for a while."

"Oh? Why's that?"

She thought quickly. "Calories. It's an easy way to cut back."

"Not that you need to worry," he said. "I love those slim curves." His voice had gone husky, making desire whisper along her nerve endings. Ruthlessly she pushed it away.

How would he like it when she was huge with child? Would he still be around or would he have removed himself, angry she had been careless or sure she was trying to trap him? Somehow she couldn't picture the Bailey she knew doing either of those things. She couldn't really believe he would abandon her.

Reminding herself to be more careful of what she said, Maureen made arrangements to see him at six. After they hung up, she decided to fix a simple meal of game hens, rice and salad. Checking the cupboards and refrigerator, she made a list and left for the grocery store. She still had no idea how she was going to drop her bombshell, but Bailey was going to be told tonight.

"Hey, something wrong? Still not feeling too well?" Bailey's fork hovered over his plate as he studied Maureen carefully. Perhaps accepting her dinner invitation hadn't been the most considerate thing to do, but he had missed being with her.

Maureen shook her head, smiling wanly, and he noticed that her cheeks were pale. "I'm fine, really."

"You look a little tired."

"I guess I didn't sleep too well." Her glance made brief contact with his before it skittered away.

Bailey bent closer, unable to resist. "That's because you were alone."

Maureen's answering smile made him want to go around the table and kiss her. Instead he made himself take another bite of the game hen, which was moist and nicely browned. "This is good."

"Thank you." Even her voice was edged with exhaustion and something else he couldn't identify as easily. Nerves, perhaps. But why?

"How's the job at that mini-mall going?" she asked, successfully distracting him. He enjoyed his work, and liked to talk about it, pleased that Maureen was interested enough to ask.

For the next few minutes Bailey described his progress in wiring a new eight-unit strip mall for electricity. Since his regular helper was busy at another job, he had hired two electricians, a journeyman and an apprentice. It was gratifying to hear Maureen's chuckle of appreciation as he described some of the mistakes the apprentice had made that day. Only in hindsight were they amusing to him.

"When we turned the overhead fan in one unit off it ran and when we turned it on it stopped," he said. "Just a small thing, but confusing all the same."

"I hope it wasn't a lot of work to correct the mistake."

Bailey noticed that she was pushing the food around her plate without eating much of it. Maybe he was boring her with shop talk. "No. He had just hooked up the wires backward." Bailey took a bite of salad and chewed it thoughtfully. "Enough about me. How have you been?"

Maureen hesitated, not quite ready to dump her news on him. Let the poor man enjoy one last meal first.

"I've been fine, but tell me how Shawn's team is doing. They won that game I watched with you."

"Shawn really likes playing first-base, and he's good at it. I can't believe how much he's matured since just a year ago." Bailey went on to describe the last game, which the team had won by a lopsided score.

Maureen was content to listen, and to watch him. His eyes glowed with enthusiasm and his mouth moved with lazy sensuality as he talked. Each one of his features had become familiar to her, as had every part of his beautiful male body. The thought made her shift uncomfortably. Would she ever know the delights of making love with him again? How would he react when she told him she had been wrong about being safe that first time? Would he believe that it had been an honest miscalculation on her part? And how could she find the courage to tell him, despite her earlier resolve?

When they had finished dinner, Bailey helped clean up the kitchen, efficiently loading the dishwasher and wiping off the table while she made coffee and put things away. Once he cornered her and stole a kiss, but when she pushed at him lightly he backed off with a lazy grin.

"Why don't you go sit in the living room and I'll bring out the coffee and that delicious-looking cake you brought?" she suggested as he hung the kitchen towel on the oven-door handle.

Bailey straightened and gave her an intense look before taking her into his arms. "I don't want to be separated from you for even that long," he said, burying his face in her blond hair.

"I promise I'll hurry."

His arms tightened and he dropped a kiss onto her upturned mouth. Then he sobered and groaned softly. "That wasn't enough," he whispered, bending his head again.

Maureen met him halfway, and the kiss they shared left her shaken, reaction twisting inside her as she clung to him. Sweet Lord, how she needed him, now more than ever.

Bailey stepped back, dropping his arms. "Remember, I got the cake at that health-food deli," he told her as casually as if they had just shared an impersonal handshake. "No sugar and not too many calories. Not that I can understand why you want to diet, but you did say you were watching it." His gaze ran approvingly over her figure. "You're perfect now."

Maureen thanked him, remembering what she had told him about the wine and coloring over yet another deception. "Go on, I'll be right out." She turned to pour the coffee and fix a tray.

Bailey eased her aside. "I'll carry this. You bring the cups." Before she could protest, he'd cut the generous wedge of cake into two pieces and put them on plates, grabbed forks and was headed toward the living room. Since they both drank their coffee black, there was nothing left for Maureen to bring but cups and napkins. Suddenly shaking with nerves, she followed him, trying to find the words to tell him that he was going to be a father yet again.

Maureen finally found the courage, swallowing a bite of cake that threatened to stick in her throat and then said, "I'm sorry that I miscalculated things so badly, but I've been to the doctor and I'm pregnant. It must have been that first time when I thought I was safe."

Bailey stared at her and she lost the sudden spurt of courage that had propelled her and bent her head to sip from her coffee cup. It shook so badly in her hand that she almost spilled its contents onto the pale carpeting.

Beside her on the couch, Bailey carefully set down his own cup. "Did I hear you right?" he asked, voice remarkably calm. "You did say that you're expecting my baby?"

Maureen forced herself to meet his gaze, dismayed at the serious set to his mouth. Any moment now, he would explode. He would walk out on her. Or perhaps he'd stand by her until she had the child, but things between them would never be the same.

"Yes. That's what I said. I'm pregnant." Her cup rattled in its saucer and she put it on the table. "I'm sorry," she said. "This was as big a shock to me as it is to you, believe me."

For a moment Bailey gazed down at his hands as if he didn't know where to look. Then he raised his head and stared full into Maureen's face. To her surprise, he was smiling. Grinning rather foolishly, she thought.

Beside her, Bailey was trying his best to take in her astounding news. He had known there was something on her mind, but he had never in his wildest dreams suspected it might be this. He knew he should be devastated by the bombshell, calculating how it was going to affect his life, the case, his relationship with Maureen. But somehow he couldn't bring himself to be that cold-bloodedly rational. All he could picture was this woman beside him round with his child, a child they had created with their passion for each other.

Some things just couldn't be orchestrated, decided reasonably and sensibly. Sometimes a man had to go on his instinct, his deep-down gut feelings, believing that a situation would work out because it would be too damned painful for it not to. Without hesitating, he took her hands in a bone-crushing grip, almost afraid to let it go.

Maureen's eyes were wide, her face a study in suspended animation, as if she were afraid to breathe until he spoke. Well, by God, if this doesn't make her suck in a lungful, he thought wryly, nothing will.

"Maureen," he said, lacing his fingers with hers, "I can't tell you how happy you've just made me."

If anything, her expression grew more wary, almost suspicious, but she didn't speak, which was just as well. Bailey didn't intend to be interrupted until he was done.

He bent his head and kissed the back of her hand almost reverently, so filled with emotion that for a moment he thought he wouldn't be able to go on. Then he swallowed and spoke the words that clamored to be spoken.

"Marry me," he beseeched, hoping that everything he was feeling showed in his face because he was too overcome to say it all to her right now. "Please, sweetheart, marry me and we'll make a real family for our children."

Chapter Nine

When Maureen didn't immediately answer his proposal, Bailey leaped to his feet, jamming his hands into his pockets. "I know this is sudden," he said. "But surely you can see that it's the only solution."

From the mutinous frown on her lovely face, he could tell that he'd taken the wrong tack. He sat back down beside her, but Maureen edged away from him and then rose and went to the window, where she looked out into the night. He ached to touch her, to wrap her in a protective embrace and tell her that everything was going to work out.

Max came over to where Bailey was sitting and butted his hand with a furry head. Absently he began to scratch behind the cat's ears.

When Maureen turned to look at Bailey, unsure what to say, the sight of him petting her cat almost made her smile. Max was usually coldly aloof to strangers, but he had taken to Bailey immediately. Maureen wished she could be as trusting as Max.

Instead, old hurts rose up inside her, reminding her to be cautious, to tread warily. Bailey hadn't said anything about love, only joining families. He was probably keenly aware of what her situation could do to his custody case, if Angela ever got around to filing suit.

"I just don't know," Maureen said, uncomfortable under his steady gaze. If he had told her he loved her, she would be in his arms now. Sadly she pushed the thought away. One relationship had been strained past endurance by a pregnancy; she didn't need another to end that way. Without love she couldn't trust Bailey to stay with her throughout the long haul, not to leave her when the going got tough.

He came over to her and put a tentative hand on her shoulder. "What did the doctor say? Are you okay?" There was concern in his voice and in his dark eyes.

"Yes. So far everything is fine. She told me that the miscarriage I'd had eleven years ago doesn't necessarily mean I'll have problems with this pregnancy."

Bailey frowned. "Miscarriage? You never told me about that. You haven't said much at all about your marriage." He moved his hand to stroke her straight hair, his fingers brushing her cheek.

"There wasn't much to tell." She shifted away from his touch, and his hand dropped to his side. "Bob didn't want the baby. He was glad that I lost it." Her voice faltered to a stop, and she squeezed her eyes shut. Then she took a shaky breath and forced herself to continue. "When I brought up trying again later, he admitted that he was having an affair and had been planning to leave me when I got pregnant. I hadn't suspected a thing." Maureen wrapped her hands around her stomach in a protective gesture. "I lost my baby and my husband on the same day."

"He didn't even wait until you'd recovered?"

Maureen shook her head.

"I'm sorry." Bailey's voice was tinged with regret. "I didn't realize what a rough time you've had. Did you love your husband?"

"I thought I did. But that was a long time ago."

"You still think about it." Bailey's perceptiveness surprised her.

"Sometimes. More so since I met you. Remembering how it was then helps me to be cautious now." As soon as Maureen had spoken the words, she wished she could call them back.

Bailey looked as if he'd been slapped. "That's unfair," he burst out. "Don't paint me with some other bastard's brush."

Maureen studied his angry face. "I'm not." She was only looking out for herself, trying to make sure she wouldn't be hurt again. Too bad she hadn't been more careful sooner.

Maureen could see from Bailey's expression that he was trying to regain control of his temper. He sighed deeply, staring at his shoes, then smoothed one thumb over his mustache.

"I don't mean to push you," he said finally. "But I really think the best thing for us would be to get married. Maybe you don't want to answer right now, and I can wait, I guess, but it's something you need to decide soon." His downward glance showed Maureen where his thoughts lay. It was the pregnancy that concerned him.

This had to be the least romantic proposal that she had ever heard. How could she agree to a marriage for all the wrong reasons? Even to him. "I don't think so," she said, firming her voice with an effort. "I appreciate the offer, but I think it would be a real mistake for us both." She did her best to ignore the thought that it would be no mistake if he loved her. Obviously that *wasn't* one of his reasons, or he would have mentioned it.

"I said you don't have to give me an answer right away. Why don't you think about it some more?" Bailey sounded anxious. Had he really wanted her to say yes?

Maureen rubbed her forehead, where a headache was beginning to build like a bank of storm clouds. "I don't need more time. It just wouldn't work for us."

For a moment Bailey looked as if he meant to argue further, but then his lips thinned to a grim line. "What are you going to do now?" he asked instead. "If you won't marry me, are you going to raise the child alone?" When she didn't answer immediately, his eyes turned dark with emotion, his brows lowering blackly. "You weren't thinking of not keeping this baby, were you?" His voice softened to a dangerous whisper. "Or not even having it?"

Maureen's mouth dropped open with shock. "Of course not! What do you take me for?"

He ran a hand across his jaw, considering. "I'm not sure. I thought I knew you pretty well, but obviously I was kidding myself." His tone was bitter.

White-hot anger filled Maureen. "Oh, I get it. If I don't do what *you* want, I'm not trustworthy, right?" She whirled away from him. "I think you'd better leave."

Bailey came up behind her, but when his hand touched her arm she jerked free.

"We're going to have to work something out," he said, fighting his disappointment. Maureen wouldn't even consider marriage. Her feelings weren't as strong as his. "Whatever *we* decide, I promise I won't desert you."

He saw her shoulders slump. Had she really thought he would abandon her? Didn't she know him better than that? Her doubts made him angry all over again, but he struggled for control.

"I wish—" he began to say, then stopped, shaking his head. There was no point in telling her how much he would have loved to have her and their child a part of his family, all belonging to each other. He was damned if he would give up, but perhaps right now the best thing to do was nothing. Maybe when Maureen had had more time to adjust, she would consider his offer rationally, but right now they were both upset and he was getting nowhere.

"What?" she asked, turning to stare into his face.

"Never mind. Maybe the best thing I can do now is to go, and let you think about my offer. It still stands, you know. We could give this baby a good home, and if I can keep Shawn and Melissa—" For a moment his throat threatened to close over the words. He swallowed. "I know that Shawn and Melissa would love this baby, and you, too."

Maureen's expression softened and he thought he saw a ray of hope there. Then she shook her head. "It wouldn't work," she said, sounding so weary he longed to take her in his arms and keep her safe. How scary this must all be for her.

This time Bailey did touch her, giving her arm a gentle squeeze, wishing he could kiss her but not quite daring it. "We'll talk again."

Maureen's chin thrust out. "I'm not going to marry you just to give this baby a name. Lots of women have children and raise them alone."

A flood of impatience made him want to shake her. "Women who have no other choice," he said shortly, brushing past her. "Thanks for dinner." He searched her face for some sign of softening, but could find none. "I'll see you later."

Maureen watched out the window as he got into his car and drove away. He'd given up easily enough, she thought. Maybe he'd just offered what he thought he had to. He was, after all, a good, responsible man. Drowning in responsibilities. Perhaps despite what he'd said, he was relieved that she had turned down his proposal.

A coldness seemed to grip her heart. In the long run you only had yourself to count on.

Bailey was so busy trying to assimilate the news that he was going to be a father again that he barely remembered the ride home. As he let himself into the kitchen through the back door, he glanced at his watch. There was still almost a half hour before Shawn and Melissa were due home.

He opened the fridge and dug a can of beer out of the back. He rarely drank, and almost never alone, but tonight he needed something and beer was all that was available. Popping the top, he leaned his head back and took a long swallow. He carried the can to the living room with him and dropped to the couch, not bothering to turn on the light. The glow from the kitchen was more than enough.

The idea that he was to become a father again was still difficult to accept. When Angela had announced the onset of her first pregnancy, both she and Bailey had been excited and happy. Shawn was a difficult baby, crying a lot and waking at night for months. Angela's second pregnancy had been an accident, when Bailey had almost given up trying to persuade her to have another child. He'd sometimes wondered, if Melissa had been anything but the sunny, smiling infant that she was, whether Angela's gradual down-slide into alcohol abuse would have come even sooner.

It was difficult for Bailey to accept that a child of his could possibly come into the world outside the circle of his influence and protection. Without his name. Possibly without a thing from him that Maureen didn't choose to allow.

For a moment, Bailey's control faltered and he was filled with a burst of churning, frustrated rage. It was inconceivable that this was happening. One moment he and Maureen were growing ever closer and he had hopes of a serious commitment. The next, she was expecting his child and they were at heart-wrenching odds. First Angela was trying to take his children from him, and now Maureen. He was only certain of one thing. He had no intentions of giving up his rights to this child. No matter how the situation affected his case, he had to do what he felt was best.

The only consolation, albeit a small one, was that where Angela had failed over and over in the motherhood department, Maureen, he was certain, would be a wonderful parent. He crumpled the empty beer can in his hand, wondering what the hell to do next.

After a few moments, Digger walked into the room and collapsed on the floor beside Bailey. The two kittens peeked around the corner, saw the dog and ran back down the hallway.

Maybe Angela and her lawyer wouldn't find out about Maureen's pregnancy. If he were lucky and Angela made a move soon, it might all be over before Maureen began to show. One thing he knew for sure, choosing between the children he had and the one on the way was more than he could do. He hoped it never came down to that.

Maureen hadn't realized how hard it would be to see Bailey at school. She avoided going to the cafeteria to meet him before class. During the evening break he waited outside her classroom door, but when she stayed in to talk to one of her students he finally walked away. When she came out after the closing bell, Bailey was gone.

Maureen walked to the staff parking lot alone, wondering if she had done the right thing in avoiding him. Perhaps she might make the wrong decision if Bailey was around to influence her, but she missed him already. Glancing up before she unlocked her car door, Maureen thought she saw his company pickup turning onto the main street, but couldn't be positive. Again Bailey had given up relatively easily, making her belief stronger than ever that he really didn't want the responsibility. Now Bailey could concentrate his energy on keeping the family he had.

Impatiently Maureen brushed a tear from her eye. What was she sniveling about now? Taking care of herself wasn't a problem. How much more difficult could it be to care for a child she already loved?

Over the next couple of weeks, when Bailey made no effort to contact her and the only sight she had of him was an occasional quick glimpse on campus, Maureen kept telling herself that she had made the right decision. Apparently he had quit going to the cafeteria, too, so she began to stop there again. Even decaf helped her to keep going. The doctor had said that extreme tiredness during the first trimester wasn't unusual, but Maureen found herself struggling with the evening classes two nights a week after a full day. It didn't seem to matter how much sleep she got; it was never enough.

At least she didn't have morning sickness, she reminded herself grimly over breakfast. Instead she had all-day sickness, a queasy feeling that sometimes stayed with her from morning till night. She was still feeling it later that afternoon as she left the administration building with one of the other teachers.

Maureen's classes were done for the day and she was eager to get home. Before she could push on the heavy glass door, someone opened it from the outside. Glancing up, she was unprepared to see Bailey in front of her, looking wonderfully familiar in faded jeans and a striped shirt.

"I want to talk to you." Determination filled his voice.

Swallowing her sudden nervousness, Maureen stepped aside and smiled at the teacher with her.

"I'll see you later, Ann. Thanks for the reading list."

The other woman, a petite blonde, glanced over her shoulder at Maureen. "Okay, 'bye." She brushed past Bailey, who was still holding the door, and thanked him. When he came up beside her, Maureen tried without success to subdue the blaze of reaction she always felt around him.

"Hi," Bailey said, studying her face. "I've been looking for you."

"What do you want?" The words came out sounding much ruder than Maureen intended.

Bailey's dark brows puckered into a frown above his brown eyes. "I want to talk. How have you been?" His gaze dropped to her stomach, and Maureen put a protective hand across it.

"I've been just fine. And no, I'm not showing yet."

An older man Maureen didn't know excused himself as she hastily stepped out of his way. As he left the building, Bailey took Maureen's arm and steered her away from the door.

"Is there somewhere less public we can talk?"

Maureen refused to return Bailey's smile, determined to remain unaffected by the way his smouldering gaze locked onto hers. "We don't need to talk." Her tone, meant to be cool, came out slightly breathless instead.

Bailey's voice lowered to an emotional whisper. "I've left you alone to get used to the situation, so we could deal with it sensibly. But I'm getting impatient. I told you I wasn't going to desert you and I meant it." His hand tightened on her arm. "If you want to stand here in the hallway and discuss your pregnancy, we will," he growled as another instructor walked by, glancing at them curiously.

Bailey held onto her as she glared back at him, unwilling to make more of a scene than they already were.

"Okay," Maureen said, relenting. "We might as well go to the cafeteria. It's pretty empty this time of day."

He nodded and dropped her arm, looking at her as if seeking reassurance that she wouldn't dart away. Tension made her movements jerky as she walked slightly ahead of him across the quadrangle in the center of the main group of buildings.

"Coffee?" Bailey asked as they approached the cafeteria serving line.

"I'm drinking decaf these days."

"I'm glad to hear it."

Maureen searched his face for any hint of sarcasm, but his expression was bland. He had probably remembered that tension was bad for the baby.

She turned to study the box of maple bars and gooey doughnuts on the counter. Her appetite had become insatiable when she wasn't feeling sick, but she was trying not to gain unwanted weight. Bailey followed the direction of her avaricious gaze and put two chocolate doughnuts on the tray with the coffee cups. For just a moment their eyes locked and she thought she saw a gleam of humor in his before he reached for his wallet and turned his attention to the cashier.

When they seated themselves in an empty corner of the room, Bailey couldn't help but remember all the other times they had met there. The expectation, the excitement and the attraction he had felt each time he waited to see Maureen again crowded him with emotions he didn't want to acknowledge. If only he could approach this dispassionately, convincing her on a rational level that marriage was the most logical solution. Instead it was all he could do to keep from sweeping her into his arms and kissing her senseless until she agreed to join her life with his. Glancing at her wary expression, he knew *that* approach would get him nowhere.

If Maureen remembered their other meetings in this room, she apparently wasn't letting them affect her as she calmly sipped her decaf. Only the chocolate doughnuts seemed to hold her interest. She kept glancing at the tray.

"Are you going to eat both of those?" she asked finally.

"No, they're for you."

Trust Bailey to understand her so thoroughly that she wasn't allowed even one secret passion, Maureen thought with annoyance as she gave up the fight and sank her teeth into one of the frosted doughnuts, sending a shower of colored sprinkles to the table. Somehow, even his thoughtfulness was irritating.

Bailey quietly drank his coffee as she demolished the doughnut, then licked the remains of the frosting from her fingers. Since she'd found out about her pregnancy, chocolate had graduated from an occasional indulgence to one of life's necessities.

"Sure you don't want the other one?" she asked gruffly, unable to resist.

Bailey grinned, sending little eddies of reaction through the calm detachment she was trying so hard to maintain. "Help yourself."

Pride should have enabled her to refuse; instead she took the pastry and made short work of it. Bailey waited until she had finished and was washing down the sinful indulgence with decaffeinated cafeteria sludge.

"Feel better?" he asked.

For a moment Maureen managed to glare, but the sight of his full lips twitching into a grin below his mustache was finally too much for her. She returned his smile, then leaned back and patted her stomach.

"I don't know what it is," she said, unthinking. "I never had a sweet tooth before."

"Not even during your last pregnancy?" His tone was dry, making the smile disappear from her face.

"I don't remember. I wasn't pregnant very long."

Bailey's lean face filled with remorse. "I'm sorry. I didn't mean to remind you of something painful."

He swept aside the empty cups and wrappers, lacing his fingers with hers. For a moment Maureen savored the heat radiating from his skin. Then she pulled away.

"No, I'm sorry," she said. "I know you didn't mean it that way."

For a moment Bailey studied her intently, the wide, clear eyes, the straight, thin nose with its slight bump above a full, passionate mouth. Today her hair, which had grown a little, was pulled back with some kind of clasp, stray wisps framing her oval face. Her blouse was ivory with a bow at the throat. He remembered that she was wearing it tucked into a slim brown skirt, her still-narrow waist defined by a wide suede belt.

He knew that beneath the expensive, simply tailored clothes she probably wore the most delicate lingerie, something silky, trimmed in lace a mile wide. His hands itched to hold her close. More erotic than any past vision was the thought of her growing bigger with his child. It was something that Bailey longed to see and to share with her on every intimate level he could imagine.

Maureen was watching him, and he wondered if his face revealed what he had been thinking. Apparently not, since she didn't react.

"Have you been to the doctor again?" he asked.

She shook her head. "Next week."

"Could I go with you?" The words surprised him; he hadn't known he was going to say them.

"You don't have to." The wary look was back.

"I know that," he said, unable to keep a trace of annoyance from his voice. "But I want to be there for you. I already told you that. And I want to pay the medical bills."

Pink filled Maureen's cheeks. "That's not necessary."

"Necessary!" he snapped. "According to you, nothing is *necessary*. But by my way of thinking, this is *all* necessary. I'm the child's father. I won't let you shut me out." He knew he was getting too angry, and he took a deep breath.

"I was there when this baby was conceived," he ground out in a low voice, leaning close. "And I remember every moment. Have you forgotten how we are together?" His voice dropped even lower. "We burn each other up."

His comments made Maureen ache with loneliness, and more. "You don't have to remind me," she told him through teeth tightly clenched to keep her lips from quivering. "I'm well aware of your role in this. But *I'm* the one carrying this child, and *I'm* the one who decides what's best for it."

"You should have gone to a sperm bank," he said baldly. The minute the words were out, he regretted them.

Maureen's face went white and she slid her chair back with a rough scraping sound. "I have a meeting." She glanced down at the debris he'd shoved aside on the table. "Thanks for the snack."

He watched her stalk away, back straight as a two-by-four, as he nibbled absently on his lower lip. *You sure blew that one, McGuire.* He probably couldn't have gotten her madder if he'd set out to make her lose her temper. Sperm bank! Where had that come from? Was he, by any chance, feeling slightly used?

As Maureen crossed the campus back to the administration building, her temper began to abate. If she was to be perfectly honest with herself, Bailey's accusation had surprised her more than it made her angry. Was that how he was feeling, like a stud?

She worked on grades and reports at home that evening, her brain returning over and over to his words, turning and twisting them to examine the idea from every angle. His accusation hadn't sounded like the sentiments of a man who was relieved to be let out of his responsibility. He sounded like a man who was hurting because he was afraid of being denied access to his child.

Maureen's pencil lead snapped and she threw it down in disgust. Nothing made sense anymore. She loved Bailey, but now they weren't even seeing each other except to exchange potshots. Either that, or he was trying to pressure her into "doing the right thing." What had happened to the loving relationship they had been building together?

If only she knew how he felt about *her*. That was the worst part. Did he really care for her, or *was* he only trying to do the right thing, the honorable thing, as a man like Bailey would be compelled to do? Maureen couldn't stand the thought that he might want to marry her *despite* his feelings and not because of them.

"What's happening with Maureen?" Janice asked Bailey when they had a few moments alone after a birthday dinner for one of her brood. "You haven't mentioned her lately."

"We haven't been seeing much of each other." He sat down heavily at her kitchen table while Janice covered the leftover food and put it in the refrigerator. Tim was supervising cleanup in the living room with all five children.

Bailey could sense Janice's hesitation, and he wished she would drop the subject. She didn't often pry, but she had told him before that she liked Maureen and hoped things worked out if that was what he wanted. At the time he hadn't been sure, but he had admitted to Janice that Maureen was special.

Janice turned on the dishwasher and went to the doorway to glance into the living room before sitting down across from Bailey at the table.

"Is this anything you want to talk about?" One hand played with her can of cola, turning it in a circle as she studied it instead of his face.

Bailey sighed and drained his cup. He had been drinking too much coffee lately and his nerves were screaming most of the time. The last day he'd seen Angela she had told him that she'd been talking to a lawyer who thought she had every chance of winning full custody. Bailey was so tired of the threat hanging over his head he had almost told her he was glad she was finally doing something to back up her empty words. Instead he'd alerted his own attorney, who had been as reassuring as possible under the circumstances, even though she couldn't give him much of an idea just how soon the case might be heard.

"It depends on so many variables," she said. "I know you're sick of hearing this, but try to be patient for a while longer."

Bailey had thanked Susan for her concern, but what he'd muttered after hanging up wasn't printable.

Then there was Maureen and his unborn child. For a moment he wondered what Janice would do if he stood up and roared out his frustration at the top of his lungs. No doubt his unshakable sister would calmly pour him another cup of java and suggest he tell her what was making him so uptight.

When Bailey glanced at Janice she was waiting patiently, her compassionate gaze now fixed on his face.

He cleared his throat. "It seems that Maureen and I made a slight miscalculation the first time we were—" he hesitated, not sure how to put it. Nothing shocked Janice, but he found it difficult to discuss such intimacies with his own sister. "—the first time we were really close," he finally concluded.

Janice's eyes widened. "Are you telling me that Maureen is expecting? A little McGuire?"

He shook his head glumly. "If she has her way, it will be a little Fletcher. She doesn't want to have anything to do with me."

"And what do you want?" Janice didn't pull any punches.

"I want to marry her." The more Bailey thought about it, the more positive he became, despite the mess the rest of his life was in right now. But how could he convince

Maureen that he wasn't trying to use *her* to help clean it up? Would she believe that he would never take advantage of her or the situation to slant a custody hearing or would he only make it worse if he tried to tell her that?

"Have you proposed?"

There was a thump and then the sounds of a child's crying from the living room, followed by Tim's voice.

"It's okay," he shouted. "Everything's under control."

Bailey couldn't help but grin. His brother-in-law was great with the kids. "I hope you know how lucky you are," he told his sister.

Janice's head bobbed. "Yes, I certainly do. And Tim would never let me forget it." For a moment her expression softened. "Now let's get back to the subject at hand before someone remembers the leftover cake on the counter." She glanced over to where the remains of the birthday concoction, decorated with circus animals, rested beneath a clear plastic cover.

"As soon as Maureen told me about the baby, I asked her to marry me," Bailey said, lacing his fingers together. "She turned me down."

Janice traced an imaginary design on the tabletop. "You men don't always have the best timing in the world," she mused. "I'm sorry. You love her, don't you?"

Bailey sighed. "Yeah, I do."

"I would have bet she returned your feelings. The few times I've been around you both there seemed to be something special going on." Janice ran her finger over a scratch on the table. "If you told her how much you love her and she still refuses to marry you, I guess all you can do is try to be there for her, as much as she'll let you. She could still change her mind. After all, this is probably a lot for her to take in all at once, too." Janice took a sip of her cola. "Is Maureen keeping the baby?"

Bailey answered absently, something she had said nagging at his brain. *If he had told Maureen how much he loved her*— But had he? He tried to remember, as Janice watched him with a puzzled frown. He knew he'd said something about making a new family. He'd been so stunned, so excited. Had he said the words, or had he just assumed she'd know?

"What is it?" Janice asked.

Bailey put the questions out of his head, to be pondered later when he was alone, when he could recall just exactly what *had* been said.

"Nothing." There was more shouting from the living room, followed by Tim's voice, not quite as patient as it had been before.

"Time to get my kids home," Bailey said. "Thanks for listening."

Janice rose. "Anytime. Keep me posted, okay? And if there's anything I can do—"

Bailey gave her a hug. "I know. Thanks."

Sitting on her couch later that evening, staring at the first page of a book she couldn't seem to get into, Maureen knew she had to come to some kind of decision, and soon. She was going to have a baby and she couldn't change that—didn't want to. What she could do was to decide under what circumstances she would raise it.

It was undoubtedly her last chance for a child of her own, and either way she meant to make the most of this unexpected gift. But what would be the best thing for the baby, raising it alone or married to a man who might or might not come to care for Maureen as she cared for him?

What if he never fell in love with her? What if the marriage failed?

By then Maureen would have let herself love Shawn and Melissa more than she did now. By then she would be so deeply involved with Bailey that losing him would be like cutting away part of herself. And what of the baby if they got a divorce? Bailey already had custody of two of his children? Did Maureen dare risk losing everything?

She wrapped her arms around herself, feeling the same gut-wrenching tension that had gripped her off and on during the day. Such stress couldn't be good for the baby or for her. She had to relax.

Maureen had risen and was headed for the kitchen to brew some herbal tea when the first cramp hit, doubling her over.

Chapter Ten

Bailey had just walked in the door with the children when the phone rang.

"Shawn, would you get that?" he asked, stepping around Digger, who was busy greeting the family after being let in from the backyard.

As Shawn picked up the receiver, Bailey hung his coat in the closet and turned to Melissa, who looked tired.

"Time for a bath and bed, honey. I'll start the water in the tub, and you get your towel and clean pajamas, okay?"

Melissa smiled up at him, shifting a doll from one arm to the other. "Okay, Daddy."

Shawn rushed in, blocking Bailey's way to the bathroom. "Dad, come quick."

"What is it? I was going to start Melissa's bathwater."

Shawn had an anxious frown on his face and his teeth worried his lower lip. "It's Maureen. I think something's wrong."

Bailey stared at Shawn's concerned face, then rushed past him, headed for the phone in the living room. "What did she say?"

Shawn followed along behind. "She just asked for you, but she sounded funny."

Bailey gave him an exasperated glance as he grabbed the receiver. "Hi, honey. What's wrong?"

"I'm sorry to bother you." Maureen's voice did sound funny, kind of strained.

"No bother," Bailey protested, surprised that she would call after the way they had parted, but glad. "You could never be a bother to me. Tell me what's going on." He could almost feel her tension. Then Bailey heard her gasp, and his fingers tightened on the receiver.

"Could you come over here?" Maureen asked. "I'm so scared."

Bailey wondered if she had heard some suspicious noises, or gotten a threatening phone call. "What's wrong?"

"I, uh, I don't feel very well."

Fear sliced into Bailey like the talons of a ravaging hawk. "Do you want me to call the doctor? Is the baby okay? Do you need an ambulance?"

He thought she chuckled weakly. "I need *you*," she said, "if you could get away. I—" Her voice broke completely, and he felt the metallic taste of terror in his mouth.

"What is it? Honey, tell me!" If Bailey could have clawed his way through the telephone wires, he would have.

When Maureen began to speak again, her voice was so low he could barely hear her. He was suddenly conscious of Shawn standing next to him, scratching his leg through the denim of his jeans. One glaring look from Bailey and Shawn's hand went still.

Bailey turned away, cradling the receiver tighter. "Tell me, honey. I'll do everything I can."

"I think I'm losing the baby. I know the signs."

He heard her sobs, and felt more helpless than he ever had in his life. "Is Mrs. Bondini home?"

"I don't know. I haven't called her." Maureen's voice sounded small and lost, like a child who didn't understand why she was being hurt.

The realization that she had thought of him first made Bailey feel warm inside, despite his fear. "Okay," he said, trying to make his voice reassuring. "You call Mrs. B., and see if she can come over until I get there. Have her call your doctor. I'm going to get a sitter and then I'll be right over." He thought furiously. "If Jennifer can't come here, I'll bring the kids with me. They can wait in the car." Maybe Janice could meet him there or something, and take them. He would deal with that when he got to it. "But I'll be there as soon as I can, okay?"

"Okay." Her voice was a little stronger, and then she moaned.

Bailey felt something tear loose inside his chest. He wished she had called him sooner, then remembered that he hadn't been home. "Call Mrs. B., okay? Remember, have her get hold of your doctor. And stay off your feet. Have you got all that?"

"Yes," she said.

"Hang on, sweetheart. We'll get through this together," he said before he hung up. He hoped to hell that Mrs. Bondini and Jennifer, his baby-sitter, were both home.

"What's wrong?" Shawn asked. "Is Maureen sick?"

"Just a sec, okay?" Bailey dialed Jennifer's number. "Go check Melissa's bathwater for me."

Jennifer's mother answered on the second ring and Bailey explained quickly without going into a lot of personal detail. Jennifer was knocking on the front door as he told Melissa and Shawn that Maureen was sick and he needed to go see her.

"Tell her I hope she gets better soon," Melissa said, looking worried.

"Me, too." Shawn's voice was gruff.

"Thanks, kids." Bailey let Jennifer in and then bid Shawn and Melissa a hasty good night.

"Thanks for coming so quickly," he told Jennifer. "I'll call you as soon as I know something."

Jennifer smiled as he pushed past her out the door. "It's okay," she said. "Don't worry about the time. My mom said if it gets late, she can come over and relieve me if you get tied up."

Bailey gave Jennifer a quick hug. "Bless you both," he said gratefully, "I appreciate it."

Moments later he pulled up in front of Maureen's apartment and leaped out of the car. He could feel his heart slamming against his chest. She had to be all right. As Bailey raced up the steps, the front door opened and Mrs. Bondini appeared. "I'm so glad you're here."

"How is she?" Bailey asked.

Mrs. Bondini shook her head, stepping outside to say quietly, "Not too good, I'm afraid. She's been spotting, and I think she's having a lot of pain. Still, they can do so much now. Her doctor will meet you at the hospital."

Before Bailey could speak, she grabbed his hand and gave it a squeeze. "Maureen's strong, but she needs you."

"I need her, too," he replied.

"Bailey!" Maureen groaned from the couch where she was lying, and he forgot all about her neighbor.

"I'm here." He took Maureen's hand as Mrs. Bondini brought her coat and purse. "Everything will be fine."

"I'm afraid." Maureen's eyes were huge, with dark shadows beneath them. Strain had cut new lines around her mouth.

"I won't let anything bad happen," Bailey promised rashly. He tried to hide his own fear. What if something happened to *her*?

"I'm glad you're here." Maureen's voice sounded tired.

He took her coat from Mrs. Bondini. "Can you put this on? Then, if Mrs. B. will open the car door, I'll carry you down the stairs."

"Do you want her in the back?"

Bailey glanced at Maureen's friend and nodded. "There's a blanket on the seat. Bring that pillow."

"I can walk," Maureen protested as he helped her on with the coat and then scooped her carefully into his arms.

"Shh," Bailey cautioned her. "Let me hold you, okay?"

Their eyes met in the kind of silent communication he had missed so much. "All right." She smiled bravely.

"I'll feed Max, and lock up," Mrs. Bondini said behind them. "Don't you worry about a thing. Mr. McGuire, would you call me when you know something?"

He turned, cradling Maureen carefully against his heart. "I will." The reflection of his own worry was stamped on her worn face. "I promise."

He could see some of the tension go out of her. "Here are Maureen's keys. I have a spare myself." She slipped them into his jacket pocket, then went ahead and opened the car door. Before Bailey set Maureen inside, she reached out to pat the older woman's hand. "Thanks for coming."

"I'll see you later, dear. You take care." Bailey saw her turn away, blinking rapidly.

Then he set Maureen down and made sure she was comfortable. "We'll be there in a few minutes," he said, going around to the driver's door.

Maureen's doctor was waiting to examine her at the hospital. Then, while she was being admitted, the doctor spoke briefly to Bailey.

"We'll do everything we can," she told him after he explained that he was the father, "but you should be prepared. It doesn't look promising."

Bailey's heart beat painfully. "Is Maureen in any danger?"

The doctor touched his arm reassuringly. "She's a healthy woman. I think she'll be fine, no matter what happens."

Bailey waited anxiously as the minutes dragged by. He called Jennifer and told her where he was and that he would be late. He bought coffee that he forgot to drink. After pacing the waiting room floor for what seemed like hours, he sank into a chair and picked up a magazine, flipping through its pages without seeing a thing.

Guilt skewered him. If he had been more careful, she wouldn't be going through this now. If he'd waited, or been prepared. He kept picturing her anguished face as she fought the pain. Again he leaped to his feet, resting his hands on his hips as he stared sightlessly out the window. A dozen memories assailed him, a collage of the happiness he and Maureen had shared. The words to a nameless prayer were running through Bailey's mind, when the doctor finally called his name.

She pushed back her bangs with a tired gesture, her expression somber. "I'm sorry," she said, eyes compassionate. "We did all we could."

"She lost the baby." Bailey felt a wave of sorrow hit him. Moisture filled his eyes, but he didn't bother to brush it away.

"Sometimes it happens that way, and no one really knows why. It's not much comfort, I know, to say that it was probably for the best."

"How is Maureen?" His voice shook.

"We've done a D-and-C, but she's awake now. We'll be keeping her here until tomorrow."

Bailey needed to reassure himself that Maureen, at least, was really all right. "Can I see her?"

The doctor studied his face. "Only for a few moments. She's very tired. I'm sure your presence will be comforting, but then she needs to rest. She's been very upset by the whole thing."

"I understand. Thank you, doctor." He held out his hand and she shook it.

"Sometimes we feel helpless, too."

When Bailey pushed open the door to Maureen's room, he could see her lonely figure huddled beneath the covers, her head turned away from him. At first he thought she was asleep, and then he heard the sound of quiet crying.

Bailey let the door swing shut behind him, and moved to the foot of the bed. "Maureen." His voice was low.

She rolled her head on the pillow and looked at him, her wet eyes reminding him of flowers crushed in a violent storm. "I'm sorry," she whispered.

With a groan, Bailey went to her side and bent over her. His fingers shook as he traced the tear tracks on her cheek. "I'm sorry, too. But it wasn't your fault, you know. The doctor said these things sometimes just happen."

Maureen's face crumpled, and fresh tears flowed down her pale cheeks. "Spontaneous abortion," she said. "What a horrid term." Her voice trembled and she stopped for a moment. "It's something in me. I can't carry a child."

Bailey sank to his knees by the side of the bed, putting his arms around her. For long moments he held her, whispering words of comfort.

"Thanks for staying." The sorrow in her voice opened fresh wounds.

"I wouldn't be anywhere else." Bailey rose, dragging a chair to the side of the bed and sitting down, gripping her hands tightly. "Did the doctor tell you that you can't carry a child?"

"No. It's just something I know."

He took a tissue from the box on her nightstand and dried her cheeks. "Don't jump to any conclusions. Wait until you can discuss the whole thing with her." He held a fresh tissue to her nose and she blew. For a moment her expression reminded him of Melissa, innocent and trusting.

"This is the third child I've lost," she said, surprising Bailey.

"I thought you'd had only one other miscarriage." It hurt him terribly to see her so sad.

Maureen wiped her eyes again and tried to stop crying. She needed to share some of the unbearable pain with Bailey. Maybe then it would lessen a little. "I had a younger brother," she said, fighting for control. "His name was Tony."

"I didn't know," Bailey said, still holding her hands.

"I haven't talked about him in a long time." For a moment she pictured him, blond-white hair, blue eyes, always laughing. "Our parents worked. Jason was always busy with sports at school. Tony was six years younger than me, but he was like my own child." Maureen swallowed past the lump in her throat.

"What happened?" Bailey asked.

"I was at a pajama party when Mom called. Tony had ridden his trike into the road and was hit by a car. He died instantly."

Bailey's voice was tender, as he smoothed his hand over her head. "I'm sorry. That must have been very hard on all of you."

She nodded. "It was. When I got married and found out we were expecting, I gave the baby all the love I'd been storing up from my little brother."

"And when you lost that baby, it hurt twice as much," Bailey said. He leaned over to kiss her cheek. "What a rough time you've had. I'm glad you told me." It wasn't surprising that she was cautious with her feelings, after what she'd been through.

"It's been so hard," Maureen murmured, blinking slowly. "So painful."

Bailey's heart went out to her, and he felt that he understood a lot more than he had. Was that why she had put off meeting his children? Not because she didn't care, but because she was afraid of caring too much? He leaned close. "You need to rest."

Maureen's fingers tightened on his. "Can you stay for a little while?" She sounded exhausted. "Dr. Pascoe said I can go home tomorrow."

Bailey leaned forward and kissed her cheek gently. "I'll stay until you go to sleep," he promised. "And I'll come back in the morning."

Maureen's eyes began to drift shut and then they blinked open. "Who's staying with your children?"

"They're okay," he soothed, stroking the back of her hand. "Jennifer was with them, and then her mom came over."

"That's nice. Will you call Mrs. Bondini?"

"As soon as you go to sleep."

"Thank you." Her voice had gotten softer. The doctor must have given her something to help her sleep. After a moment her hand relaxed in his, but he didn't let go. She murmured something and he leaned closer.

"What did you say?"

"I loved this baby already," she whispered, and fresh tears seeped out from beneath her lashes.

Bailey had trouble swallowing past the lump blocking his throat. "So did I, sweetheart."

When he got back to the hospital the next morning, after reassuring Shawn and Melissa that Maureen was feeling much better and then getting them off to school, Mrs. Bondini was sitting by Maureen's bed.

"I couldn't stay away," she said, rising as Bailey came in.

"Go ahead and sit back down," he told her, crossing to kiss Maureen lightly. "How are you feeling this morning?"

Maureen gave him a lost look. "Okay."

Bailey's smile was forced. He'd spent much of the night thinking about her and their relationship and the child they'd lost before ever knowing it.

"I'm sorry," Maureen said again, as she studied the slight puffiness around Bailey's dark eyes, and the lines of exhaustion on his lean face. Would he blame her, somehow? So far he had been so kind, but she wondered what he was really thinking.

Mrs. Bondini came forward and bent over to give Maureen a hug. She smelled of lavender and cinnamon. "I fed Max before I came. I have to stop at the store on my way home. Can I get you anything?"

Maureen concentrated hard. "A loaf of bread, I guess, and a quart of two-percent milk." It was hard to remember such ordinary things, when all she wanted to think about was the baby.

"No problem. I'll leave you two now, and I'll be home all day if you need me later."

Maureen thanked her, and so did Bailey.

"She's nice," he said after Mrs. Bondini had left.

"Yes," Maureen agreed, thinking of all the times she had been there to feed the cat, or listen, or give some sage advice. They took turns looking out for each other. "She's a good friend."

"Have you called anyone else?"

For a moment Maureen wasn't sure what he meant. "About being here?"

Bailey nodded.

"No, I hadn't gotten around to telling anyone at school about the baby. I guess now I might as well leave it that way." She thought about how different everything would have been, if she and Bailey were married. Then she realized that it all would have ended up the same. No baby.

"I'll call my brother later." She toyed with the edge of the sheet. "I guess that, in a way, this simplifies things," she said experimentally.

Bailey's face took on a closed-up expression. "Don't think like that," was all he said before a male nurse came in.

"Time to check your temp and blood pressure," the young man said cheerfully. "How are you feeling?"

"Okay," Maureen said, wishing mightily that the nurse hadn't come in at just that moment. She wondered what, if anything, Bailey had been about to add to what he had said. Was he relieved, after all? He might feel some loss, but in the long run he had to be thinking that this was better for both of them.

The nurse took Maureen's temperature and then started to check her blood pressure, as she watched Bailey, who stood at the window. His hands were shoved into the pockets of the slacks he wore this morning with a sport shirt, instead of his usual jeans. She wondered if he was supposed to be at work, or if the clothes were in her honor.

As soon as the nurse left, Maureen asked him if he should be somewhere else.

"No, I took the morning off. Thought I could give you a ride home." He didn't look at her when he spoke.

"Thanks, but you don't have to if you really don't have the time. I can call a taxi, or I'm sure Mrs. Bondini would come back and get me."

Bailey turned and glared at her. "I said it's okay." His tone was even and patient, gratingly so.

Suddenly Maureen realized that she felt like picking a fight with him. She wanted to yell at somebody and get rid of the pressure that seemed to be building up inside her. Instead she turned over, facing the doorway. "The doctor said she'd be here around eleven, and she'd probably let me go home then."

Bailey circled the bed so he was again looking down at Maureen. "That's fine. Are you sure you're up to leaving?"

"I'll be okay." She realized the annoyance she felt wasn't really directed at Bailey, it was just one more reaction to her loss. She had gotten attached to the baby in a few short weeks; after her initial fears about being pregnant, she had begun to look forward to having a child of her own. That would never happen now. Fresh tears threatened to overflow, and she blinked rapidly.

"What about school?" Bailey wasn't looking at her, he was watching the door. Probably wishing that Dr. Pascoe would get there early.

"I'm taking a week's sick leave." Maureen hated the idea of being idle that long, but the doctor had insisted. With nothing to do but brood, the days would drag by.

"That's probably a good idea," Bailey said absently. He didn't suggest that she spend some of that time with him.

Where did the two of them stand now? Maureen wondered. There was really no more reason for him to go on seeing her. The thought was an infinitely sad one. She still loved him, and they'd gone so quickly from being happy together to this.

To her surprise, Bailey glanced at his watch and then crossed the room and shut the door. Coming back to the bed, he pulled the chair over and sat down, clearing his throat.

"While we have a little time, there's something I need to ask you," he said. His expression was somber, almost grim, and his eyes didn't meet hers.

Here it comes, Maureen thought anxiously. Some stupid question, and then he'll say there's really no reason for us to keep seeing each other now that I'm no longer pregnant. Maybe I *will* take a taxi. How can he expect me to ride home with him after this?

"Go ahead," she told him, bracing herself. She rested one hand on her stomach protectively, then remembered that there was no longer any need, and shifted it to rest on the bed beside her.

Bailey seemed to be in no hurry to speak. To Maureen's surprise, he covered her hand with his and then turned it over, linking their fingers. His head was bowed and she looked at his dark, thick hair, a few gray strands woven in with the rest. She longed to touch it one last time.

"I know we've been through a lot," he began slowly. His fingers tightened and he raised his head to look at her with eyes full of pain and something else she couldn't recognize. "So much that neither of us expected. Do you think we could go back to what we had? Or go on?"

When she remained silent, he let go of her hand and rose. "I guess I mean, *can* we go on? We had something special, and over the past few weeks it's slipped away."

Hope began to glow inside Maureen, warming her for the first time since she'd felt the cramps and known she might lose her child.

Bailey turned to her again, then began to pace restlessly. "Hell," he almost growled. "I don't know what's happened to us, but I know that I care about you, and I don't want to lose what we have."

Some of Maureen's growing excitement seeped away at his careful words, but at least he wanted to go on seeing her. He wasn't ready to give up. Not completely. For now, that had to be enough.

She waited until Bailey was looking at her again. "I'd like to go on seeing you," she said.

Bailey's beloved face softened in a smile, and she knew she was doing the right thing.

"Besides," Maureen couldn't resist adding, "who else could get you through your Spanish final?"

"So which color do you like best?" Maureen asked Melissa. They were looking at bathroom rugs. After Maureen had recovered from her hospital stay, she decided to completely redo the guest bath at her condo, and had invited Melissa to go with her and help to pick out a new color scheme.

Melissa studied the rose-and-blue combination that the store clerk had suggested, and then went back to the mint green rug and peach towels she and Maureen had put together. "I like this," she said finally. "You can get some of those peach teddy-bear soaps we saw, and the green wicker wastebasket."

Maureen hadn't been sure if Melissa would care about going to the mall with her, but the little girl seemed pleased she'd asked, and they had had a good time so far looking in the toy store and the bath shop. Next they were going to lunch, and then home.

"Good idea," Maureen said to Melissa. "I'm glad I brought you with me, or I would have ended up with something as dull as the brown-and-cream I'm replacing." She had invited Bailey to bring the children over one afternoon and they had met Max, who was on his best behavior, purring when they petted him. The four of them had watched a rented movie and shared a delivered pizza.

"The bathroom was pretty bad," Melissa agreed, with the honesty of a child. "I'm glad you decided to let me help you fix it."

Maureen chuckled at the memory of Melissa's obvious relief that her carefully chosen cream, chocolate and natural wicker were all going to the Goodwill. "It will be pretty for when you come to visit me," she said. "You can wash your hands with the teddy-bear soap."

"And dry them on the new towels," Melissa added.

"That's right, you can. We'd better get a couple more sets."

"Can I stay overnight sometime? You said there's a bed inside your couch."

Maureen was touched by Melissa's willingness to make friends. "Actually, the couch folds out to make a bed. I'll show you how it works." Since Maureen had lost her own baby, she and Bailey had spent a lot of time with his children. He seemed to sense that she took comfort in their company. Melissa, especially, soaked up Maureen's attention and Shawn, still reserved, at least didn't seem as resentful as he had been.

"Are you sure you wouldn't be bored if you spent the night at my condo? I don't have any toys for you to play with, you know."

"I could watch television and play with your cat," Melissa said eagerly. "Maybe we could make cookies."

Maureen thought of Mrs. Bondini's collection of cookie cutters that she took out when her own grandchildren came to visit. Perhaps Maureen could borrow them, along with a couple of foolproof recipes.

"Sure," she said to Melissa. "As long as it's okay with your dad." And some time when your mom doesn't have you, she thought, feeling a little jealous. Today Maureen had to have Melissa back by one-thirty so Angela could take both children for the rest of the weekend. "We'd better buy this stuff and go eat lunch," she said, noticing the time.

"Please stay," Bailey insisted when Maureen tried to leave after taking Melissa home. "Angela will be here in a few minutes, if she's on time. Then I could go over with you and help you fix up the new bathroom." His eyes gleamed, making promises that Maureen wasn't yet physically able to keep.

"You know I can't—" she began hesitantly as Melissa went to find Shawn and bore him with a description of the bathroom items she and Maureen had purchased.

Bailey took Maureen's hands in his and shook his head slowly. "I know *we* can't yet," he emphasized in a teasing voice, "not until after your doctor's appointment next week." He took a deep breath and folded their clasped hands between them as he pulled her closer. "But we could still cuddle and smooch—" he punctuated his sentence with a quick kiss on her mouth "—and drive each other slightly crazy."

Maureen snuggled closer, until awareness of the condition of his body made her glance into his face with surprise.

"I can't help it," Bailey murmured. "When I get around you I want you. A man can't hide that." He bent his head to kiss her neck, making her giggle. "But that doesn't mean I can't wait." His grin absolved her of any guilt for not being able to make love with him yet. "And I will wait. I really don't mind. But I still need to be close to you, and give you just a little taste of what you've been missing." Again his head dipped and he kissed her, this time sending his tongue past her lips to caress hers briefly before he pulled back.

"And to torment me!" Maureen exclaimed, returning his smile. Since he'd told her at the hospital that he wanted to go on seeing her, they had become even closer than before.

It wasn't always easy. Sharing a little of their pain and bitter disappointment had gone a long way toward absolving both and smoothing the path to a deeper sense of togetherness. If Maureen occasionally wondered where they were headed, she was learning to be patient. Bailey hadn't mentioned marriage since her miscarriage. Despite the new closeness between them, that convinced her he'd only proposed because she was pregnant.

"So, will you stay?" Bailey asked, bringing her back to the present.

Maureen was curious about Angela, his ex-wife. He had told Maureen a little more about his failed marriage, and she'd shared with him some of her memories of Tony. The only picture she'd seen of Angela was the wedding photograph Melissa showed her one day. This would be a perfect opportunity to satisfy some of her curiosity about the woman, as well as to spend some time with Bailey.

"I'll stay," she said, bringing another smile to his mouth. Impulsively she reached up and placed her lips on his for a moment, her hands gripping the front of his shirt. Before he could react, she pulled away.

"What was that for?" he asked, bemused by her spontaneous gesture. Maureen had been rather reserved since he'd first taken her home from the hospital, and even though he wanted to give her time to adjust, sometimes he wondered if she still cared for him. Now his body responded to her kiss with a flare of hunger that surprised him with its strength. His hands curled around her upper arms, holding her close, while his chest absorbed the cushiony feeling of her breasts pressed against him. Maureen's breath caught, but she didn't struggle.

After a long moment Bailey let out a shuddering sigh and released his hold, easing her away from him. "Sorry," he rasped in a thickened voice. "I guess my control is shakier than I thought." Feeling guilty, he glanced around, but the children were still in Shawn's room. He could hear their voices.

Maureen raised her hand and rested a palm against his cheek. "Don't be sorry. It's nice to be wanted."

He smiled his appreciation of her words. "Perhaps you'd rather I didn't come over?"

Maureen knew what he was asking. Did she trust him to be alone with her at her apartment? "That's silly," she assured him. "I know you wouldn't—"

A shout of laughter from the bedroom reminded her that they weren't alone.

"You wouldn't do anything to hurt me," she finished. "And I *do* like the idea of being alone with you." Bailey just might be in for a surprise, she decided. She had a few tricks up her sleeve she hadn't shown him yet.

Bailey watched the self-satisfied smile curve her mouth, and wondered what she was thinking.

Angela eyed Maureen with a tight smile. "Nice to meet you," she said in a breathy voice. White jeans hugged her curvaceous figure and a silky blue blouse contrasted with her long red hair.

Maureen couldn't help but wonder how much the other woman knew about her own relationship with Bailey. She wished she had thought to ask him before.

"You, too," Maureen returned. "I can see who Melissa takes after."

She had said the words without calculated thought, but when she did, Angela almost preened. "She does look like me, doesn't she, despite the dark hair?" Angela turned and put an arm around her son. "And Shawn is going to be as handsome as his father." She sent Bailey a fluttering glance from beneath lowered lashes.

Maureen couldn't resist a look at Bailey, who was watching Angela with an amused expression. "He's got some of your stubbornness," he said dryly, reaching forward to ruffle Shawn's hair. "He's always been very independent."

Shawn grinned self-consciously. "Whatever works, right?"

"That's right," Bailey agreed. "As long as you don't overdo it."

"Who, me?" Shawn asked him in a teasing voice as Bailey grabbed him in a gentle headlock and they wrestled briefly.

Maureen was always impressed by Bailey's openness with his kids, and the easy affection they shared. Her own father had been a quiet, aloof man who was always working. And Bob, her husband, had been too self-centered to make a good parent. She realized that now.

Bailey took the time to listen and to answer his children's questions thoughtfully. It was easy to see that he was a loving father. For a moment Maureen mourned her baby's not having the chance to know him.

Angela gestured impatiently to the pile of bags and other possessions by the front door. "Do you kids both have everything you need? Pillows? Tomorrow we're going to a friend of mine's for lunch, so I hope you're taking some decent clothes with you." She flicked a glance at Bailey, as if to gauge his reaction.

Maureen could see that both children were wearing clean jeans and T-shirts, with fairly new athletic shoes. Their hair was combed and they were well-scrubbed, just as always. Had Angela meant to imply that they usually wore rags unsuitable for visiting, or had the jab been unintentional?

"Have them back by six," Bailey told her, ignoring her words. "So they can get ready for school next week."

"Okay, okay. You're the boss." Angela wore a curiously smug smile. "For now, anyway."

Apparently Bailey chose to ignore her remark. Instead he hugged Melissa and then Shawn, who wriggled out of his father's embrace, looking embarrassed.

"Be good and mind your mom," Bailey told them both. Then his attention shifted to his ex-wife, and Maureen saw the hard glitter in his eyes. "Take good care of my kids," he told her.

Angela's cheeks flushed a deep red that was extremely unattractive with her fiery hair. "I always take good care of *my* children." She lowered her voice as Shawn and Melissa ran ahead to her car, a new sporty model that was painted bright red with a racy black stripe running its length. "And they're going to be all mine real soon."

"What do you mean?" Bailey asked.

Angela's eyes flashed and she tossed back her hair. "You'll be hearing from my lawyer the first of the week. I've filed for custody."

Chapter Eleven

Before Bailey could respond, Angela glanced at Maureen, who quickly schooled her expression. "Interesting meeting you," Angela told her.

Not sure how to take that, Maureen, unsmiling, said, "You, too," as Angela herded the children and their parcels to her car. Maureen glanced at Bailey, whose expression was a study in frustration. He turned and their eyes met.

"She knows I can't have this out with her in front of the children," he growled. "Damn it!"

Maureen stepped closer to him as he waved at Melissa, who had turned to wave another goodbye.

"Neat!" Shawn exclaimed as he stood looking at Angela's car, unaware of the storm brewing around him. "When did you get it?"

"It belongs to a friend of mine," Maureen heard Angela reply as she opened the driver's door. "You ride in front now, and then Melissa can later."

"The friend we're going to meet tomorrow?" Shawn asked as he walked around to the other side.

Angela shut her door and Maureen didn't hear her reply.

"Well," Bailey said with false heartiness, "how about if I feed Digger and we get out of here for a while?" To Maureen his complexion seemed pale beneath its normal tan, and his mouth had a grim set to it.

"Sure," she said, wishing there was something she could say to take away some of the heartache and worry he must be experiencing. "Let's stop at the deli, and then go to my place." Maybe she could take both their minds off the long-awaited custody fight, at least for a little while. Not that she was doing a good job of keeping her own mind off the lingering sadness of her miscarriage; she still thought of the baby a hundred times a day.

An hour later they walked into Maureen's apartment carrying sacks of poor-boy sandwiches and cans of cola. Bailey seemed calm enough, but each time Maureen tried to bring up the children he changed the subject. Apparently he wasn't ready to talk about it yet.

"Are you hungry?" Maureen asked him as they dumped the sacks on her kitchen counter.

"Actually," he replied, looking slightly surprised, "I'm starved."

"Me, too." Maureen got a jar of pickles from the fridge and put paper plates and napkins on the table. "Let's eat."

Bailey pulled out a chair for her, then dropped into the one next to it, a long sigh escaping as he handed her one of the thick pastrami-and-cheese sandwiches they'd bought. Silently he unwrapped his own and took a large bite.

Maureen followed his lead, eating most of her sandwich before she broke the silence that had settled around them like a damp fog.

"When are the children coming back?"

Bailey fished a pickle out of the jar. "Tomorrow, at six." His white teeth bisected it, his eyes not quite meeting hers.

Maureen shrugged and took a swallow of pop before finishing her sandwich. When they were both done eating, she rose and began to gather up the empty wrappers and plates. Bailey shoved his chair back and put their pop cans in the bag she kept beneath the sink.

"Do you want to know what I thought of Angela?" Maureen asked him as she wiped off the table.

Bailey's voice was flat. "I guess so."

"Well, pardon me!" She put her hands on her hips and did her best to look offended. It wasn't easy; she had an idea how he felt, knowing he'd hoped all along that Angela would never get around to filing. Maureen had begun to believe that, too.

Bailey came over to where she was standing and pulled her close to his hard body. "I don't want to talk about Angela," he said softly. "I don't want to talk, at all." His head lowered and his mouth covered Maureen's in a kiss that sent shivers down her spine.

She slipped her hands around his waist under the hem of his knit shirt and began to trace patterns on the warm skin of his back. It was silky and taut beneath her fingers.

Bailey groaned, then took her mouth again and deepened the kiss. After a long moment, he bent and scooped her into his arms. When he began striding down the hallway to her bedroom, Maureen leaned back to look into his face.

"What are you doing?" she asked.

Bailey paused, dark eyes holding hers. "Are you feeling okay?"

She nodded.

"Do you trust me?"

"Absolutely." Maureen didn't have to hesitate. With Bailey she felt safe, as well as utterly feminine and highly desirable. If only he loved her, too. With a burst of determination, she thrust the traitorous thought aside. She had already decided to be patient and to take what he gave her without wishing for the moon.

Maureen ran a hand around his neck and slid her fingers into the back of his thick hair. Bailey raised his head and rubbed it back and forth.

"Mmm," he sighed as she sifted through the silken strands. "I just need to hold you for a little while." Then, as he shouldered his way into her bedroom, she released the top button of his shirt.

"What are *you* doing?" Bailey's voice had suddenly deepened.

Maureen peered up at him, smiling provocatively. "Undressing you."

"Oh. You know that we can't—"

She placed a finger across his lips. "I know."

For a moment, Bailey looked as if he were about to add something, then he set her gently down on the wide bed and eased her backward. "Don't stop now," he said, stretching out beside her.

Looking at his face above her, Maureen almost lost her nerve. Then, as his expression softened and he flashed the now-familiar dimple, she relaxed. This was the man she loved, the man who needed her loving. He had been there for her when she had needed him the most.

Maureen drew his head down to hers.

After a moment she stopped kissing him long enough to finish unbuttoning the placket of his shirt and pull it over his head. Beneath it his chest was beautifully bare, the silken skin hot to her touch.

Maureen swallowed and reached for his belt buckle. Bailey's hands immediately covered hers.

"Are you sure you know what you're doing? My control around you is never invincible." He read the answer in her eyes. His darkened to black, his cheeks flushing, and then he slowly lay back on the bed.

When Maureen's loving hands unfastened his belt and slowly undid his zipper, Bailey shut his eyes and tried to stifle a groan. When he felt her breath and then her hair and finally her lips tickle his chest, he stared up at her. She'd removed her blouse and only a skimpy lace bra covered her breasts. Through the sheer fabric he could clearly see the hard press of her nipples.

When Bailey licked lips gone suddenly dry, wanting to taste her, Maureen removed her bra and leaned closer, drawing her breasts gently over his face.

Fighting for control, Bailey drew first one and then the other inside the heat of his mouth and sucked gently. Her quick indrawn breath made his body tighten like a bow.

Fighting for control, he tried to sit up. "This is crazy," he rasped as Maureen pushed him firmly back down. "I thought I could handle it, but you're driving me straight out of my mind. We have to stop."

"Trust me." Her voice drifted over him like the lightest of kisses.

As Bailey tried to relax, to somehow keep a tight rein on his burgeoning desire, Maureen's hand stole across his chest and down over his flat abdomen. His skin jumped beneath the caress.

"Let go," she murmured, slipping her fingers into the open fly of his jeans and lightly tracing the waistband of his shorts. "Give yourself to me."

Her words were so soft that Bailey thought he'd dreamed them. He sucked in a breath. Only when those loving hands wandered inside the band of elastic to touch him intimately did he believe the words had been real. A swirling red haze filled his mind and all he knew was her voice and her touch.

"That's it," she murmured sweetly.

With a groan that turned into a sigh, Bailey gave himself up to Maureen's sweet, ardent loving.

With her lips and hands, she showed him what selfless love was all about. When he finally collapsed, completely spent, she rose and lay her body along his bare one, cradling him close.

After a while Maureen sat up and tugged down her slacks, kicking them away. When Bailey's galloping heartbeat had slowed to a bearable rhythm, he reached down to pull up the afghan that was folded at the foot of the bed. Covering their bodies, he slid his arms back around her. His sleepy brown eyes stared intently into hers. As long as he had Maureen, he was not an empty man.

"You're...unbelievable," Bailey whispered, tangling his legs with hers as he tried hard to concentrate, to fight the sudden, overwhelming exhaustion that threatened to smother him with sleep. There was something he wanted to say. "I can't begin to tell you how much I . . ."

Bailey's eyes drifted shut and his breathing evened out, but his arms remained firm around Maureen as he fell asleep.

Beside him, she groaned silently, his unfinished thought making her desperately curious. Then she gazed into his unguarded face and her heart threatened to overflow with the love she felt for him. Love that washed away some of her sadness. As she continued to study Bailey, his lips moved silently. Maureen reached up to press a kiss against his mouth and then, pulling the afghan up to her chin, she snuggled down next to his big, warm body. In seconds she, too, was asleep.

After he left Maureen and went home, Bailey waited impatiently for Angela to drop Shawn and Melissa off as the numbers on the clock flashed six-thirty and then seven. He called her apartment every fifteen minutes but there was never an answer. He thought about calling the police; he thought even more about wringing Angela's neck. She'd said something about taking the children to lunch with a friend; she had probably forgotten the time.

Bailey jammed his hands into the back pockets of his jeans and resumed his pacing. It was hell coming home from such an unbelievable afternoon with Maureen, satiated and relaxed, only to begin stewing over the whereabouts of his kids.

Picking up the receiver again, Bailey punched in Maureen's number. She had promised to go to bed early since she had a full schedule the next day, but Bailey had to hear her voice before he flipped out completely. Just thinking about what she had done brought heat to his face and a foolish grin to his mouth. He had tried to tell her, but she'd smiled and kissed him, sealing the words inside. Even now, Bailey wanted to pour out his heart, but instead he glanced out the window to the empty driveway as he listened to the phone ring, cursing Angela under his breath.

Maureen was watching an old movie on television, Max curled up in her lap, when the telephone interrupted. Probably a friend from school.

"Hi, sweetheart," Bailey's deep voice greeted her after she had pressed the mute button on the television control and picked up the receiver. "Just wondered how you are."

Maureen snuggled down on the couch and cradled the receiver against her ear. "I'm fine," she sighed, picturing the expression on his face before he'd left her. Loving was the only word to describe that look. "After you went home I took a long shower, and now I'm watching an old Errol Flynn movie called *Footsteps in the Dark*. What are you doing? Did the kids enjoy their visit with Angela?" Maureen was surprised he'd even had time to call during what he called "Sunday Night Madness," getting lunches and homework, baths and bed all accounted for.

Bailey's voice had been soft, but now it took on a definite edge. "I don't know how they liked their visit. Seems like they're still on it."

"I thought Angela was supposed to have them back by six," Maureen said, sitting up straighter. Surely nothing had happened. Maureen couldn't bear it if those children were hurt in any way. She had come to love both of them almost as much as she did their father.

"She was. Unfortunately time has never meant that much to my ex-wife." Bailey's voice was grim, hiding the worry she knew he must be feeling.

Maureen glanced at the clock on her VCR. "They're over ninety minutes late. Shouldn't you call someone?"

"Who?"

"*I* don't know. *I'm* not a parent." She felt helpless, and frustrated. Bailey undoubtedly must feel a lot worse. "Try not to worry too much, I guess," she heard herself telling him. Dumb!

"I always worry when she has them." His voice was dry. "Even when she's on time." His rough sigh made Maureen ache to smooth away the lines she knew were etched into his forehead. "I suppose she just forgot the time, but I wish she'd try a little harder," he said, exasperated. "It always takes a while for the kids to come down after they've seen her, and we have school to get ready for."

Maureen switched the phone from one ear to the other. "You're probably right. She just wasn't watching the time. I bet she'll be there any minute now. You know Angela, she isn't going to do anything that would hurt her case." Maureen could have bitten her tongue. He didn't need to be reminded of that right now."

"Who knows what she'd do?" Bailey grumbled, sounding a little less uptight. "She's never been what you'd call predictable."

Maureen wished he didn't have so many worries, so many responsibilities. "Anything I can do?"

"No, thanks. It helps just to hear your voice."

She could picture Bailey smoothing his mustache with his left thumb, something he did when he was thinking. For a few more minutes she tried to raise his spirits, until he finally said he'd better get off the phone in case Angela tried to call. Reluctantly Maureen hung up, after making him promise he'd let her know when the kids got home.

Bailey replaced the receiver reluctantly and again glanced out the window. To his surprise, headlights cut through the gathering darkness. Car doors slammed as he rushed outside.

He could hear Angela's voice as his anger and worry struggled for release. Patience, he told himself. At least give her a chance to explain.

To Bailey's surprise, it was a police cruiser and not Angela's new sports car that sat in his driveway. His heart threatened to choke him.

"Didn't we have a lovely time at Burt's house?" Angela asked Melissa as Shawn began unloading their bags from the backseat.

"We're late," he said, ducking around the patrolman who was climbing out from behind the wheel. "Dad's going to be mad."

"Oh, pooh! He's an old stick-in-the-mud," Angela replied in a singsong voice. "We're only a little late."

Bailey moved closer to the car as Melissa shot around the patrolman to give him a hug. "Hi, Daddy."

He hugged her back. "Are you okay? What's going on, officer?"

"We got to ride in a police car," Melissa said. "It was neat."

Bailey wasn't even aware of his answer to her as he glanced at Shawn, breathing a silent prayer of thanks that both children were unharmed, at least physically. "You two go in the house and unpack. I'll be there in a few minutes."

For a moment Shawn looked as if he wanted to argue, but then he glanced at Angela and bent his head. "'Bye, Mom."

Angela swept over to give each child a smacking kiss, as Bailey and the officer looked on. As soon as the back door shut behind them, Bailey turned to the policeman.

"Now," he said, voice grim. "What the hell is going on here?" He'd seen enough to know that his charming ex-wife was a little short of being sober. Bailey knew the signs, and it wasn't the first time since she'd come back that he'd seen them.

"I understand that this woman is your wife," the policeman said, looking slightly confused.

"Ex-wife," Bailey corrected him, frowning at Angela, who had the temerity to giggle.

The policeman nodded, comprehension dawning. "I see. We stopped the car that she and your children were riding in because it was swerving dangerously."

This time the furious look Bailey sent Angela promised retribution. Her smile faded and she took a step backward.

"Burt Lewis, the driver, failed to negotiate the field-sobriety test I administered to him, so I took him to the station."

The rage that filled Bailey when he heard how carelessly Angela had treated his children threatened to overflow. For one of the few times in his life, he felt capable of physical violence. "Go on."

"Mrs. McGuire had also been drinking, so we impounded the car. Since I was going right by here, I offered to give your ex-wife and children a ride." The officer shifted uncomfortably, then said, "I'm sorry. I suppose that Mrs. McGuire resides somewhere else. I didn't realize."

Angela stepped forward and Bailey silenced her with a glance. "I'll take her home," he said.

Angela began to protest, but the officer looked relieved. "I'll be on my way, then," he said.

Bailey thanked him for the safe deliverance of Shawn and Melissa, then watched as the cruiser drove away. Barely controlling his temper, he turned to Angela, who wore a defiant expression.

"Don't think you're going to lecture me about this," she said, taking the offensive. "I got my lecture for today." She glared angrily in the direction the policeman had gone. "I wasn't even driving," she added pettishly.

Bailey's fingers curled around her elbow. "Come in the house," he said. "I'll see if I can get a sitter and then I'll drive you home."

"You don't have to," she said, pulling loose of his grip. "I can call a cab."

"You and I have some talking to do," Bailey said, a little of his suppressed anger spilling over into his voice. "Get inside."

Ten minutes later, after Jennifer had arrived and Bailey told the children good night, he drove Angela to her apartment in silence. She kept sneaking sidelong glances at him, but Bailey had no intention of discussing the situation with her until he could give it his complete attention. Let her stew!

Pulling up in front of her building, he unsnapped his seat belt and glanced at her, ignoring the way her lower lip trembled. "Come on."

Bailey waited until she was out of the car and then followed her into a modern apartment that he was surprised to see was only partially furnished. Angela had led him to believe that she was completely settled in.

"Not planning to stick around long?" he asked, glancing at a leather couch, side chair and lamp, the only pieces of furniture in the room.

"Of course I am. It takes time to furnish an apartment."

"You always did travel light," he couldn't resist adding.

Angela glared and flounced into the kitchen. "Do you want a drink?"

"No, and neither do you unless it's coffee."

She glared again, but she came back into the living room empty-handed and sank onto the couch. "I'm sorry we were late," she said, surprising him.

He raked a hand through his hair. "You know it's not your being late that I'm the most angry about. How could you let some friend of yours drive with the kids in the car when he'd been drinking?" Bailey was doing his best to remain calm.

Angela twisted her hands together. "What was I supposed to do?" she asked in a whiny voice that set his teeth on edge. "I'd had a little, too. Burt seemed okay to me."

"Burt," Bailey repeated. "New boyfriend?"

"He's just a friend." She tossed her head. "He has a house on the beach and I thought it would be fun for the kids."

You wanted to see him, so you dragged the kids along, Bailey thought as he studied her. Angela's gaze shifted away from his and she began to pluck at the fabric of her gauze slacks with one hand.

He rose, shoving his hands into the pockets of his jeans. "You could have had an accident," he said, voice rising.

"Didn't you even think? I would have come to pick the kids up. You should have called me. Do you know how worried I've been since you didn't show up on time?" He realized he was shouting, and lowered his voice. "Then to see them come home in a police car. Thank God they weren't hurt."

Angela's eyes filled with tears, and Bailey bit off a curse. This was pointless. He stepped in front of where she sat, and bent down toward her. "Don't you ever do anything like this again," he ground out, shaking a finger in her face. "Or I'll do my very best to see that your visitation rights are curtailed."

"You can't do that!" There was genuine fear in her eyes. The tears spilled over and ran down her cheeks.

"Can't I? Watch me!" Bailey was so angry he was shaking. "I thought you said you'd stopped drinking?"

She looked away. "I did!" she exclaimed. "I just had a little this afternoon."

Bailey was too disgusted to even argue with her. It was like trying to reason with a child. Maureen would never act so irresponsibly where the children were concerned, and she wasn't even a parent. Why did someone like Angela, who had the maternal instincts of a fish, have to be their mother?

"Remember what I said," he told her. If Angela was thinking about her custody suit, she had the good sense not to mention it. Shutting the front door carefully behind him, Bailey walked to his car.

All the way home he battled grim thoughts and vivid scenarios of how the afternoon could have ended if an alert policeman hadn't pulled Angela's boyfriend over. When Bailey got back to his house and sent the sitter home, he visited first Melissa's and then Shawn's room to give them an extra hug and a good-night kiss, and to re-assure himself one last time that they were both safe and well, under his care.

"So I called Susan and told her about it, and she said she'd get a copy of the police report," Bailey told Maureen as they sat together on her couch early the next evening. "Maybe it will help our case, even though Angela wasn't driving. Susan couldn't promise anything."

Maureen watched him as he raised his iced-tea glass and drained it, wishing she knew what to say to make him feel better and stop worrying. The case wouldn't go to court for several weeks, and Maureen was already wondering how either one of them was going to stand the waiting. Bailey was already as tense as a coiled spring. Even when he'd kissed her when he first arrived, his whole attention didn't seem to be with her.

"I'm sure this will all help," she said, choosing her words carefully. "Didn't you say that Angela had a drinking problem she told you was in the past?"

Bailey nodded, staring at Maureen intently as if he hoped she could say something to reassure him. "Yeah. I tried to question the kids without arousing their suspicions, to see if I could find out whether she'd been drinking at other times they were with her, but they just don't know."

Maureen caught his hand and held on tightly as he stopped in front of her. "Things will work out," she said fiercely. "The judge will see how much you love your children, and how hard you've worked to give them a good home. He'll understand, and you'll win. You just have to!" She tried to look encouraging, knowing that the children's welfare wasn't always the deciding factor in a case. How could Maureen stand to see him lose those precious kids, when she knew how important they were to him? When she had a good idea what kind of a mother Angela was?

Bailey dropped back down beside Maureen, taking her in his arms. "You're really something," he murmured. "You let me go on like a selfish idiot, when you've just lost a child yourself, and you even try to bolster my spirits." His eyes darkened and he bent his head. "Forgive me."

Maureen shifted away before his mouth could cover hers. The mention of the baby she had lost had caught her unprepared for the sharp pain that pierced her heart.

"I'm sorry," she gasped, pulling out of his arms. "I thought I had it all under control."

Bailey made no move to touch her. "No, I'm the one who should apologize," he said quietly. "It was insensitive of me to mention your miscarriage so casually. After losing Tony when the two of you were so close, and then your other baby, you can't expect to put this behind you easily."

Maureen turned tear-filled eyes to look at him. Perhaps he really did understand. She touched his face with her hand. "It was your loss, too."

"Yes, and I miss what might have been." Bailey's face darkened with regret. "More than you know," he added so silently that Maureen wasn't sure she was even meant to hear it.

So why don't you speak? her heart cried out. *If you love me, tell me. We could still have a future together.*

Beside her, Bailey stood once again. "I'd better go," he said tersely. "I have errands to run before I get home." Again he'd put distance between them.

Maureen tried to find the words to assure him once again that he would win the case, but her mouth refused to say them. How she wished the damned hearing was over and done with, one way or the other. How she wished that she and Bailey were truly together, and that *she* were the children's mother.

Maureen walked Bailey to the door. This time when he bent to kiss her, she returned his embrace, sliding her arms around his neck to tangle her fingers in his hair, opening her mouth under his and trying to show him without words how much she loved him. The smile he gave her before turning away held some of the warmth she had missed seeing on his handsome face.

On the way home, Bailey decided that he could no longer postpone talking to the children about the custody case. Angela had made veiled references to it when they'd last been with her, and Bailey knew they were confused and worried. He hadn't wanted to unduly upset them, but their mother had made it impossible for him not to bring it up.

When Bailey got to the house, Shawn was in the kitchen working on a model, and Melissa was watching a tape of *Bambi* on television while Jennifer did homework.

"We need to talk," Bailey told both children after Jennifer left. "Melissa, why don't you turn off the TV for now, and we'll sit here in the living room." He settled into the recliner, hoping for the inspiration to explain things without adding to their confusion.

Melissa crawled into Bailey's lap and Shawn slipped to the floor in front of the couch, clasping his hands loosely around one bent knee. His expression looked as if he were bracing himself for whatever bad news Bailey was about to tell them.

"It must be nice having your mother back after all this time," Bailey began, watching their faces carefully.

"It sure is," Melissa burst out. "I missed her."

Her words made Bailey wonder if he had been wrong about the children finally beginning to adjust before Angela showed up again. Perhaps they'd only been waiting for her to return.

Shawn was more cautious with his answer. "Yeah," he said noncommittally after a moment. "It's okay."

"That's fine," Bailey hastened to assure them. "She's your mother and it's perfectly all right for you to love her. She loves you both very much." How he wished she loved them enough to do what was right and to leave them with Bailey, who had given them a stable home!

Shawn was frowning, his mouth set into a stubborn line. As Bailey watched him, he slowly shook his head.

"What's on your mind, son?"

At first Bailey thought he wasn't going to answer. Then Shawn squared his shoulders and took in a deep breath. For a moment, Bailey had a glimpse of the young man Shawn would soon become.

"Mom said she wanted to be a family with us and you again," Shawn said quickly, as if he would lose his nerve if he didn't get the words out fast. "She said you're the one holding back on us all being together."

Now it was Bailey's turn to hesitate, as he wondered how much to tell them, and the best way to put it. "I told you once before," he said finally, "that I don't feel that special way toward your mother anymore, the way that married people need to feel about each other. She'll always have a place in my heart as your mother," he felt compelled to add. "But we won't get married again.

We're not going to all live together, but you can see her often.''

Bailey glanced down at Melissa, who was listening intently. "It was really unfair of your mom to let you think it might happen," Bailey concluded. He always tried hard not to criticize her in front of them, but she had brought this on herself.

"What if you hadn't met Maureen?" Shawn demanded. "I bet then you'd be willing to give it a try."

"I like Maureen," Melissa said, as Shawn turned to frown at her. "She's nice."

"But she's not our mom," Shawn said.

Melissa's face got red, and Bailey could see an argument coming. "Wait a minute, kids. I know that Maureen isn't your mom, and she isn't trying to take your mom's place. She just wants to be your friend, that's all. Like she's my friend." He almost stumbled on those words, knowing he wasn't being completely honest, but now sure wasn't the time to elaborate on that to the children or to Maureen.

Melissa smiled, but Shawn muttered something under his breath that Bailey supposed he should be glad he couldn't hear.

"Maureen has nothing to do with what's going on between your mom and me," he said. "But what I really wanted to talk to you about is the custody case your mom and her lawyer are taking to court." He'd done his best to convince Shawn that Maureen wasn't to blame, but he wasn't sure he had succeeded.

The expressions on both children's face grew solemn.

"What's custody?" asked Melissa.

She stuck her thumb into her mouth, something Bailey hadn't seen her do in years. Gently he pulled it back out.

Then he explained about custody and visitation rights as simply as he could.

"There's a boy at school whose parents have joint custody," Shawn said importantly. "He has two bedrooms, one in each house, and lots of toys."

Melissa scooted forward on Bailey's lap. "That sounds fun."

Bailey felt as if he were losing control of the conversation, but perhaps it was better for them not to be worried until the case was settled. "We wouldn't share custody," he felt compelled to explain. "Your mother wants total custody, which means you'd live with her and visit me."

Melissa pulled out the thumb she'd jammed back into her mouth. "I wouldn't like that. My dolls are here."

"Don't we have anything to say about it?" Shawn demanded.

"The judge might want to ask you some questions, but it won't be scary. Susan will be with you, and I will be if I can. Susan will explain to the judge how much I want you both to stay with me. Your mother's lawyer will try to persuade him that you'd be better off with her. Then the judge will have to decide where he thinks the best place for you to live is."

"That sucks," Shawn said clearly.

"Yeah," Melissa echoed. "Sucks."

Bailey gave her a hug, then leaned forward to grab Shawn's hand. "I want you two with me," he promised. "And I'll be doing everything I can to convince the judge of that." He studied their anxious faces, wondering if he could have done a better job explaining or if he would have been smarter not to say anything at all.

"I want to stay here with you, Daddy," Melissa wailed, tears beginning to slide down her cheeks.

"So do I." Shawn looked ready to cry, too.

Bailey's own eyes grew damp, and he blinked the moisture away. Feeling totally frustrated, he held both children to him, promising himself he'd somehow manage to keep them, and just as soon as that issue was settled, he'd straighten things out with Maureen. Once and for all.

Chapter Twelve

Maureen was putting the last touches on her makeup when the phone rang. "Get that for me, would you?" she said to Max, who was sitting on the corner of the bed watching her in the vanity mirror.

Max stared unblinking. Maureen gave him a smile and reached for the phone herself. Classes that day had gone well, and she was going to dinner with Bailey. Her mood, still often sad, was lighter.

Maureen picked up the receiver. "Hello."

Bailey's tone reminded her of the concert they had missed because of Melissa's fever. "I'm sorry," he said, voice weary, "but I'm going to be late. Angela was supposed to pick up Shawn and Melissa a half hour ago, but she hasn't shown up or called."

"I hope nothing's wrong," Maureen said automatically. She knew the children would be disappointed and her heart went out to them. Now that Maureen had gotten to know both of them, she knew that Melissa's reaction would be to pepper Bailey with questions, while Shawn would withdraw into a moody silence.

"Nothing's wrong but Angela's screwed-up sense of timing," Bailey grumbled. "That woman is going to drive me around the bend."

"I'm sure she'll be there any minute," Maureen said, trying to calm him. After the last incident, which Bailey had described over coffee at the college cafeteria, she thought Angela would be on her best behavior, at least until the hearing. Apparently she didn't operate under the same guidelines as Maureen might, but she was lucky Bailey had agreed to let her take the children again at all, when they didn't have a strictly formal agreement. Sometimes Maureen thought he carried his sense of fair play too far. She might have been tempted to be more protective, but she had to remind herself that Bailey was their father and knew what he was doing.

"I want to see you," he said, "and soon. I've been looking forward to this evening for a week. Dinner and then dancing with you in my arms is one of the best ways to spend an evening that I can think of."

The warmth and longing in his voice made Maureen wish he was beside her so she could hold him close, feeling the gentle strength of his body as his big hands caressed her.

"If Angela disrupts our plans," he continued, "I'm liable to wring her scrawny neck."

"Have you tried to call her?" Maureen had bought a new dress for the occasion, a strapless dream of fuschia satin with a fitted bodice and full, short skirt that made her legs look long and sleek. With it she wore a matching bow in the back of her hair, which she'd pinned into a romantic upsweep, and crystal earrings. As she turned in front of the mirror, they glittered in the light.

"There's no answer at her apartment, and the real-estate office said she got off hours ago. I'd call Jennifer, but her whole family's gone camping, and the other sitter I use has plans, too."

"Well, let's give Angela another half hour before we panic," Maureen said, trying to be cheerful. "Call me then, or whenever she gets there."

"I'm going to see you tonight," Bailey promised. "With or without the kids." Then he said goodbye reluctantly.

His words warmed Maureen, who caught herself smiling dreamily at her reflection as she replaced the receiver. It was true that Bailey had been moody and tense over the last week, but she knew the custody case hung heavily on his strong shoulders. Despite the strain, he had still managed to be loving enough so that Maureen was beginning to hope they had some kind of future after all. His love-making had been more ardent than ever after their forced wait until she recovered from the miscarriage, and afterward he'd held her and told her how much she meant to him.

Bailey hadn't yet spoken the three words she wanted most to hear, but Maureen was beginning to hope he might. That possibility was the only thing that made the loss she still felt over her baby even remotely bearable. If Bailey did love her, there might be another chance for a child. Even without one of her own, Maureen had discovered that the children he already had went a long way toward fulfilling her maternal instincts. If only he didn't lose them to Angela.

When the phone rang a half hour later, Maureen crossed her fingers before answering.

"How about a change in plans?" Bailey asked. "Since there are still three of us here, let's put on our jeans and get some burgers at that drive-in down toward Seattle where the carhops still wear roller skates."

Maureen swallowed her disappointment and wondered how the children felt about their mother's latest stunt. "Sure," she told Bailey. "Burgers sound good to me, as long as you're part of the agenda." At least she would get to see him, even if they would have two pint-sized chaperons.

"Thanks for being so nice about it." Bailey glanced at Shawn and Melissa, who sat on the living-room couch like two small thunderclouds. "Do you mind driving over here, so we don't have a car problem later?"

"I'll change and be there in twenty minutes," Maureen promised.

"Come on, you two," Bailey said when he got off the phone. "Lighten up. As soon as Maureen gets here, we're going to get hamburgers and then we'll see what's playing at the movies."

"Oh, boy," Melissa said, sliding off the couch. "That sounds good."

"What if Mom comes over?" Shawn demanded, grabbing Melissa's sleeve. "She'll be worried if we aren't here."

Bailey tried to be patient. "She's an hour late, son, and I've called everywhere I know to look for her. I don't think she's coming, but I'm sure she'll explain later."

"Mom could be hurt," Shawn said, "and you don't even care! I want to stay here and wait for her." Releasing Melissa, he sat back and crossed his arms over his chest.

Tightening his jaw, Bailey counted to ten. "Tell you what," he said, "we'll leave a note on the door. If she does come here she'll know you waited for a long time, and meanwhile we can still go out to eat."

Shawn thought it over a minute and then, to Bailey's relief, he nodded. "Okay. I guess that would work."

"Goody!" Melissa said, clapping. "I want to see Maureen, and get onion rings."

Close to a half hour later, Maureen rang the bell. Feeling a little self-conscious in front of his children, Bailey gave her a kiss on the cheek, then stepped back.

"You look great," he said, gazing appreciatively at her tight jeans and royal blue pullover, covered by a red parka with grey stripes on the sleeves.

"You two sure look ready for an evening of burgers and a movie," Maureen said to the children with a smile while Bailey watched, pleased that she was so much more comfortable with them than she had been in the beginning. "I like your jeans, Melissa. Isn't acid-washed denim great? Shawn, is the picture on your shirt from one of the Saturday-morning cartoons?"

"Yeah," he mumbled. "Captain Lightning. It's my favorite show."

"He's got pajamas with them on the front, too," Bailey added.

"Dad!" Shawn exclaimed, obviously embarrassed by the revelation.

"Sorry," Bailey saw Maureen turn away to hide her grin. Apparently nine year olds weren't comfortable discussing their nighttime attire. He would have to remember that.

"What do you two like on your burgers?" Maureen asked after they'd all gotten into Bailey's car. She had turned to face the rear seat.

"Plain!" said Melissa. "No yucky mayonnaise and pickles and ketchup and relish and—"

"We get the picture, princess," Bailey said dryly.

"I don't care." Shawn's voice sounded bored.

"Did you know the waitresses skate to the cars with your food?" Maureen asked him.

"Yeah."

She sighed, trying not to be discouraged as Bailey reached out a hand to squeeze hers. Shawn seemed to resent her presence more than ever, and she was already trying so hard!

Bailey tuned the radio to a golden-oldies station to get them in the mood, he said. Maureen turned back around and for the rest of the trip they listened to the music, Bailey sometimes singing along in a deep, pleasant voice. When they got to the drive-in, all of the spaces for cars were full.

"Let's eat inside," Bailey suggested. "They have booths and a collection of real old-fashioned juke-boxes."

"Sounds good to me," Maureen said, realizing who messy it could be to eat in the car with two children. "How about you, kids?"

Melissa agreed and Shawn shrugged, so they went inside and crowded into a booth. Old movie posters and record-album covers from years ago decorated the walls.

Bailey handed around plastic menus.

"I see the prices are up-to-date," he said to Maureen, smiling, then asked Melissa, who was pretending to study her menu, what she would like.

"I want a taco," Shawn grumbled. "But all they have is hamburgers."

Bailey gave him a long look, complete with raised eyebrows.

Shawn colored and glanced back at his menu. "I guess a bacon burger would be okay."

After milk shakes and burger baskets, with onion rings on the side, they found a movie about animals that sounded appropriate for their varied age group. On the way back home, Melissa fell asleep and Shawn remained quiet, looking out the window.

"Not a bad evening, for such a quick change of plans," Maureen said softly to Bailey.

His gaze dropped to her mouth. "Not quite what I'd had in mind. Did you really enjoy yourself?" He returned his attention to the road.

"Yes, it was fun." Maureen realized she was telling the truth. Despite Shawn's moodiness, the evening had been fun. When she was with the three of them, Maureen found herself pretending they were a family, even telling herself that other people seeing them would think she was Shawn and Melissa's mother, Bailey's wife. The thought was at first exhilarating and then depressing. Maureen could admit, at least silently, that it was a position she'd give almost anything to fill.

"Shall I fix some coffee while you tuck the kids in?" she offered as they pulled into Bailey's driveway alongside her car.

"Good idea." He leaned closer, kissing her cheek before he opened the door. "We won't be too long."

The note Bailey had left for Angela was still taped to the door. Shawn went over and ripped it down, examining it closely. "Mom hasn't been here."

Maureen looked at Bailey, whose expression was grim. "You can call her in the morning," he said.

"I'm hungry," Shawn announced as soon as they walked into the house.

"You should have eaten more when you had the chance," Bailey said, remembering the snacks he'd bought at the show. "It's past bedtime."

"I can't go to sleep with my stomach growling," Shawn argued. "It will keep me awake."

"Okay." Bailey gave in abruptly. "Have an apple while Melissa's getting ready in the bathroom. Just be quick about it."

Shawn ran to the kitchen, while Melissa gave Maureen a sleepy hug. "I'm glad you came," she said, her high, sweet voice melting Maureen's heart.

"Me, too, honey. Sweet dreams." She kissed Melissa's soft cheek and watched her walk down the hallway.

"Don't forget to brush your teeth." Bailey turned to Maureen. "That's one of the key phrases a parent is supposed to say, along with clean your plate, pick up your room, and go to the bathroom before we leave home."

"Sounds like you've got all that parenting stuff down pretty good," she teased. "I'll make the coffee."

Before Maureen could get to the kitchen, a piercing wail stopped her in her tracks. Shawn!

"What's wrong?" Bailey shouted, racing past her.

Maureen followed quickly. When she got to the kitchen, Bailey had grabbed a towel and had it wrapped around Shawn's hand. A butcher knife lay on the counter, next to a partially cut-up apple. Shawn was crying.

"It's okay," Bailey said. "Now let me look at the cut."

Slowly he unwrapped the towel, as Maureen's stomach knotted into a tight ball. Shawn was sniffling, trying to be brave. Maureen saw the red stain and put a bracing hand on Shawn's shoulder.

"I think this will need stitches," Bailey said, face grim. "You're lucky you didn't take off a finger with that big knife."

"I'm sorry, Dad." Shawn's voice was faint.

Bailey rewrapped his hand. "Don't worry about that now." As Melissa darted into the room holding a toothbrush, Bailey's dark eyes sought Maureen's. "Could you stay—"

"Of course," she agreed quickly.

"The emergency room can take a while on a weekend."

"No problem." Maureen patted Shawn's back before dropping her hand. "You're going to be fine."

He managed a weak smile through his tears. "It hurts."

"I know," she said. "I'm sure the doctor will give you something for the pain."

"Hold the towel tight," Bailey told Shawn. He grabbed his car keys and jacket, while Maureen draped Shawn's parka over his shoulders. She wanted to give him a hug but didn't quite dare. Instead she squeezed Bailey's arm. "Everything will be okay," she said.

"Thanks." He smiled distractedly, then put an arm around his son as they went out the door.

"Is Shawn really going to be all right?" Melissa asked Maureen. "He hardly ever cries."

Maureen swept the pieces of apple into her hand and tossed them into the garbage. Then she set the big knife in the sink. "Cuts always hurt," she said. "Your daddy's taking him to the hospital so they can fix his hand all up."

Melissa nodded wisely. "They've gone there before. Shawn broke his arm last year, and once he fell and cut his forehead and the doctor sewed it up with black thread."

Apparently kids and emergency rooms went together. "Have you ever had to go to the hospital?" Maureen asked, taking Melissa's hand and leading her to the living-room couch.

"Once when I was little, but I don't remember it," Melissa said, crawling into Maureen's lap. "Will you stay with me until they get home?"

"Sure, honey. How about if you get into bed and I'll read you a story?" She hoped that Melissa had some books in her room. Maureen hadn't told a bedtime story from memory since she used to put her brother Tony to bed when they were both children.

"Do you think my mommy and daddy will get married again?" Melissa asked her when they were halfway through a book about a dragon who was afraid of fire. "Daddy says no. Shawn thought they would, but now he won't talk about it."

Maureen thought a moment before trying to answer the question. "You know they're divorced," she said finally, sitting closer on the edge of Melissa's bed. "Divorced people can be friends, but they don't very often get back together. How will you feel if your daddy and mommy don't get married again?"

It was Melissa's turn to think for a moment. Her little fingers smoothed the hair on her doll, tucked into bed beside her. "It would be okay, I guess, if you came to live with us instead," she said finally. "That would be kind of like having a mommy here, wouldn't it?"

Maureen was deeply touched, her eyes filled with sudden tears that she tried to blink away. "Thank you, sweetie. I know you already have a mommy, but I'd like very much to be your friend. Would that be okay?''

"Could you come and live with us?" Melissa asked.

Maureen took a deep breath. "That's something your daddy and I will have to decide after we get to know each other lots better," she said carefully, hoping that Melissa didn't repeat any of this conversation to Bailey. "First we have to see what happens with the custody hearing your daddy talked to you about."

"I hope he wins," Melissa said softly. "Mommy's fun, but I like living with Daddy."

"Your daddy loves you very much," Maureen said, pulling the covers up and smoothing the bedspread.

Melissa yawned, covering her mouth with her hand. Then she reached up and gave Maureen another hug. "I love you," she murmured sleepily. "Will you come back sometime and finish the book?"

Maureen kissed her forehead. "Sure, sweetie. I love you, too." Melissa's eyes were shut, and Maureen wasn't sure if she heard or not. Walking back to the living room, Maureen wished she had told Bailey to call her. Shawn's cut had looked deep and she hoped it wouldn't damage any of the tendons or ligaments near his thumb.

An old movie in black-and-white was half over when the doorbell rang. Startled, Maureen glanced at the clock and then shushed Digger, who had begun to growl. With the dog right behind her, she cautiously opened the door.

"I guess I'm a teeny bit late," Angela said, pushing her way in. "Why are you here?" Her voice was slurred and she blinked owlishly at Maureen, who shut the door and hoped the loud voice wouldn't wake Melissa.

"I'm here because Shawn cut his hand. Bailey took him to the emergency room," Maureen replied. "Just as a precaution," she added when Angela's face twisted with worry.

"Is my baby okay?" she demanded, grabbing Maureen's arm in a death grip. "Are you sure?"

Maureen gently disengaged Angela's hand. "He'll be fine. Would you like some coffee?" She had made a pot after Bailey left, then didn't have any. "I'd like a cup myself."

Angela followed her unsteadily to the kitchen, and Maureen knew that she did not want this woman raising Shawn and Melissa. Mother or not, Angela wouldn't be good for them.

"So what happened to you tonight?" Maureen asked as she set two full mugs on the kitchen table.

Angela picked hers up, almost spilling it before she sat down. "Oh, things came up," she said, waving the mug and sloshing the coffee onto the table. "You know how that goes."

"No, I'm afraid I don't." Maureen handed her a napkin to mop up the mess. "Shawn was very worried. So was Melissa." Maureen's dislike of this woman was growing by the minute.

As the hands of the kitchen clock dragged, Maureen tried awkwardly to make conversation, pressing a refill on Angela when she had finished her coffee. Maureen wished she would leave, but knew she was in no condition to drive.

"I'm going to call the hospital," Angela said, lunging to her feet. "What's the number?"

"I don't know," Maureen told her. "I'm not even sure which hospital they went to."

Angela stared, then dropped back into her chair. "Not very much on top of things, are you?"

Maureen had to bite her lip to keep from making a sizzling rejoinder. Instead she quietly sipped her coffee.

"I've been seeing a wonderful man," Angela said after a few moments of awkward silence. "He's crazy about me." Her expression was almost anxious, a distinct contrast to her self-assurance when Maureen first met her.

Maureen tried to smile at the news. "That's nice." She was dying to ask why Angela wanted custody when the children had such a good home with Bailey, but it just wasn't her place, no matter how much she loved them.

"He wants me to go to California with him. He has a terrific job waiting for him there." Angela frowned into her empty mug, as if she could see some message printed there.

"Does he like children?"

Angela frowned. "What? Oh, you mean my kids." She thought a moment. "Yeah, kids are okay with him."

Again they lapsed into silence as Maureen glanced at the clock. She hoped that Bailey and Shawn would be home soon. This awkward conversation was giving her a grandmother of a headache.

"Would you like more coffee?" She looked at Angela, and then stared harder. The bright head was bowed and tears mingled with mascara were making dark tracks down her cheeks.

"What's wrong?" Maureen asked. "I'm sure that Shawn will be just fine."

Angela blinked and took a napkin from the holder on the table, dabbing at her face.

"I'm such a fraud," she said in a low voice that Maureen hardly recognized. The husky drawl was gone, the pain easy to hear.

Without thinking, Maureen covered Angela's hand with her own. "Want to tell me about it? I'm a pretty good listener."

Angela was silent for so long that Maureen decided she wasn't going to speak. Then suddenly it all came pouring out on a wave of anguish that Maureen couldn't help but sympathize with.

"I told Bailey I'd quit drinking," Angela said. "But I think he knows I haven't. I was so sure I'd licked it, you know?"

"I understand."

"I go to a bar and someone always buys me a drink. That's how I met Burt. I start with plain soda water, but pretty soon we get to talking, and then I decide I'd be having more fun if I just had one drink." Angela's head went down and she sniffed loudly. "I thought if I got the kids back I wouldn't be so lonely, then I wouldn't drink."

Maureen wanted to say something, but didn't interrupt.

"That's why I threatened the lawsuit. I thought Bailey would take me back, instead of risking the kids." She shrugged, trying to laugh lightly. "That didn't work. He said he didn't want me. It took me a while to believe him." She stared hard at Maureen. "He's a terrific guy," she said, shaking one finger. "Don't you hurt him."

"I won't," Maureen said. "I love him." It felt so good to say the words out loud, to finally tell someone.

"I thought so. You'll be good for him." Angela fell silent, thinking. "Do you love my kids, too?"

"Yes, I do."

Angela bobbed her head, as if she had settled something in her mind. "I'm dropping the case," she said, fresh tears filling her eyes.

At her astounding announcement, Maureen straightened. "What did you say?"

"I'm dropping the case." Angela's voice wavered and she choked. Then she took a deep breath and clasped Maureen's hand. "I love them," she said, voice breaking. A sob shook her, and Maureen almost cried, too, at her obvious pain.

"I know you do."

Angela wiped at her eyes, sending more of her makeup across her cheeks in a smudgy streak. Maureen handed her another napkin.

"I thought I could take care of them, but I can't," Angela wailed as she crumpled the napkin in her hand. She put her head down on her hands, fresh sobs shaking her shoulders. "I just can't. They're better off here, but, oh God, it hurts."

Maureen got to her feet and put a hand on Angela's shoulder, trying to soothe her with long, comforting strokes. She thought how hard it would be to voluntarily give up the children you loved for their own good. "You're very courageous," she said softly.

Angela raised her head. "Do you think so?"

"Absolutely." Woman to woman, part of the same vast sisterhood, Maureen realized that silent tears were coursing down her own cheeks in appreciation of Angela's pain.

Maureen doubted that Angela had undergone any kind of complete character transformation, but for once, when it really counted, she was putting the children before her own selfish desires.

"I think I have some idea of what this is costing you," Maureen said. "And I hope you don't change your mind."

Before Angela could reply, the door burst open and Shawn and Bailey walked in. Maureen hadn't even heard the car. Shawn's hand was heavily bandaged, but he wore a smile that faded when he saw his mother.

"What happened?" he demanded, rushing to her.

Angela, whose face was streaked and whose hair was a tangled mess, managed to smile. "I'm okay," she said, "but I heard you tried to amputate your arm. How is it?"

Bailey glanced from her to Maureen, brows raised. Maureen tried to smile reassuringly. Bailey frowned and looked back at Angela. "What the hell is going on?" he asked, obviously frustrated.

"Shawn first," Angela said, voice firm. Maureen marveled at how quickly she had regained control.

Shawn told them all about the emergency room and the four stitches the doctor had put in his hand. "It didn't cut anything important," he said. "The doctor told me it wasn't as deep as Dad thought."

"We were lucky," Bailey added. "But you've got school tomorrow. Say good night, and be sure to take one of the pain pills they gave you. I'll be in to check on you in a few minutes."

For a moment Shawn looked as if he meant to ask Angela some more questions, but then he glanced at his dad. "Okay." He hugged his mom and smiled at Maureen. For a startling moment his grin reminded her of Tony. "I had a good time tonight," Shawn said, surprising her. Then he raised his hand. "Except for this."

After Shawn left the room, Bailey poured himself a cup of coffee and dragged out a kitchen chair. "So," he said to Angela. "You want to tell me what the hell happened to you tonight, and why you're here now?"

Maureen wanted to ask him to take it easy, then bit her tongue and leaned back. "Perhaps I should go," she offered.

"No way," Bailey said, glancing at her. "At least, not if you don't mind staying." There was an unreadable message in his eyes, and she felt warmth fill her cheeks as she agreed to stay.

"Now," Bailey said, redirecting his attention to his ex-wife, "explain."

To Maureen's surprise, Angela did, calmly and directly. "You know I'm still drinking," she said to him. "I know I haven't fooled you."

He nodded.

"I've just been telling your girlfriend here that I'm dropping the lawsuit."

Bailey's expression was so stunned it was almost comical. He glanced at Maureen, who smiled encouragingly, then back at Angela. "Are you sure?"

She nodded. "You've done a wonderful job with our children," Angela told Bailey softly. "It would be wrong of me to try to take them away."

Bailey felt such a roaring in his ears that for a moment he couldn't speak. "I don't know what to say."

Angela stood. "Just say you'll let me see them sometimes."

Bailey and Maureen rose, too. "Of course." He was almost babbling in his excitement. "We'll work it out. With you so close—"

"I'm going to California," Angela interrupted. "Don't think less of me, Bailey, but there's no place for me here." She glanced toward Maureen, but Bailey didn't see any animosity in Angela's gray eyes. What on earth had happened between the two women while he'd been gone?

In the light of what she had just given him, Bailey couldn't find the words to question her. "Promise me one thing," he said finally. "You know you can't quit drinking all by yourself. See someone, get some help." He touched her arm, remembering how important to each other they had once been and feeling sad for her. "You can do it, I know you can."

Angela smiled, walking toward the door. "Thanks, honey. I'll think about it. Meanwhile, give my kids a kiss for me, and don't let them forget how much their mother loves them." Her eyes filled with fresh tears, and Bailey found his own throat tightening with emotion.

"I will," he promised solemnly, squeezing her hands.

Angela turned to Maureen, and Bailey watched with surprise as the two women embraced, both smiling tearfully.

"Good luck," Maureen told her. "And thank you. It's a very brave thing you're doing." She and Angela exchanged a look brimming with shared understanding.

"Good luck to you, too," Angela told her.

She gave Bailey a hug he was able to return without hard feelings and then, before he could say anything else, she left. Moments later, he heard the car start, headlights playing briefly against the window before the sound of the engine faded into the night.

"I guess I need a moment to absorb all that's happened," Bailey said to Maureen, who was waiting silently in the doorway to the living room. "Let's sit down."

She followed him to the couch, and curled up beside him as he finished his coffee. "Did she really tell me she was dropping the custody suit?" he had to ask after a short silence.

"Yes," Maureen replied. "She told me that she's going to California with her boyfriend. She really loves those kids. I think that's why she did what she did."

Bailey smoothed a hand over Maureen's hair, letting his fingers thread through the silken strands. "I never thought she could be that generous, or that noble," he mused, breathing in Maureen's perfume. "I guess I underestimated her."

"I felt badly for her," Maureen said.

"You know what it's like to lose the children you love," Bailey agreed. "You probably understand her pain even better than I do."

Maureen was silent, and he wondered if she was thinking of the children she'd lost, first her brother and then her two babies. His arm tightened around her as he realized he was finally free to tell her how he really felt.

Maureen felt him tense, and pulled away. He probably wanted to be alone to savor the sweetness of his victory. His worries were over, and his little family would stay intact. "I should go," she said, trying to rise.

Bailey's hand clamped on her wrist. "No way, lady!" Immediately he lowered his voice. "Not until we talk."

Maureen shifted to face him. "I can't tell you how happy I am for you," she said carefully, trying not to think that he might not need her in his life anymore. He had his children back.

"You could make me even happier," Bailey said, taking her hand in a warm, firm grip.

Maureen went rigid. She couldn't stand it if he was about to ask something mundane. She tried to pull her hand away, but his grip tightened. Anxiously she searched his dark eyes, looking for some clue.

Then Bailey smiled. His face, so dear to her, relaxed into gentle, tender lines, much of the harshness she'd seen there for so long just melting away. He raised her hand to his mouth and kissed it. As always, reaction leaped up Maureen's arm like heat lightning, and her heart began to race.

"I should have told you this when I proposed before," Bailey said gravely. "I guess I just assumed you would know, which was kind of silly, and then it was too late. Maybe you were right to say no. I didn't feel I had the right to ask you again until my own life was in some kind of order."

Maureen squirmed anxiously beneath his intense gaze. What was he trying to say?

"I couldn't bear for you to suspect, even for a moment, that I was looking for a wife to strengthen my case," he said, the word wife making her heart stop, and then resume with a thunderous beat.

"Are you looking for one now?" Maureen asked bravely.

Bailey's smile widened. "First things first, okay?"

Maureen colored with embarrassment, afraid she'd jumped to the wrong conclusion. When she ducked her head, Bailey crooked a finger beneath her chin and gently coaxed her gaze back to his.

"I love you," he said. "I've loved you for a long time, and so intensely that I foolishly thought you knew." He took a deep breath. "I come as a package deal. I need to know if you love me, too, and whether you could come to love my children." For the first time, the strain was there in his voice for Maureen to hear.

A wave of such intense happiness washed over her that for a moment she couldn't speak. "I already love you," she said finally, when Bailey had begun to look anxious. She slipped her hands around his neck. "And I know that I love your children, too. The thought of your losing them has been pure hell."

Groaning with relief, Bailey bent his head and kissed her, his mouth warm and hungry. Then he straightened abruptly.

"Does that mean that you'll be my wife?" he asked. "That you'll marry me as soon as we can arrange it, and live with me forever? I need you desperately."

"I'd like that very much," Maureen confessed, so full of love she was afraid she'd burst with it. Then she hesitated, glancing shyly away.

"What is it?" Bailey demanded. "What's wrong?"

She turned back to look at him. "Nothing," she said. "We can talk about it later, if you want, but I was just wondering if you'd mind trying for another baby?"

For a moment, Bailey sat stock still. Maureen was just about to tell him it didn't matter, when an expression of pure joy blazed across his face. Maureen thought she saw moisture in his eyes as he swallowed.

"Honey, I'd love to have a baby with you. I can't think of anything that would make our lives together more perfect. If the doctor says it's okay, it's sure okay with me." Then a shadow crossed his face. "But don't be disappointed if it isn't meant to be. Having you and the kids is going to make me a very happy man."

Before Maureen could tell him how his words made her feel, he kissed her again. All their love for each other seemed to come together in that one kiss, as their lips and arms and hands clung tightly, sweetly.

"Tell me again," Maureen murmured as Bailey finally lifted his mouth from hers.

"I love you."

It was there in his voice and shining in his eyes, everything he felt for her, everything and more than she had ever dreamed of finding. "I love you, too." Before she could kiss him again, a sound in the kitchen made them raise their heads.

"Hi," Shawn said, silhouetted in the doorway. "How come you're sitting out here in the dark?"

Maureen could feel Bailey shaking with laughter beside her. "How come you're up?" he asked, reaching to switch on a lamp.

"I was getting a drink. My hand hurts a little. Where's Mom?"

"She's gone, son."

"Oh, yeah. I guess it's pretty late."

Bailey's arm tightened around Maureen. "No, I mean she's leaving town again. She told me to say goodbye for her."

There was a moment of silence. "I figured she was getting restless," Shawn said. "I guess it was time. Where's she going?"

"California."

Maureen was grateful for the easy way Shawn accepted the news. She hoped he wouldn't end up blaming her. At some point, Bailey would have to talk to him some more, but not tonight.

Shawn came into the room and looked at Maureen. "Are you leaving, too, or are you going to be sticking around?"

Looking for direction, Maureen glanced at Bailey.

"Tell him," he said.

She tried to read Shawn's feelings on his face but couldn't. "No," she said after a moment. "I'm not going anywhere." She held her breath for his reaction.

Shawn's expression was serious. "Good," he said. "I'm kinda glad. I like having you around." Then his face turned a dusky red and he looked away, as if he'd revealed too much.

Maureen was too surprised by his reply to speak, but Bailey apparently wasn't. "Maureen has agreed to marry me," he told Shawn.

"When?"

"We were just getting to that when you came in." Bailey's voice was dry.

"Oh, sorry. Does that mean you'll be our stepmom?" Shawn asked Maureen.

"Yes, I guess it does," she replied carefully. "I'll do my best to be a good one."

To her surprise, Shawn came over and gave her a self-conscious hug. "Welcome to the family," he mumbled into her shoulder.

Over Shawn's head, Maureen's gaze collided with Bailey's. His expression was brimming with love and approval. Maureen knew then that she had made the right choice. She finally had her family.

* * * * *

Double your reading pleasure this fall with two Award of Excellence titles written by two of your favorite authors.

Available in September

DUNCAN'S BRIDE
by Linda Howard
Silhouette Intimate Moments #349

Mail-order bride Madelyn Patterson was nothing like what Reese Duncan expected—and everything he needed.

Available in October

THE COWBOY'S LADY
by Debbie Macomber
Silhouette Special Edition #626

The Montana cowboy wanted a little lady at his beck and call—the "lady" in question saw things differently....

These titles have been selected to receive a special laurel—the Award of Excellence. Look for the distinctive emblem on the cover. It lets you know there's something truly wonderful inside! DUN-1

Take 4 bestselling love stories FREE

Plus get a FREE surprise gift!

Special Limited-time Offer

Silhouette Reader Service®

Mail to
In the U.S.
3010 Walden Avenue
P.O. Box 1867
Buffalo, N.Y. 14269-1867

In Canada
P.O. Box 609
Fort Erie, Ontario
L2A 5X3

YES! Please send me 4 free Silhouette Special Edition® novels and my free surprise gift. Then send me 6 brand-new novels every month, which I will receive months before they appear in bookstores. Bill me at the low price of $2.74* each—a savings of 21¢ apiece off cover prices. There are no shipping, handling or other hidden costs. I understand that accepting the books and gift places me under no obligation ever to buy any books. I can always return a shipment and cancel at any time. Even if I never buy another book from Silhouette, the 4 free books and the surprise gift are mine to keep forever.

*Offer slightly different in Canada—$2.74 per book plus 69¢ per shipment for delivery. Sales tax applicable in N.Y.

335 BPA 8178 (CAN)

235 BPA R1YY (US)

Name _____ (PLEASE PRINT)

Address _____ Apt. No. _____

City _____ State/Prov. _____ Zip/Postal Code _____

This offer is limited to one order per household and not valid to present Silhouette Special Edition® subscribers. Terms and prices are subject to change.

© 1990 Harlequin Enterprises Limited

PASSPORT TO ROMANCE
SWEEPSTAKES RULES

1. **HOW TO ENTER:** To enter, you must be the age of majority and complete the official entry form, or print your name, address, telephone number and age on a plain piece of paper and mail to: Passport to Romance, P.O. Box 9056, Buffalo, NY 14269-9056. No mechanically reproduced entries accepted.

2. All entries must be received by the CONTEST CLOSING DATE, DECEMBER 31, 1990 TO BE ELIGIBLE.

3. **THE PRIZES:** There will be ten (10) Grand Prizes awarded, each consisting of a choice of a trip for two people from the following list:
   i)   London, England (approximate retail value $5,050 U.S.)
   ii)   England, Wales and Scotland (approximate retail value $6,400 U.S.)
   iii) Carribean Cruise (approximate retail value $7,300 U.S.)
   iv)   Hawaii (approximate retail value $9,550 U.S.)
   v)   Greek Island Cruise in the Méditerranean (approximate retail value $12,250 U.S.)
   vi)   France (approximate retail value $7,300 U.S.)

4. Any winner may choose to receive any trip or a cash alternative prize of $5,000.00 U.S. in lieu of the trip.

5. **GENERAL RULES:** Odds of winning depend on number of entries received.

6. A random draw will be made by Nielsen Promotion Services, an independent judging organization, on January 29, 1991, in Buffalo, NY, at 11:30 a.m. from all eligible entries received on or before the Contest Closing Date.

7. Any Canadian entrants who are selected must correctly answer a time-limited, mathematical skill-testing question in order to win.

8. Full contest rules may be obtained by sending a stamped, self-addressed envelope to: "Passport to Romance Rules Request", P.O. Box 9998, Saint John, New Brunswick, Canada E2L 4N4.

9. Quebec residents may submit any litigation respecting the conduct and awarding of a prize in this contest to the Régie des loteries et courses du Québec.

10. Payment of taxes other than air and hotel taxes is the sole responsibility of the winner.

11. Void where prohibited by law.

COUPON BOOKLET OFFER TERMS

To receive your Free travel-savings coupon booklets, complete the mail-in Offer Certificate on the preceeding page, including the necessary number of proofs-of-purchase, and mail to: Passport to Romance, P.O. Box 9057, Buffalo, NY 14269-9057. The coupon booklets include savings on travel-related products such as car rentals, hotels, cruises, flowers and restaurants. Some restrictions apply. The offer is available in the United States and Canada. Requests must be postmarked by January 25, 1991. Only proofs-of-purchase from specially marked "Passport to Romance" Harlequin® or Silhouette® books will be accepted. The offer certificate must accompany your request and may not be reproduced in any manner. Offer void where prohibited or restricted by law. LIMIT FOUR COUPON BOOKLETS PER NAME, FAMILY, GROUP, ORGANIZATION OR ADDRESS. Please allow up to 8 weeks after receipt of order for shipment. Enter quickly as quantities are limited. Unfulfilled mail-in offer requests will receive free Harlequin® or Silhouette® books (not previously available in retail stores), in quantities equal to the number of proofs-of-purchase required for Levels One to Four, as applicable.

OFFICIAL SWEEPSTAKES
ENTRY FORM

Complete and return this Entry Form immediately—the more Entry Forms you submit, the better your chances of winning!
- Entry Forms must be received by **December 31, 1990**
- A random draw will take place on **January 29, 1991**   3-SSE-1-SW
- Trip must be taken by **December 31, 1991**

YES, I want to win a PASSPORT TO ROMANCE vacation for two! I understand the prize includes round-trip air fare, accommodation and a daily spending allowance.

Name_____

Address_____

City_____ State_____ Zip_____

Telephone Number_____ Age_____

Return entries to: **PASSPORT TO ROMANCE**, P.O. Box 9056, Buffalo, NY 14269-9056

COUPON BOOKLET/OFFER CERTIFICATE

	LEVEL ONE Booklet	LEVEL TWO Booklet	LEVEL THREE Booklet	LEVEL FOUR Booklet
Item	1	1 & 2	1, 2 & 3	1, 2, 3 & 4
Booklet 1 = $100+	$100+	$100+	$100+	$100+
Booklet 2 = $200+		$200+	$200+	$200+
Booklet 3 = $300+			$300+	$300+
Booklet 4 = $400+	____	____	____	$400+
Approximate Total Value of Savings	$100+	$300+	$600+	$1,000+
# of Proofs of Purchase Required	4	6	12	18
Check One	____	____	____	____

Name_____

Address_____

City_____ State_____ Zip_____

Return Offer Certificates to: **PASSPORT TO ROMANCE**. P.O. Box 9057, Buffalo, NY 14269-9057

Requests must be postmarked by **January 25, 1991**

✂- - - - - - - - - - - - - - -

ONE PROOF OF PURCHASE   3-SSE-1

To collect your free coupon booklet you must include the necessary number of proofs-of-purchase with a properly completed Offer Certificate   © 1990 Harlequin Enterprises Limited

See previous page for details